HOLLOW

ROAD TO BABYLON

SAM SISAVATH

Published by Road to Babylon Media LLC
www.roadtobabylon.com

Edited by Jennifer Jensen, Wendy Chan, and Shavonne Clarke
Cover Art by Deranged Doctor Design

ALSO BY SAM SISAVATH

THE RED SKY CONSPIRACY SERIES

Most Wanted

The Devil You Know

ABOUT HOLLOW

PARADISE FOUND...AND LOST.

Lara left it all behind. The battles, the blood, and the sacrifices. She's settled in a small seaside village along the Texas-Mexico border under an assumed name, determined to live out the rest of her life in obscurity.

She isn't starting over alone. Keo is by her side. Together, they have made a good life for themselves. It's an unexciting life. A quiet life. A perfect life.

Unfortunately, the world doesn't leave you alone just because you want it to. The arrival of desperate men ruins everything, and Lara is forced on a journey across the countryside with Keo hot on her trail.

Keo has sacrificed too much to just let Lara go now. His skills might be a little rusty, but all it takes is one good kill to get the juices flowing again.

In *Hollow*, book 7 in the continuing *Road to Babylon* series, paradise is a hard place to find but even harder to hold onto.

ONE

He opened his eyes to gunfire.

Pek-pek-pek!

No, not gunfire.

Pek...pek...

The vibe was all wrong. Even the scar along the left side of his face wasn't tingling, and it usually did when there was gunpowder anywhere in the vicinity.

...pek...

Not gunfire. Not even close.

...pek-pek-pek...

Just rain pelting the roof above him.

...pek-pek-pek...

Persistent rain, yes, but nothing to get excited about. Rain was part of the everyday world, but the slightly chilled breeze in the room wasn't. Not a lot, just enough for him to notice that something had changed.

...pek-pek-pek...

Keo got out of bed and padded across the room, barefoot and in his boxers. Rain was falling in sheets outside. They'd forgotten to bring down the wooden slabs that covered the windows before dozing off. It was a hot summer—hotter than usual, according to the others—and AC was a luxury that no one had these days. Fortunately, the rain had chased the mosquitos away, if only temporarily, but water had pooled inside the building in turn.

He actually enjoyed the cold water as he pulled back the sticks to lower the wooden cover and let it fall back into place, grabbing it at almost exactly the last second so it wouldn't slam and wake her. He moved over to the next window and repeated the process.

As he was closing the second window, lightning lit up the night sky in the distance. He paused temporarily to count.

One Mississippi...

Two Mississippi...

Three Mississippi...

He got to *ten* before thunder *boomed* and the rainfall grew in intensity, like machine-gun fire hitting the rooftop above them.

Like machine-gun fire, but *not* machine-gun fire.

That was another world. Another life.

Pek-pek-pek...

...pek-pek-pek...

Rain. Just rain. That was all.

"That sounded close," a voice said from behind him.

Keo glanced back. "Two miles."

"Two miles?"

"Two miles."

"You sound pretty sure of that."

"I counted."

"Counted what?"

"The seconds between the lightning and thunder. That's how you measure the distance. Five seconds for every mile."

He walked back over. Lara lay on her side, hugging one of her big, fluffy pillows. She'd let her hair grow out, which he approved of. Soft, crystal-blue eyes watched him from across the semidarkness of the room. Not that he needed light to see her; Keo had every inch of her face and body memorized.

"Sounded closer," she said.

"It wasn't."

"That's why I said *sounded*. See the difference?"

He smiled and said, "Nope," and walked past her.

"Where you going?"

"Going to do a quick check."

"Hurry back."

"Yes, ma'am."

He left the bedroom door slightly open behind him and walked across the similarly dark living room. Not that Keo thought someone would have sneaked in while they slept, but you never knew with a driving rainstorm out there. Although, it had been months—two months and three weeks, to be exact —since the last stranger wandered into their area. Three men and two women, and after they were done with trading, had left never to be seen again.

Two months and three weeks. That was a long time. So what was he so worried about?

Just in case...

They had solar-powered LED lanterns—one in the

bedroom and one in the living room—but Keo didn't bother grabbing them to light his way. He could see just fine even with the windows closed out here. That was good; at least he remembered to do that before bed. He hated the idea of letting his guard down, but months with nothing even remotely smelling like danger had convinced him sleeping with the windows open was okay. Especially since it was hot as hell out there.

Persistent *tap-tap-tap* sounds (not the rain, but something else) echoed around him, but he couldn't locate where they were coming from. There was definitely more than one. He wasn't too alarmed about these sounds either, because he knew what they were even if he couldn't see them. There were holes along the ceiling that he'd been meaning to caulk up since the last rainstorm gave them away, but he had never gotten around to it.

Put it on the To-Do list, along with everything else.

Then: *Jesus, I sound like a suburban dad.*

The front door was still locked, the deadbolt still in place. He unlocked it, then opened the door and looked out at the patio and beyond.

The village was being pounded by the storm, the other houses within view just as dark as theirs. The ocean was fifty meters to his right, and he could make out stronger than usual waves pounding the beaches tonight. That meant more water near the shallows, which would mean he and George wouldn't need to venture too far out to find fish tomorrow morning. Not that he minded the solitude of the ocean.

Keo closed the door and locked it again before walking back across the living room. He had left wet footprints from the bedroom along the wooden floors, but they would dry in a few hours. The puddles from the leaks in the roof would be more troublesome, and he made a mental note to look for them the first chance he got.

For real, this time.

Yeah right, pal.

Lara was sitting on the bed, scribbling notes on that old notebook of hers, the bedroom LED lantern on the nightstand turned on low. She glanced up when he returned. "Everything okay?"

"Everything's fine."

"What made you want to check?"

"Nothing." Then, because he could see his response didn't satisfy her, he added, "Just in case."

She smiled. "Just in case, huh?"

He returned it. "Just in case."

Lara put the notebook and pen down. "What time is it?"

It was a good question. They didn't have clocks in the house, and he couldn't remember the last time he'd worn a watch.

"Past midnight," Keo said.

It was just a guess, but it was probably close. It *felt* like past midnight. There was a time not long ago when he could pinpoint, if not down to the minute, then the hour, by just feeling the light, or lack thereof. But that ability had been dulled by his new life.

Is that good or bad?

Good, he answered himself.

He nodded at the notebook on the nightstand. "You've been looking at that thing a lot these days."

"Marie's pregnancy," Lara said.

"She okay?"

"Probably." She bit her lip, the way she always did when she was lost in thought. "I just have to be sure of some things."

He slid back into bed. "Sounds serious."

"It's not. I just want to cross all my *T*'s and dot my *I*'s." Lara cuddled up against him, resting her chin on his naked chest, before making a face. "You're sticky."

"It's hot, babe."

"Maybe you should go outside and take a shower in the storm." She dramatically sniffed him. "And you smell bad. I'm getting a pretty strong fish odor."

"Well, we are in a fishing village..."

"Excuses," Lara said. She slid her legs against his and ran the sole of one foot up and down his leg.

He gave her a curious glance. "What are you doing?" Then, because he didn't want her to stop, "Not that I'm complaining or anything."

She laughed. "Nothing." She sat up before gliding casually over until she was straddling his waist.

"Nothing, huh? You call this nothing? Watch yourself, woman."

She smiled down at him. "Ophelia asked me a question this morning that I've been thinking about all day..."

Keo put his hands on her hips, then moved them down slightly until he found the hem of her nightgown. He slid the smooth fabric up along her thighs, high enough to expose her cotton panties. She didn't do anything to stop his progress, so he took that as permission to cup her ass in both hands.

"What did she ask you?" Keo said.

"I don't know if I should say."

She leaned down and kissed him lightly on the lips. He

recognized a frisky Lara when he was presented with one, and she was definitely being frisky tonight.

"But you've been thinking about it all day," Keo said.

"Uh huh."

"So what is it?"

"She asked..."

"What?"

"She asked..."

He pinched the hem of her panties and snapped them back against her waist. Her skin was a lot tanner these days, but that only complemented her eyes more.

"Hey!" she yelped.

Lara slapped at his hands and shot him an annoyed look. But she didn't get off him, so he kept both hands on her bottom.

"What did Ophelia ask?" Keo said.

He caressed her naked thigh, liking the feel of it. Which was like saying water was wet. He couldn't remember a time when he didn't like touching her. Maybe he'd gone soft in his old age, though truth be told, there was never anything "soft" when she was around him. Like now, sitting on top, knowing full well the reaction she would get.

"She asked if we were ever going to have a baby," Lara said.

He raised both eyebrows. He wasn't sure what he had expected, but that...was probably not it.

"Hunh," he said.

"That's an interesting response."

"Is it?"

She shrugged. "I was expecting something...else?"

"Like what?"

"I don't know. That's why I added the inflection at the end. Something...else? See the difference?"

"Ah."

He stared up at her, and she watched him back. She didn't look angry, just a little...what was it? Curious? Had he given her the right response? If not, then what was she hoping to hear from him? Six months after they found the village, and every day of it spent together, and he still had difficulty reading her needs.

"What did you tell her?" Keo asked.

"I told her I didn't know, that it never came up. It hasn't, right?"

"Not as far as I know."

"So I wasn't wrong."

"Have *you* ever thought about it?" he asked.

She sat back slightly. "Not really."

Not really? he thought.

"What about you?" she asked, focusing on him intently. "Have you ever thought about it?"

"Not really, either," Keo said.

"No?"

He shook his head.

"Never?" she asked.

"Not that I can recall."

"You and George never talked about it?"

"Lara, I fish with the guy. We don't exactly do a lot of talking when we're out there."

"So what do you guys do for all those hours?"

"Mostly we sit and stare at the water and drink beer."

She smiled. "That's it?"

"That's pretty much it. George isn't much of a talker and neither am I. And neither is Dusty, as it turns out."

"Dusty's a dog. He can't talk."

"He can. We just can't understand dog."

"Oh, that makes sense."

She stopped talking but didn't look away from him. Keo had a feeling this was where he was supposed to fill in the gaps.

Shit, I'm bad at this.

"Have you ever thought about it?" he asked.

"About having a baby?" Lara said.

He nodded.

"When I was younger," Lara said. "Every girl does. She's weird if she doesn't. I'm guessing it's not the same with guys."

"It's not."

"Right. Anyway, I haven't thought about it in a long time. Not until this morning, anyway."

"When Ophelia opened her big, fat mouth."

Lara smiled. "She was just being herself."

"She was being nosy."

"Like I said, she was just being herself."

"But her question prompted you to think about it all day today?"

"Uh huh."

"*All* day?"

"Mostly all day."

"Did she know that?"

"No. I kept that part to myself."

Keo glanced over at the nightstand, at the notebook on top of it. "That's not filled with baby names, is it?"

She rolled her eyes dramatically. "Of course not."

Keo noticed the way she was gazing at him, but not *at* him. Lara could be intense, but these days she had mellowed out by a huge degree. He assumed he had, too, but obviously there was no way for him to know.

And yet, when he looked up at Lara, he thought he saw something...

"Wait," Keo said, "you're not...?"

"I'm not what?" Lara said.

He placed one palm on her stomach but didn't look away from her. "You're not...?"

She shook her head and pursed a smile. "No. I'm not pregnant."

"Oh." Keo sighed. Then, smiling, "Good."

"'Good?'" She narrowed her eyes. "What does that mean? 'Good?'"

Uh oh, Keo thought, and quickly said, "It doesn't mean anything."

He knew it was the wrong response when she didn't stop staring daggers down at him. Also because she wasn't wiggling her body on top of him anymore.

"Oh, I think it means something," Lara said. "What does that mean? 'Good?'"

"It means...good."

"Meaning?"

He sighed. "I don't know what you want me to say."

"You don't want to have a baby with me?"

"I didn't say that."

"What are you saying?"

Alarm bells went off inside Keo's head. "I... I'm just saying..."

"What are you just saying?"

"I'm just saying..." He shook his head. "I just never thought about it, that's all."

That was probably not the answer she was hoping for, but it seemed to soften her somewhat, and Lara put away the knives.

Thank God.

"Never?" she asked, in a noticeably less antagonistic voice.

"You know what I used to be, what I used to do."

She nodded.

"When you're in that world, doing the things I used to do, you don't think about bringing a child into it," Keo said. "It's just not something that comes up, because you know better. You've seen how people are. To one another. To their enemies. Even to their friends."

"You're not in that world anymore, Keo."

"Have you *seen* the world around us, Lara? Six months ago, you were leading an army and trying to stop a bunch of warmongering fucks from slaughtering innocent civilians. Six months ago, I was killing those same fucks so they couldn't hurt you. It's not the world it used to be, but that doesn't mean it's any better. There are just less rules now."

"You really believe that, don't you?"

"Don't you?"

"No."

"After everything you've seen? Everything you've been a part of? You still want to bring a life into this world?"

"I don't know. I haven't decided anything. It was just something that came up..."

"Just came up, huh?"

"You put two women in the same building long enough, baby talk comes up. There's no conspiracy here, Keo."

"Okay, but when you do figure this out, can you at least tell me first so I'll know how to respond?"

"Now what would be the fun in that?"

"I just don't want to be murdered in my own home, that's all."

"As long as you say the right things, you won't be."

"That's the trick, isn't it?"

Lara climbed off and lay down next to him. Keo turned over onto his side so he could look at her.

She smiled back at him, but it wasn't a full smile. It was an *I'm sorry I brought the topic up* smile.

Keo brushed his hand against her cheek and leaned over to kiss her. "I'm sorry. I know that wasn't the answer you were hoping to hear."

"It's my fault for bringing it up."

"It's not."

"It is."

"It's not." He pulled her over and wrapped his arms around her warm body. "I love you. You know that."

"I know," she said softly.

"If you want to have a baby..."

"I don't want to do anything you don't want to do."

"I just want to make you happy."

"I know you do. That's why I love you." She leaned up slightly, just enough to kiss him on the lips, before resting her head against him again. "I want to make you happy, too. If this doesn't, then we don't have to talk about it again."

"I'm not saying I don't ever want to have a baby."

"No?"

"I'm a guy. It's in my genes to spread my seed around."

She laughed. "Just as long as you don't tell me where

you've been spreading it. I know how to use a scalpel, you know."

"Ouch," Keo said.

He tightened his arms around her. She was warm against him, but maybe the hot summer air had a little something to do with that.

"Does this mean I'm not getting lucky tonight?" he asked after a while.

"Go to sleep," Lara said. "You have fish to catch tomorrow."

"Maybe I should take a sick day. I'm definitely smelling too much like fish lately."

He couldn't see it, but he thought she might have smiled when she said, "Don't worry; your natural BO more than masks the fishy smell."

"Oh, wonderful. Here I am, worried for nothing."

She pushed in even closer, their legs entwining on the bed. The blanket was somewhere on the floor, not that they needed it with the humidity.

Keo listened to the *pek-pek-pek* of rainfall on the rooftop while Lara breathed calmly against him. Eventually, she fell asleep, her breathing turning into soft snores, but he remained wide awake.

He thought he could hear the leaks in the living room outside the bedroom door, but that was probably just his imagination. It was raining too hard outside for him to hear much of anything beyond what was in the room with him right now. Which was all that mattered anyway.

Him. Her. Them.

Pek-pek-pek...

...pek-pek-pek...

Then, from far away, a monstrous *boom!*

Lara moved slightly against him, subconsciously reacting to the harsh sound of thunder. Or, at least, Keo thought it was thunder. For a second or two, he thought he'd heard something exploding, but he was pretty sure it was just his imagination.

It's just rain and thunder.

Just rain and thunder, that's all.

TWO

Dusty was perched on his hind legs at the bow of the boat, looking straight into the sunrise as if he expected something to show up this time that hadn't before in the last hundred or so mornings they'd been out here. When the sun finally revealed itself and all that anticipation proved to be for naught, the brown dog slid his chin down to the warm deck of the eighteen-foot boat and commenced his usual routine of licking himself to pass the time.

"Is it me, or does he do that every time?" Keo asked.

George chuckled. "It's you."

"You sure?"

"Yes."

"I think you're lying, George."

"Pretty sure I'm not."

"Uh huh," Keo said.

He looked back over at his fishing lines, the rods sticking out of individual holders along the side of the boat. All three remained taut as the sailboat drifted aimlessly. George sat in

t of his own poles on the other side, his back to Keo's. Four
more trawling lines lagged at the rear, but like the three in
front of Keo, there was no action.

Keo glanced up occasionally to check the loose sail flaps
fluttering against a light breeze above them. They'd tied the
fabric up to drift, but Keo was already thinking about moving
to a new location. Maybe try a spot they hadn't before, or head
even farther out. Maybe he'd give it another hour and see what
George thought.

"Looks like school's going long this morning," George said
after a while. "All the kids are stuck in class."

Keo smiled. "Stuck in class, huh?"

"You know. Schools of fish?"

"Yeah, I know, George."

"Just wanted to make sure. There's nothing worse than a
good joke going to waste."

Keo wasn't sure how "good" that joke was, but he let the
old man have his moment.

"You want a cold one, kid?" George asked.

"Already?"

"Good a time as any."

"Sun hasn't even been up for ten minutes yet."

"It's been up longer than that in Asia."

"You make a good point."

He heard the tab on a can popping open behind him.
According to George, beer didn't actually expire; the stamped
expiration date was just a trick by beer sellers to get more business, back when money still mattered. Keo didn't entirely
believe him, mostly because the beers they'd drank weren't
always as flavorful as he remembered.

"Here," George said.

Keo reached over and took the open can from George. It might not have been as fresh as when it came off the assembly line six (or was that seven now?) years ago, but at least it was cold. You could keep a lot of things chilled by putting them in a gym bag and allowing them to soak in the Gulf of Mexico. Besides two beers, there were some bottles of water tapping against the hull of the sailboat.

"Some tadpole told me last night that you and the missus had a convo about kids," George said.

Keo groaned. "Does this tadpole's name start with an O?"

"It might."

"She tell you everything?"

"Pretty much."

Ophelia, the culprit who had brought up the subject of kids to Lara and stopped Keo from getting lucky last night, was also George's wife. Not that there were any documents or even a priest around to make the whole thing official. Not these days.

"So, you gonna knock her up or what?" George said when Keo kept quiet.

"You make it sound so romantic."

George chuckled, then took a second or two—or ten—to drink his beer. That left the *whump-whump* of the sails above them to fill in the silence. There was somewhat of a breeze, but not enough to keep Keo's shirt from sticking to his sweaty chest.

Finally, George said, "You should start thinking about it. You're getting up there in years, kid. Edna ain't a spring chicken herself."

Keo grinned, knowing George wouldn't notice. It still made him smile when someone referred to Lara as Edna.

When they were together and people called him Bob and her
Edna, they would almost always exchange a private, amused
glance.

"You should tell her that," Keo said.

"Which part?"

"The part about Edna not being a spring chicken
anymore."

"Hell no. You think I'm suicidal?"

Keo pictured Lara taking a swing at George, who was
more than thirty years older than her but looked even older
with his leathery, tanned skin. It was the result of too much
time shirtless in the sun. Even now, George was topless while
Keo had on a long-sleeve shirt to keep the sun from
baking him.

"You're thinking about it, aren't you?" George asked.

"No," Keo said.

"Liar. You're thinking about it."

"You and Ophelia don't have any kids."

"We don't, but I did, before everything."

"You never told me that."

"You never asked."

"Fair point." This time, it was Keo who waited for the
other man to continue, and when he didn't, "So what
happened?"

"Same thing that happened to everyone who didn't make
it," George said, and didn't say anything else.

He didn't have to. Keo had heard the same stories before
from countless people. Only the names ever changed. He was
one of the "lucky" ones—he didn't have very much to lose to
The Purge. Once upon a time, he'd had a simple motto: "*See
the world. Kill some people. Make some money.*" That had

gotten him through a lot of tough times. He had no one, and that was just the way he liked it.

But that wasn't true anymore. The Purge changed everything for everyone—including him. A lot of women had come into his life after the monsters came out of the shadows, but they were never like Lara. No one had her spirit, that something he couldn't explain but which drew him the first time he saw her; and all the days, weeks, months, and years since had only reinforced his first impressions. He'd left her behind and spent five years trying to forget her, but all it took was one day of being with her again to remind him why he couldn't stop thinking about her.

And now she was his, and he'd never been more content in his life. He wondered if that would change if they did have a child. She wasn't wrong when she said he wasn't knee-deep in the blood and bullets and bodies of his old life anymore. But he'd also had a point when he'd responded that the new world wasn't all unicorns and rainbows.

He was pretty sure he had a point, anyway, but thinking about it now, this morning...

"Yeah, you're thinking about it," George was saying. "You're definitely thinking about it now."

"I'm not," Keo said.

"Liar, liar, pants on fire."

"Whatever."

"Remember, if it's a boy, you should think about naming him George."

Keo grunted. "Over my dead body."

George laughed, and they didn't say very much after that.

Keo concentrated on the fishing lines in front of him. It'd been about fifteen minutes since they baited the hooks, and still no bite. It would have been a disaster if the two of them catching fish every day was necessary to the village's survival. The truth was, nothing they caught—or didn't catch, like today —out here was really going to impact whether the others ate or not tonight. If anything, this was busy work, something to occupy all the free time he suddenly found himself with.

His thoughts strayed back to Lara. He remembered the look on her face when he had responded to her questions last night. He realized, now, that she'd been trying to feel him out on the subject and was clearly disappointed with his answers.

It was too late to change his answers now, but that didn't mean he couldn't make up for it later tonight. The *how* was the tricky part.

Twumph as something fell into the water on the other side. Keo glanced over and spotted an empty aluminum can floating away from them. George, already done with his beer.

"You ever heard of 'Don't mess with Texas?'" Keo asked.

George let out a loud burp. "Factually incorrect. We're more in Mexico waters than Texas's."

"Don't mess with Mexico."

"She's already been messed with. Same for every other country out there. You finished with that beer? Want another one?"

"Not yet."

"What's the hold up? You got something else better to do?"

Keo chuckled. George had a good point.

He was raising his can to his slightly dry lips when he heard something echoing in the distance.

Was that...?

It was very faint, which made it difficult to guess what had caused it or where it had come from.

Keo lowered the beer. "You heard that?"

"What?" George said. "You got fish on that side?"

"No. Not fish."

Keo put the can down and stood up. The sailboat rocked slightly, and Dusty, at the bow, glanced curiously over at him.

George, sunlight glinting off his almost bronze face, also looked over. "What is it?"

"I heard something," Keo said.

"What?"

Keo shook his head and kept quiet, trying to pick up the sound again.

"Kid?" George said. "What did you hear?"

"I'm not sure."

And he wasn't. At least, not with 100 percent certainty.

Keo looked northwest, in the direction of the village. Not that he could see any traces of it in the distance. They were at least ten kilometers, if not more, down the Gulf. They hadn't dropped anchor, and the boat had been drifting, letting what little wind there was take them wherever it wanted.

"It was probably nothing," George said.

Maybe, Keo thought.

"Here," George said, and popped another tab on a beer.

"I haven't finished the first one yet."

"So what are you waiting for?" George asked, taking a sip from the second beer, deciding that he liked it, and taking a bigger drink.

Keo sat back down. The rods sticking off his side of the boat were still arched slightly, but not enough to signal that a fish had taken one of the baits. It was starting to look like one of those days—

Dusty popped up onto his legs and whirled around on the

bow. That startled Keo, and he stood up again before following the dog's gaze as he looked backward, toward the northwest—

Smoke, rising lazily in the horizon.

"What is that?" George asked as he also stood up next to Keo.

It was a thin wisp of smoke, rising higher and higher.

Something was burning on land, along the shoreline...

The village. It was coming from the village.

"We're heading back!" Keo shouted, before snapping open the back storage compartment and pulling out the battery.

"Hey, hey, calm down, kid. We don't know what's happening," George said.

Keo ignored him and attached the wires to the trolling motor clipped at the back of the craft. George kept the battery charged using solar panels, though according to him he'd never managed a full charge. But there was enough juice that when Keo flicked the power switch, the motor came to life and the propeller began spinning.

George was standing next to him when Keo said, "George, sit your ass down. We're going now!"

The older man hurriedly sat as the boat began moving. The motor provided forty-five pounds of power, which meant they weren't going to be skipping back to the village at any great speed. Still, it was going to get them home much faster than if they'd only had the wind to rely on. Which, at the moment, was mostly missing.

The boat finished its turn, and Keo pointed it forward—northwest, back toward the village. Dusty hadn't moved from the bow, not that Keo was afraid the dog might fall off given their current speed. (*Dammit! Can't this thing go any faster?*)

If anything, it looked like the animal was enjoying finally moving again after being still for so long.

Keo couldn't say the same.

The smoke—he could make out more of it now, rising higher into the crisp summer air—was the result of a fire.

George was clutching to the side of the hull, even though he didn't really have to. They weren't moving fast enough to risk tossing either one of them into the water.

"You said you heard something earlier?" George asked. "Before the smoke?"

"Yeah."

"What was it? What did you hear before, kid?"

Keo didn't answer him.

"Kid," George said. "What did you hear before we saw the smoke?"

"A gunshot," Keo said. "I thought I heard a gunshot."

He expected to hear gunfire as they neared the village, especially with the low whine of the trolling motor buzzing away in one ear. But he didn't, and Keo wasn't sure if that was a good thing or not.

It's good. Isn't it?

Maybe...

The smoke had continued to grow in size, and by the time they had the beach in sight, it had already jumped from one building onto two others. It didn't help that the houses sat side-by-side, with only ten meters or so of grass and sand between each one. Flames were now roaring into the sky, and Keo thought he could feel the heat all the way out here in the water.

He glanced toward the leftmost part of the beach and at his and Lara's home. It was at the end of the column of buildings and had, for the meantime at least, been spared by the fire. Even as he thought that, the flames jumped again and lit up a fourth building, adding to the already thick smoke gathering above the shoreline. The same clouds of smoke that were growing wider with every second.

This is bad. This is very bad.

"Jesus Christ," George whispered next to him.

Keo looked over at the older man. "Take the lever, George."

George scooted over and grabbed the long stick that controlled the motor powering them—slowly, way too damn slowly—back home. "What're you gonna do, kid?"

Keo didn't answer. He was too busy running forward and jumping up onto the bow to stand next to Dusty. The dog glanced over as if to say, *Hey, what are you doing up here?*

He ignored the animal and got ready.

"Bob!" George called over from the stern. "Bob! Hey, Bob!"

Keo could hear him just fine; he just didn't feel like answering. He watched parts of the middle section of what he'd come to call home burning in front of him instead. He could already smell the smoke, and Keo began breathing through his mouth. Dusty let out an annoyed series of barks next to him.

Yeah, I don't like it either, dog.

The village was really just a group of houses built a few meters beyond the sandy beaches, each one with a generous porch. They had been constructed from the ground up after The Purge by people like George, the ones that made this place home long before Keo and Lara had shown up. Whether they had done it on purpose or not, George and his friends had created something uniquely simple. It was that simplicity that Lara loved so much; and because she loved it, so did Keo.

He went into a crouch, one hand on his bent knee, the other on the deck to maintain his balance. The sheathed Ka-Bar was secured in his front waistband. It was the only weapon George kept on the boat, and they used it primarily to filet fish. The old timer didn't even know the proper name for it; he'd always just called it a knife.

But it was all Keo had at the moment. What he wouldn't give for a pistol. Better yet, a rifle.

Better yet, a couple of rifles...

The billowing smoke continued to thicken, spreading out across the cloudless sky above. As they neared the beach—two hundred meters and closing—Keo could make out people moving in front of the homes. The other villagers, fighting the fire. They had formed a jagged line from the grassy area to the beach and were passing buckets of water up and down.

He concentrated on where the fire was spreading from. The building in the very center... The clinic. Whatever had happened, it had started at the clinic first, then jumped to the other structures.

Lara...

Keo stood up as the beach rushed toward them.

Fifty meters...

Forty...

Thirty...

He got up and took a couple of steps closer to the front. Dusty smartly remained where he was.

Twenty...

Ten!

Keo jumped at almost the last second and landed in a crouch on the beach. He was up on his feet and running a second later, reaching down to make sure he still had the Ka-Bar—not that he expected to need it right away, as the faces of the people fighting the fire before him came into view. Familiar faces. People he'd come to call friends over the months.

His heart sank at the sight of burning homes.

They're not going to stop it. It's going to keep jumping and take down all the houses.

Keo thought about all the work that went into building this place, to turn this stretch of nothing into a community. As simply constructed as the buildings in front of him were, they were still their *homes*. Not just his and Lara's, but George and Ophelia's, and the forty other people. The thought of losing this—losing everything over the course of a single afternoon—made him angry.

For him, for them, for all of them.

The first person that turned around when they heard the boat approaching was Ben. His and Susan's home was next to Keo and Lara's, and they were good neighbors and even better friends. Ben was covered in sweat and smoke and soot as he handed a metal pail to Peter, another neighbor, and hurried over to meet Keo halfway.

"Bob, Jesus, there you are," Ben said. "You saw the fire from all the way out there?"

Keo nodded. "What happened?" he forced himself to ask,

even though the real question he wanted to ask Ben was, *Where's Lara? Where is* Lara?

"I don't know," Ben said, shaking his head. He wiped at a layer of sweat with the back of his hand. Both his arms were black with smoke, and Keo could smell burning hair coming from the older man. "I don't know what happened, Bob. Me and some of the guys were in the woods hunting when we saw the smoke. When we got here..."

"Edna?" Keo asked. "Where's Edna?"

Bob shook his head again, blinking his eyes rapidly against the sting of smoke wafting everywhere around them. "I don't know. I don't know anything. We haven't had time to get any information with the fire spreading so fast."

Keo hurried past Ben and up the beach, passing the line of people sending bucket after bucket of seawater up from the ocean. But even as they desperately scrambled to fight the wall of flames, Keo already knew it wasn't going to be enough. They weren't going to stop it. There weren't enough people and not enough resources. The ocean was big and vast and had an endless supply of water, but it wasn't going to march up the sands and pour itself over the flames for them.

He stopped in front of the clinic—or what was left of it. There was nothing but a red and orange inferno now. He wouldn't even know there used to be a building there if he didn't have prior knowledge. There was just a roaring fire in its place, and it was going to keep burning until all the wood was gone.

And the whole village was built from wood...

Someone grabbed Keo's arm from behind, and he spun around. Ophelia, her face black and covered in soot, which only seemed to heighten the comically widened whites of her eyes. She was a tall and thin woman, wearing jeans and a white T-shirt. There was dirt on the front of her wet shirt, and she was clinging to a beat-up metal pail.

"Bob, oh God, Bob," Ophelia said. She was hyperventilating, the bucket trembling along with the rest of her. "She's gone, Bob. She's gone."

"Who?" Keo said. Then, when Ophelia didn't answer fast enough—A second? Maybe just a second and a half of hesitation?—Keo grabbed her by the shoulders and shook her, shouting to be heard over the flames and activity around him, "Who is gone, Ophelia? Who is gone?"

The woman stared back at Keo, her lips quivering. "Edna. They took her, Bob. They took Edna..."

THREE

The fire didn't stop. If anything, it only increased and kept spreading, jumping from building to building. The closeness between houses, one of the many things that made living here so welcoming because you could just step out onto your porch and talk to your neighbor without raising your voice even a little bit, was now the problem.

Their problem, not mine.

Right now, Lara's all that matters. Just Lara.

Just Lara...

He wanted to tell the others that it was hopeless, that they weren't going to contain the fire, but he didn't. This was their home, more than it was his and Lara's, and he had no right to tell them not to waste their sweat and blood, and potentially their lives, trying to save what they had built.

Ben and a few others had wisened up and broken from the even-more-ragged line of firefighters stretching across the beach. They were now trying to salvage what they could from the still-untouched buildings. The problem was that all that were left were the homes; the clinic, along with the supply warehouses, were in the middle, and they had been the first ones to catch fire. Their contents were now feeding the ever-expanding blaze.

Keo wasn't thinking about all the clothing and extra materials and dry meats they had stored in the communal buildings at the moment. His entire attention was on what was left of the clinic, little more than a husk now. It had never been an especially large structure to begin with because there was never any need for anything too big. Most mornings it was just Lara, with Ophelia assisting. Before Lara arrived, the clinic was used for storage.

"It's like working at the world's most boring hospital," she had told him after their first couple of weeks here.

"That's good, right?" he'd said.

"It should be, but I don't know. It feels..."

"Lacking?"

"More like too easy."

"I like too easy. Especially my women."

That had gotten him a nice punch on the shoulder. He still remembered the conversation, months later, as he turned away from the charred remains and jogged up the beach toward their house.

He ran past Ben, coming out of his own home with a couple of men—Stephen and Miguel—helping to carry some furniture. Keo wanted to tell them to concentrate on more important things, but he didn't waste the energy.

Ben saw him running by and called after him, "Bob! Bob, you need help?"

Keo turned, and still backpedaling, shook his head. "Save what you can, Ben. Don't worry about me."

"What about Edna?" Ben said. "I haven't seen her around. What did Ophelia say happened?"

"I'll find her. You just save what you can!" Keo said, and turned and jogged up the steps to the porch and into his house.

He hurried through the living room, making a beeline for the kitchen. The green army duffel bag they'd brought with them when they first arrived was still in the back of the pantry where Lara had stashed it. He pulled it out now, then crouched and dug through some boxes at the bottom until he found it: a brown pack with *Property of U.S. Army* stenciled on top. He took out the Ka-Bar and slit the box open, then grabbed bundles of unopened MREs and shoved them into the bag.

He remembered the conversation with Lara about the Meals Ready-to-Eat, food that was designed for soldiers to pack on the calories while in the field. They had given almost everything they had salvaged from the army truck to the others, like an offering for welcoming the two of them in. Lara hadn't wanted to hide away the extra box, but Keo had insisted.

"You never know when we might need it," he had said.

"I know, but..." She had shaken her head and pursed a smile. "I don't want to start this off on the wrong foot."

"Just in case," Keo had said. "Just in case..."

She had relented after that. Maybe, because like him, Lara knew that not everything always worked out the way you planned it, and *just in case* was always a good mantra, even in safe times.

He didn't have nearly enough room to take everything, but he put enough into the bag to last him for a week, if necessary, though he didn't think it would be. There was plenty of "food" out there on the land, waiting for someone to hunt it down. But MREs were easy, and he wasn't going to bypass easy right now.

Keo hoisted the duffel over his shoulder and headed for the bedroom. He stopped temporarily to glance back at the inferno still raging outside the open door. Even from his living room, he could see and feel the heat. The warm air had gotten noticeably hotter, and he was already sweating after the brief jog, his heartbeat slightly accelerated, more than it should have been. He blamed it on living the good life, where the hardest thing he had to do was jump up and down from George's boat in the mornings.

Yeah, that's it. It's not because you got lazy and fat or anything.

Definitely not.

In the bedroom, Keo went straight to the closet and pushed aside the clothing—at least 90 percent of it was Lara's—to reveal the gun rack at the back wall. He ignored the shotguns and went for the AR-15 rifle. He grabbed four spare magazines for it and tossed them into the bag before going for the Brugger & Thomet MP9. The submachine gun once belonged to a man who had tried to kill Keo. Lara thought it was bad luck to hold onto a dead man's weapon, but Keo couldn't care less. A lightweight submachine gun with a built-in suppressor was a dream if you could find one, especially if you had to carry it for long periods. Keo was only taking the longer and heavier AR, too, because you never knew when you'd need to make a long-distance shot.

The first-aid kit box that Lara always kept around was in the nightstand on her side of the bed. Keo jammed that into the now too-full bag. He thought about taking something out to lighten the load but decided against it. Too full was better than not full enough, in this case. Besides, he could always throw some away as he went.

He heard footsteps behind him and thought it was either Ben or the others come to warn him about the approaching fire, as if Keo didn't already know. The air was even hotter now than a few minutes ago, and he could smell the smoke getting thicker.

Except it wasn't Ben but George. The older man stood at the doorway, watching Keo as he unhooked the tactical belt and slipped it around his waist, then filled the holster with the Glock pistol. He put the sheathed Ka-Bar behind his back to make room for spare magazines for the handgun and MP9.

"O told me what happened," George said. "With Edna and Marie. You're going after them?"

"That's right," Keo said.

"You don't even know where they went."

"Northwest."

"O told you that?"

"No, but it's the only possible direction."

"How you figure?"

"If they'd gone south along the shoreline, we would have spotted them when we were coming back home. They could have gone north up the shoreline, but after what they did— what they took—that's unlikely."

"Why is that unlikely?"

"They essentially attacked the village, George. They wouldn't make it so easy to track them after that. Heading north up the shoreline would be too easy. So they would have gone northwest, where they have the entire state to get lost in."

"But you're just guessing, right?"

"Uh huh."

"What if you're wrong?"

"I'll improvise. I'm good at that." Keo hiked the duffel bag over his shoulder and snatched up the AR from the bed. He hurried past George, who followed. "Is your house safe?"

"It's gone," George said. "Almost everything's gone out there."

"They're not going to stop the fire, George. It's too big and too strong, and there aren't enough people to carry buckets from the ocean."

"Yeah, I kinda came to that conclusion myself."

They walked outside and stood on the porch. Ben and the others were still running in and out of Ben's house carrying out clothes and the kind of junk Keo didn't understand why they were wasting their time saving. But who was he to tell Ben what he should or shouldn't do? The man had different priorities.

Keo's, right now, was Lara.

Just Lara.

"O told me there were a dozen guys," George said.

"That's what she told me, too," Keo said.

"And they have guns. That's a lot of guys with guns, Bob."

"Not for long," Keo said.

Pop-pop-pop! coming from somewhere in front of them.

Gunfire?

No, not gunfire. It was the wrong sound; more like glass shattering.

"Shit," George said.

"What was that?" Keo asked.

"The solar panels on my roof that I've been using to charge

the batteries. I guess that means I'm going to need a new house."

"Forget the house, George," Keo said, and stuck out his hand. George shook it. "Houses can be rebuilt. Take care of Ophelia. That's what's most important."

George nodded and forced a smile. "Go get Edna and Marie back."

Keo nodded and hopped down the steps. He spun around and backpedaled, looking back at George. "Scratch Dusty for me!"

"Will do!" George said, waving back at him.

Keo turned and ran down the beach, away from the others and the fire raging uncontrollably behind him. Soon, the flames would reach his and Lara's house and consume everything. That was fine. Like he had told George, homes could be rebuilt, but it was everything else that he couldn't afford to lose.

Lara...

He replayed what Ophelia had told him in his head:

"I don't know who they were," she had said. "They showed up after you and George left, looking for a doctor. Someone told them we had one in the village."

"How many of them were there?" he had asked.

"About ten? Maybe a dozen. I didn't get a good count, but I think there was about a dozen of them in all."

"How did they get here?"

"They had horses. And they were pulling two wagons."

"No cars?"

"No." Then, looking as scared as he'd ever seen her, "I'm sorry, Bob. We couldn't do anything. They had guns."

So did everyone here, Keo had wanted to say but didn't.

Having guns and using them were two different beasts. The people in the village had all survived The Purge, but they'd never had to deal with the kind of monsters that walked in the sunlight. Most of the weapons they had were used to hunt wild game in the nearby woods, and even then they weren't especially proficient at it. But that hadn't mattered, because there was just so much meat to be had out there after The Walk Out thinned the ghoul ranks, leaving the animals to enjoy a buoyant resurgence.

So he didn't blame the ones who were around when the men took Lara for not fighting back. Killing a deer or a rabbit was not the same as putting the iron sights on another human being and pulling the trigger.

"Bob!" a voice called from behind him.

He was almost a hundred meters from the village when he stopped and looked back. A figure was running after him, the wall of flames and the dark, black smoke clouds in the background like the harbinger of some ruthless storm.

Harbinger? It's already here.

This is *the storm...*

Seeing the place go up in flames from a distance was different. He wasn't sure what he was feeling. Maybe a little of regret, maybe some sadness.

And then he thought about Lara, and none of it mattered.

The runner slowed down as he neared Keo. It was Yuli, Marie's husband. Keo should have guessed the man wouldn't be staying put, either. Yuli was a city kid from somewhere in Mexico City, but he'd proven to be semi-decent in the woods with a gun. He wasn't much of a fisherman, though. No one in the village was, except for George.

Yuli stopped in front of Keo and leaned over with his

hands on his hips to catch his breath. He was carrying a Remington bolt-action rifle behind him and was shouldering a well-worn backpack that looked just as stuffed with supplies as Keo's. And like Keo, Yuli had on cargo pants, boots, and a long-sleeve T-shirt that stuck to his skin by a generous supply of sweat. Keo could feel beads of the stuff stinging his eyes and swiped at them.

"George told me where you're going," Yuli said when he'd finally gotten enough wind to talk. "I'm coming with you."

Keo stared at the kid. He wasn't really a kid, but he was younger. Yuli was in his late twenties, with short hair and dark eyes. He and Marie were expecting their first child, and Keo thought about what Lara had told him last night:

"She okay?" he had asked her.

"Probably," she had answered. *"I just have to be sure of some things."*

And now Marie was gone, all because she was in the wrong place at the wrong time.

"Why did they take Marie?" Keo had asked Ophelia.

"I don't know," Ophelia had said. "I think because she was there when they showed up. I was looking in on Cassandra at the time."

Wrong place at the wrong time, Keo thought.

For Marie, anyway. It wasn't the case for Lara.

"They showed up after you and George left, looking for a doctor. Someone told them we had one in the village," Ophelia had said.

That wasn't unusual. The village did regular trades with other beachside towns in the area. Lara had even gone to a few of them to help out from time to time, so people knew about her. Which meant Lara had been taken because of what she knew—medicine—and not because of *who* she was. That was really the only upside—and that was being charitable—to her abduction. Lara, like Keo, had enemies. Too many, in fact.

"Don't tell me to go back," Yuli said when Keo didn't say anything to him. "'Cause I'm not going back. No way in hell, man. They took my Marie, too. I'm getting her back. Her and my child."

Keo nodded. "Wasn't gonna tell you to go back, kid."

"Good, because I'm coming with you."

"It's a free country, or so I've been told."

Keo turned and began walking.

Yuli fell in beside him. "You know where they're going?"

"Northwest."

"That's it?"

"That's it."

Yuli didn't say anything, and they started jogging for a few minutes in silence. Keo wasn't too worried about the Mexican keeping up. He was young and in good shape, and he didn't seemed to be having any trouble carrying the pack and rifle. He wasn't wearing a gun on his hip, but maybe that was just as well. Keo preferred the amateurs he worked with not to be *too* armed; you never knew when they might accidentally shoot you as well as the enemy.

Keo glanced over his shoulder at the village one final time. The fire had intensified and had jumped again. It had almost completely swallowed up all the houses, with only a few left untouched. One of them was Keo and Lara's at the very end.

"Mine's already gone," Yuli said. "I had to grab the rifle and supplies from Ben's. That's gone too by now, probably."

"Probably," Keo said.

The tree lines towered in front of them on the other side of the field of grass. Another half kilometer, and they'd reach it, but Keo was expecting to find something else before then. He began to slow down after about twenty more seconds of jogging, and Yuli did the same.

There, the two-lane country road. If he didn't already know it was there, he would have missed it entirely. The overgrown stalks of grass hid the asphalt from view, and a person who wasn't aware of its existence would literally have to step onto it to know it even existed out here. It stretched south and north but had an eventual curve that would take anyone traveling along it in a northwestern direction. You had to leave the road to get to the village, but you could see the place—especially the homes—from here.

"Come on," Keo said, and stepped up onto the road.

Yuli trailed behind him. "You don't think they went into the woods?"

Keo shook his head. "No."

"Why not?"

"Ophelia said they had wagons. That's not optimal for traveling in the woods. Wheels are made for roads. Besides, they took Lara because she was a doctor. That means they have wounded with them."

"The wagons," Yuli said. "You think they're carrying their wounded in the wagons."

"One or both of them, yeah."

"So they would try to avoid bumpy grounds as much as possible."

"Exactly."

It didn't take long for Keo to confirm his theory with actual proof. About two hundred meters later, Keo saw tire tracks abandoning the field and climbing onto the road. Along with those were horse hooves. Not all of the animals were using the asphalt; most stayed on the softer ground nearby to lessen wear and tear on their feet.

"I guess you were right," Yuli said.

"Yeah," Keo said.

They continued along the gray top, following the obvious tire prints. Rubber tires. There were two, just as Ophelia had said, traveling in a line with two horses apiece pulling them.

Maybe twelve men, all on horseback, and four more horses to pull two wagons. That's a lot of horses. Where did they get all the horses?

Horses weren't easy to come by these days. There were plenty of the animals running wild out there, but you had to know where to find them, and then later, break them in. Those weren't easy tasks. The village had one horse in all the years since The Purge, but they'd lost it when the animal got ill. Since then, they'd been reliant on manpower for everything, and it was fortunate they didn't have to go very far for their food.

Maybe that was one of the problems with the village. It was just too easy of a life. They could hunt if they wanted, or fish when they didn't. You didn't really need to do both; it almost entirely depended on what you felt like eating in a given week. There were always enough hunters like Yuli and Ben to take care of the meat, and Keo and George, and a few others with boats, to bring in the fish. They hadn't needed to learn to farm or do much of anything else to get by. Every now and then, they would put together an expedition to see what was still out there that was worth bringing back home.

Life had been good. Maybe *too* good. For him and for Lara, but it'd been even longer for people like George and Ophelia.

Yuli, too. Marie, his wife, had just celebrated her twenty-second birthday two weeks ago.

After about ten minutes of steady jogging, the road began to curve away from the shoreline as Keo had expected. The two lanes would take them around the woods and from there, join up with a bigger stretch of four-lane highway. Anyone pulling two wagons with them would stay on asphalt for as long as possible, especially when they were hauling wounded.

The problem was that the abductors had a good two-hour lead. That was according to Ophelia's best guess, anyway. And that was just *one* of the problems. The other—and maybe bigger one—was that they were moving faster. Keo could run for a long time, if he had to, but there was a reason horsepower was now the dominant and preferred mode of transportation in a post-Purge world. They could go for longer distances before they got tired.

Where the hell did they get all the horses?

It was a good question, and Keo reminded himself to ask them when he finally caught up to the bastards. Because he would catch up. He had no doubts about that. It might be today or tomorrow or a week from now, but he would catch up.

"Bob," Yuli said after a while. He sounded winded but hadn't stopped matching Keo stride for stride.

Keo glanced over at him.

"You ever shot anyone before?" Yuli asked.

"Yes," Keo said. "You?"

Yuli shook his head and gave Keo an almost apologetic, forced smile. "Never had to." Then, sucking in a deep breath, "I ever told you what I did before all of this?"

"No. What did you used to do?"

"I was a journalist. Or, well, I got a degree in journalism, anyway. Never really got around to getting the career started before, you know, everything happened."

A journalist?

Then: *Swell.*

"I guess I've been lucky," Yuli continued. "Despite everything, I haven't had to kill anyone. What about you?"

I haven't been that "lucky," Keo thought, but he said, "What about me?"

"You never said what you used to do before all of this."

"No one ever asked."

"That's a rule in the village. We don't pry about what you used to be before The Purge. If someone wants to tell, they'll tell. I know what Edna used to be. She was a doctor."

Medical student, actually, Keo thought, not that it was Lara's fault she never finished medical school. It was hard to get the credits necessary to graduate after The Purge. Keo didn't think it was worth the time to correct Yuli, though, so he didn't.

"But we don't know anything about you," Yuli continued.

They jogged up the curving road in silence for a moment, the only sounds the *tap-tap-tap* of their boots on the hard pavement, along with Yuli's increasingly labored and loud breathing. Soon, Keo was going to have to ease up, because Yuli seemed determined to stay with him even if it killed him rather than admit he needed some rest.

Maybe Yuli was expecting Keo to reciprocate by revealing his own past, and when Keo didn't, the younger man said, "So. What did you use to do before all of this?"

"This, that, everything in between," Keo said.

Again, Yuli waited for Keo to continue, and when he

didn't, the Mexican said, "Are you fucking with me right now?"

Keo grinned. "Just a little bit."

"Okay, fine. You'll tell me when you feel like it, I guess."

Don't hold your breath, Keo thought, but he said, "By the way, my real name's Keo."

"Keo?" Yuli said.

"Yeah."

"You mean, your name isn't Bob?"

The way Yuli had posed the question made Keo think the young man actually *did* believe his name was Bob. Keo found that a little difficult to swallow. He was pretty sure everyone, but especially George and Ophelia, knew that his name wasn't Bob and Lara's wasn't Edna. They couldn't look *less* like a Bob and an Edna.

At least, that was what Keo always thought. Maybe he was wrong?

"No," Keo said. "It's Keo."

"Oh," Yuli said. Then, a few seconds later, "So what kind of name is Keo, anyway?"

"Everything else was taken," Keo said.

FOUR

They hadn't gone more than an hour, with over five kilometers left, before they could bypass the woods that had sprung up to both sides of them, when Keo sniffed it.

Smoke.

But it wasn't coming from the burning village behind him. No, the smell tickling at his nostrils was originating from in front. Burning kindling and cooking venison. Someone had made camp.

Keo grabbed Yuli by the elbow and nodded, leading the younger man off the road and into the tree line. Yuli, smartly, stayed quiet until they were inside the woods and out of the open before speaking.

"You see something?" he finally asked.

"No, but I smell something," Keo said.

Yuli raised both eyebrows. Apparently, he hadn't smelled anything. "You sure?"

"Yeah," Keo said. He pushed against a tree and leaned out, looking northwest up the road, searching for—

There. Small wisps of smoke appearing out from the tallest trees about a hundred meters up ahead. Inside the woods, not out in the open. Keo stared for a moment, replaying all the times he'd been out here with Ben and the others.

"I see it," Yuli said, leaning out from behind his own tree next to Keo's. "I don't smell anything, though. You must have a really good sense of smell."

Either that, or you have a really bad sense of smell, kid.

He said, "It's the camping ground. The same one we've used during the hunts."

"I don't see anyone," Yuli said. He was leaning closer to the tree line, trying to get a better look up the road. The wagon tracks, along with the unshod horse hooves, continued on ahead of them. "You think it might be them?"

"Could be anyone. Them, or someone passing through."

"That would be a hell of a coincidence if it's someone else."

"That's why they call it coincidence, kid."

"Huh?"

"Exactly," Keo said. He pushed off his tree and started forward, sticking to the woods. "Come on. Watch your step, and don't make any unnecessary sounds."

Keo unslung the Brugger & Thomet MP9 and flicked the fire selector to semiauto. The submachine gun was lightweight and designed for close-quarter combat. It was also equipped with a suppressor that would allow him to take action with minimal noise. Keo had yet to find a gun, even the superbly built MP5SD, that was completely silent. If he needed to do some long-range shooting, the red dot scope on top would help. Of course, the MP9 wasn't meant for that kind of work; that was what the much-heavier AR Keo had brought along was for.

Yuli followed closely behind him, making a little too much noise for Keo's liking. It could have just been Keo's imagination, but it seemed like the Mexican was going out of his way to step on every dry leaf and branch in the woods. Keo could have sworn he had told the younger man to watch his step.

"Watch your step" must mean something else in Mexico.

"What if it's them?" Yuli asked. He had dropped his voice to almost a whisper, so at least he was doing that right.

"Then we'll do what we have to," Keo said.

"Which is what?"

"Get the women back."

They walked silently for a moment—or, at least, Keo did. Yuli was still snapping too many twigs and, at one point, might have detoured slightly just so he could struggle through a thick bush. That's what it sounded like to Keo anyway, who grimaced every time he heard another unnatural *pop* or *crack* or *snap*.

"I mean, what will we do to get the women back?" Yuli asked.

The answer was obvious to Keo, but apparently it wasn't to the younger man.

He asked, "Why did you bring that rifle, Yuli?"

"Because I might need it," Yuli said.

"That's your answer."

"Oh," Yuli said.

They walked the rest of the way in silence, with Keo keeping both eyes open for signs of people in front of them. Even Yuli had begun to watch his steps a little bit more. He was still making noise (*Dammit, he's still making way too much noise*), but it wasn't quite as loud as before. The point was that the kid was trying, if not entirely succeeding.

The aroma of burning venison became more obvious the farther they treaded through the heavy woods. Keo stopped a couple of times, thinking he'd heard voices, but there were never any to be found. Fortunately, Yuli was smart enough to know what Keo was doing and never asked unnecessary questions during those moments of dead silence.

They continued on, Keo with the MP9 in front of him, his forefinger in the trigger guard. It occurred to him that it'd been a while since he'd actually used the weapon. The submachine gun previously belonged to the last man Keo had killed. That was more than six months ago, though it seemed like a lifetime now.

Time flies when you're living the good life.

And that was exactly what he'd been doing with Lara at the village. It really was a fine existence, even if the first couple of weeks had been filled with nervous energy as they both kept waiting for something to show up and ruin things. Whenever a stranger appeared on the road or along the beach, or even a strange craft showed up in the waters nearby, Keo kept thinking about the MP9 resting in the gun rack at the back of their closet.

The Brugger & Thomet had an additional pistol grip underneath the barrel. and Keo clutched it with the fingers of his left hand now. He was reasonably certain he could use the weapon with some proficiency, even though he'd never really practiced with it.

A gun was a gun, was a gun.

Voices, finally, drifting between the trees in front of them. Keo quickly went down on one knee. Yuli did likewise behind and slightly to the right of him. Or, at least, Keo assumed the young man did; he never actually glanced back to confirm, but he did hear Yuli shuffling around back there, then going quiet.

Two voices talking, but they were still too far for Keo to make out words. He remained where he was, breathing calmly, and spent the next few seconds regulating his heartbeat, which was going noticeably faster than usual. It had been a while since he'd had to do this.

Six months, pal. You got over six months with Lara. That's more than you could have asked for.

He finally glanced back at Yuli, crouched behind him. "Stay here," Keo said, not quite whispering.

Yuli gave him a questioning look.

"And watch your fire," Keo added before the Mexican could respond.

Then he was on his feet and moving forward again.

He didn't look back to make sure Yuli had followed his orders. He couldn't hear any movements back there—and he would have if Yuli had gotten up. Keo hoped the former journalism student stayed back there. The last thing he needed right now was to keep one eye out for a civilian during a firefight with what might be twelve guys, even though he didn't think there were twelve guys (*Or more*) in front of him right now. It sounded like two. Three, max.

Shit. I hope it's two or three.

The voices got louder as he neared, but he still had difficulty making out what they were saying. The conversation was casual, friendly. No one was raising their voice for his benefit.

"—done?" one of them was saying.

Keo stopped and went into a crouch again, this time behind a large bush. Two massive trees squatted in front of him like sentries, but Keo had a good angle with which to see into the campground.

It was really just a circular clearing where he, Ben, and the others had spent time over the months after a hunt. They'd used the area to skin their kills and cook them before returning to the village with the rest of the meat. There had been warm beer and someone—maybe Daniel—had sneaked a half-full bottle of Japanese sake with them one time. To this day, Keo didn't know where the rice wine had come from, but he remembered they'd tossed it into the woods before heading back.

The campground was about fifty meters from the road, with enough trees and greens in-between that you couldn't spot the asphalt from in here and vice versa. There was a makeshift fire pit in the center of the clearing, which was where the smell of cooking venison was coming from. Three figures sat on logs placed strategically around the fire while a spotted fawn, its head still attached, turned over on a spit.

As Keo watched, one of the three stood up and applied what might have been homemade sauce from a jar onto the animal's burning skin. "Almost," the man with the brush said. He finished up, then sat back down and put the jar away in a well-worn backpack.

Keo watched them closely, trying to decide if these were three of the people he was looking for. He observed them in silence, listening to them talking and passing around canteens and small bags of dry meat. He also paid attention to the way the two men treated the lone woman among them. A couple of rifles leaned against the logs next to the men, but none of the three were wearing sidearms. At least four backpacks lay on the ground nearby, along with a half-made tent. A second tent had yet to be erected. That meant the woman was coupled up with one of the men.

He replayed back everything Ophelia had told him about the ones that had taken Lara and Marie, and it didn't match what he was seeing here.

Goddammit, it's not them.

Which left him with...what? Not much, but he was sure the abductors were still on the road and would have passed this trio earlier. How much did they see? How much could they tell him? Right now, he could use all the intelligence he could get.

"Hello!" Keo called out.

One of the two men grabbed his rifle—a camouflaged AR—and stood up, turning to face Keo—or at least the two trees in front of him and the bush he was crouched behind. The second one was slower to react, but he also reached for his rifle —a bolt-action with a big scope on top—and also looked around. Unlike the first man, who was much older—late forties, with a large beard dotted with gray streaks—this one didn't know where to look but quickly joined his friend in staring toward Keo's direction.

The woman also stood up, but she was unarmed and moved behind the younger man for protection. Keo guessed he knew who the couple was now.

"Who's out there?" the older one shouted.

"Friendly," Keo shouted back.

"We'll see about that!"

Keo held up his hands, one holding the submachine gun high in the air so it could be seen. "Don't shoot!"

"Come on out so we can see you!" the older man shouted.

Keo did, standing up slowly. "I'm not alone. Got a friend somewhere behind me, waiting for the all-clear."

"He should come out, too," the man said.

Keo turned his head slightly and shouted, "Yuli! Come on out! Keep your rifle over your head when you do!"

It took a while—about thirty seconds longer than Keo would have liked—but Yuli finally appeared holding his bolt-action over his head.

Keo turned back to the campers. "Can we come in?"

The older man lowered his rifle, then looked back at the young one and the woman, and gave them a nod. The couple relaxed.

"Come in, if you want," the older one said.

Keo stepped around the bush with Yuli and walked into the campground. He glanced around him just to make sure there was no one else hiding out there.

"It's not them?" Yuli asked.

"No," Keo said.

"Then why are we wasting our time?"

"They might have seen something."

The three campers hadn't sat back down; instead, they watched Keo and Yuli approach with caution. The older one was as grizzled up close as he'd looked to Keo from afar, with a big scar under his chin to rival Keo's own. The two young people were in their mid-twenties, the man even younger than Keo had thought when he'd first seen them. The girl was blonde and pretty, but she only came out from behind the man when the older one gave the *Okay* nod.

Keo extended a hand toward the one with the AR. "I'm Keo. This is Yuli."

"Roger," the man said, shaking their hands. "This is Clark, and that's his wife, Bella."

Clark, the younger man, gave them a *hey* nod.

"Take a load off," Roger said.

The three sat back down. Keo and Yuli shared one of the logs while Roger moved over to join Clark and Bella on the other one.

"What were you guys doing sneaking around out there?" Roger asked.

"We weren't sneaking around," Yuli said.

Well, technically we were, Keo thought, but he said, "We're from the village near the shoreline farther south."

"There's a village nearby?" Bella asked.

"You didn't know?"

"No."

"I guess you were right," Clark said to Roger.

Off Keo's questioning look, Roger said, "I told them I might have smelled some smoke from the south—near the ocean. We were going to check on it after we ate." He looked from Keo to Yuli, then back again. Or, more precisely, the submachine gun Keo had slung in front of him. "Something happened back there? You guys look pretty heavily armed to be hunting deer."

"We're looking for someone," Keo said. "A group of some-ones, actually. They might have passed you by on the road. Twelve men or so on horseback, pulling two wagons with them."

Roger exchanged a look with Clark.

"You saw them," Yuli said.

The older Roger nodded. "They were heading up the road when we were coming down. We rushed inside the woods to avoid them. If we hadn't, we wouldn't have stumbled across this area. This place yours, too?"

"We've used it before," Keo said. He didn't bother telling them that he, Ben, and the others had put the fire pit together and even cut down the trees they were sitting on now. He said instead, "What made you avoid them? The others on the road?"

"We usually avoid people on the road when we can," Clark said. "It's better that way. And these guys..."

"What did you see, exactly?"

"Like you said, about a dozen guys or so, with two wagons," Roger said. "They were even heavier armed than you two. MOLLEs, packs, and I think one of them had a 249 SAW, but I could be wrong. Definitely a squad weapon of some type, though."

Keo smiled. He'd thought Roger looked like a former grunt, and hearing him talk proved it. "You ex-army?"

"Yeah," Roger said. "What gave it away?"

"Your vocabulary."

"Hunh."

"Sounds like you got a pretty good look."

Roger reached into his pack, which was sitting nearby, and took out a pair of binoculars. "They didn't see me, but I got a good enough look at them through these to know there was no point in introducing ourselves."

"We've had bad experiences with people on the roads," Clark said.

You and me and the whole wide world, kid, Keo thought.

"They kidnapped two women from our village," Yuli said to the trio. "Did you see them, too?"

Bella looked over at Clark, and the young man put a hand on her arm and squeezed.

"Didn't see them," Roger said. "But the wagons they were pulling were covered."

"Covered how?" Keo asked.

"You said they were wagons, but they looked more like utility trailers to me, the kind you used to be able to rent to move things. They'd put some kind of tarp over them, as far as I can tell, probably to keep out the weather and protect whatever's back there."

Like someone who needs a doctor. That's why they're going to stick to the roads as much as possible.

He said out loud, "Did you get a look at what was inside those wagons?"

"Sorry," Roger said, shaking his head. "After I spotted all the hardware they were carrying, we hightailed it in here and let them pass by. That was"—he glanced down at his watch —"almost three hours ago."

Three hours. Shit. He had assumed a two-hour lead, but three?

Keo stood up. "They continued northwest up the road?"

"Last time we saw them," Roger said.

"Who were they?" Clark asked.

"I don't know," Keo said. Then, back at Roger, "You saw what they looked like. What else can you tell me about them?"

"Besides the hardware?" Roger said. "They were wearing dark clothes underneath their vests. They looked paramilitary, but I didn't wait for them to get closer before I skedaddled."

"Did you happen to get a head count?"

"No, but twelve sounds about right."

"All on horseback?"

"As far as I could tell, yeah."

"Okay," Keo said. He turned to Yuli. "Come on. They have three hours on us."

Keo and Yuli started off, but they hadn't gotten to the edge of the clearing when Roger called after them, "Hey."

Keo stopped and looked back at the grizzled vet.

"One more thing," Roger said.

"What's that?" Keo said.

"Whoever they were, they looked like bad news, like they'd been through the shit. You know what I mean?"

Keo nodded. "Yeah."

"Good luck."

"Thanks."

He and Yuli turned and started walking again before quickly picking up their pace back toward the road.

Twelve men or so. Heavily armed. Hard-looking enough to spook even a vet like Roger.

Keo wasn't sure how he was feeling about all the new information, but he did know one thing: They were going to stay on the road. He had been sure about that before, and he was dead certain of it now.

And that, thank God, was going to make it easier to track them down.

"You think they had Marie and Edna in the back of one of those trailers?" Yuli was asking him.

"I don't know," Keo said. "Probably. It would be too much of a hassle to make them walk. It would just slow them down."

"That makes sense," Yuli said. Then, "What did Roger mean back there?"

"Which part?"

"When he said those guys we're chasing looked like they'd been 'through the shit.' What's that mean?"

"He means they looked dangerous, that we're not chasing after a bunch of former CPAs that picked up a gun one day and decided to call themselves bad boys. It means that when you get one of them in your sights, you pull the trigger without hesitation. You understand?"

Yuli didn't answer him.

Keo stopped and turned, grabbing Yuli by the arm. The younger man looked alarmed—or maybe he was just surprised by how fast Keo had moved and how aggressive his grip was.

Keo glared at him. "Do you *understand* me, Yuli?"

Yuli nodded. "Yes."

"Are you sure?"

"Yes."

"Are you *sure*."

Yuli didn't answer the third time quite as readily.

Eventually, the younger man nodded and said, "Yes. I understand you, Bob. I mean, Keo." He gave Keo a nervous smile. "I'm not sure I'm ever going to get used to not calling you Bob."

Keo let go of Yuli's arm and gave him what he hoped was a reassuring pat on the shoulder. "You can keep calling me Bob, if you want. I've always been happier as Bob than I ever was as Keo anyway."

He turned and jogged off, and Yuli ran after him.

Three hours' head start, Keo thought even as he picked up his pace. *Three friggin' hours. Swell.*

FIVE

"This might not work."

"It'll work."

"But it might not."

"It'll work."

"Why are you so sure?"

"Because you want this. And because you want it, I want it, too. So I'll make it work."

She had smiled at him. *"You're too good to me."*

"And don't you forget it," he had replied.

That back and forth had occurred during their first night at the no-name village, sleeping in George and Ophelia's living room because they didn't have their own house yet. The building they would eventually call home was then under construction but was supposed to be another storage area. When Keo and Lara showed up, the others had decided to make it theirs. They had done it voluntarily, after only a brief meeting, and Keo had been surprised by how well they were being treated. Lara, too, prompting the conversation. He had meant it when he told her he'd make it work.

And it had worked...for a while.

"Hey, hey, slow down. Can we slow down for a moment?" Yuli was saying from somewhere behind him.

Keo downshifted to allow the younger man to catch up. Yuli had looked to be in pretty decent shape, but maybe Keo had overestimated him. Either that, or Keo had really picked up his pace and hadn't realized it. He was still breathing normally, so he couldn't have been going that much faster.

"You okay?" Keo asked.

"Let me catch my breath for a second. Just a second," Yuli said. They stopped to allow him to do just that. "I haven't had to run this much since... Ever."

"You went out with us to hunt."

"Yeah, but I never had to run like this." Yuli squinted at Keo from behind some sweat. "You used to do marathons or something?"

"No."

Keo took the opportunity to scan the area around them. They had left the woods—along with Roger and the others— behind. There was now nothing but open Texas asphalt in front of them and brown grass melting underneath the harsh sun to their left and right. The temperature had increased the more distance they put between them and the ocean, and Keo was already drenched in his own sweat, his clothes clinging to his skin even more now. He swiped at the layer of perspiration on his face with the back of his sleeve.

He had been out this far a few times in the last six months, mostly to search the nearby towns. He knew for a fact there were two such places up ahead. The closest was called Ryder, and the one after that was Silver Hills. Neither place had been occupied for years, and there hadn't been much to find that was useful, though they'd always returned with clothing, bedding, and various miscellaneous things to spread among the villagers.

"I've never been out this far before," Yuli was saying.

Keo looked back at him. The younger man was still bent over at the waist, sheets of sweat dripping to the hot road at his feet.

"Never?" Keo asked.

Yuli shook his head. "You have, though."

"A few times, to look for supplies."

"You mean 'useless junk?'" Yuli said with a grin.

"One man's junk is another man's treasure," Keo said. He glanced up the road for a bit before turning his gaze to Yuli. "You ready?"

"I guess so." He straightened up, hands still on his hips. "How can you keep running for so long with all that stuff and not get tired?"

Because someone I love is out there, and the people who took her have a three-hour head start on me.

He said, "Let's go," and began jogging up the road again.

Yuli followed. Or Keo assumed he was back there some where. Keo was starting to think the Mexican was going to be more of a burden than help. He would have liked the extra gun Yuli had the potential to provide, but the more he thought about it, the more he was beginning to doubt even that. Yuli may have a rifle, and he might know how to use it, but if he couldn't pull the trigger when Keo needed him to...

He glanced back at the younger man.

Yuli gave him a forced smile, as if to say, *Yeah, I'm still here,* but Keo didn't fully believe him.

"Keep up," Keo said.

"I will," Yuli said, pursing his lips to show his determination. "I'm not going anywhere. They took my woman too, remember?"

"Less talk, more running."

And they did.

———

Two hours since they left the burning village.

An hour since they met Roger and his two companions.

And there was still no visible confirmation of Lara's abductors, who had a three-hour head start on them, and were moving on horsepower. That was the real problem. Horses got tired, but not nearly as quickly as men.

Gotta pick up more speed.

Gotta pick up more speed somehow.

Keo unslung the AR rifle and tossed it to the side. It landed in the grass, where each and every blade was bent over halfway against the heat radiating down from the harsh sun. The weapon didn't completely disappear into the thicket, but if you didn't know it was there, you would probably walk right past it.

"What are you doing?" Yuli asked from somewhere behind him.

"Lightening my load," Keo said, swiveling the bag from behind to in front of him.

He took out the spare magazines for the AR and tossed them into the grass, too. The lack of a rifle saved him approximately eight pounds, six and a half-ish for the AR itself, and an extra pound for the full thirty rounds in the magazine. After ditching two more spares, he now had ten less pounds to hump. He had to be satisfied with the MP9 and the Glock at his hip. He considered ridding himself of one of the Glock's spares and leaving just one but decided against it. The same for the submachine gun's two magazines.

There were also the MREs and two bottles of water. He'd stuffed as many into the bag as he could back at the house. Keo quickly dismissed the thought of getting rid of them, too. You could survive without bullets, but not without water or food. He could hunt for both, yes, but that would take time that he didn't have.

"I should keep my rifle, right?" Yuli asked.

"Probably," Keo said.

He slowed down just enough for the younger man to catch up. Yuli was straining, his tanned face beet red from the heat and near exhaustion. The bolt-action was slung over his back, and he had the thumb of his right hand hooked around the strap to keep it tight against his body so it didn't bounce around back there. He had his left hand around one of the backpack's straps to do the same to it.

Keo took the opportunity to pull out one of the bottles of water and take a sip, just enough to quench his thirst. "What's in that thing?" he asked, nodding at Yuli's backpack.

"Some food, water, and ammo for the rifle," Yuli said.

"How much ammo?"

"A box full."

"The pack looks heavy."

"Not as heavy as the rifle." Taking his cue from Keo, Yuli pulled out a canteen from his pack and took a sip.

"Keep up," Keo said, and ran off.

"I'll keep up, don't worry about me," Yuli said.

We'll see about that, Keo thought, but didn't say out loud.

They ran for another hour, with some rests in-between for Yuli's benefit. Keo's legs were sore, and his back was starting to ache from carrying the duffel bag, but the idea of letting up didn't even register in his mind. For over six months, he'd done nothing but fish and hunt and eat a steady diet of what he caught or killed on land and in the water. When he wasn't doing those things, he was swimming in the Gulf of Mexico, revisiting his love for the water. It didn't hurt that he hadn't been shot or stabbed or punched in all that time and was able to allow his body to heal from the times when he had been shot, stabbed, and punched. He might not have been in the best shape of his life—he was older, for one, and you could never beat Father Time—but it was pretty damn close.

The same, unfortunately, couldn't be said for Yuli. The younger man kept sweating more and more and eventually began to lag behind Keo again. Keo had to stop a couple of times just for Yuli's sake, and each time Keo weighed the pros and cons of leaving him behind. Was Yuli's rifle really worth all the seconds and minutes he was losing to Lara's captors? Yuli, to his credit, never complained and never asked for a break. Keo always took the initiative for the young man's sake.

They'd been running for hours, but it felt like much longer. The road never seemed to end and neither did the swath of sun-burnt grass around them. The sky was inconveniently cloudless, giving them zero protection against the rough sun. Keo's clothes were drenched, and he was leaving boot prints in the form of puddles of sweat on the hot asphalt. Of course, those same prints quickly vaporized minutes later against the unrelenting heat—

Keo stopped, and Yuli almost bumped into him.

"What is it?" Yuli said, alarmed.

Keo didn't answer him. He was too busy staring at the road —or more precisely, at the cluster of dirt left behind by what looked like three or four unshod hooves. He couldn't tell the exact number because the prints overlapped, but he could tell they had stopped here and gathered around briefly for some reason.

"Keo?" Yuli said.

Keo looked over at the field of green to their right. Silver Hills was somewhere out there, connected to the highway they were standing on now by a spur road that would become visible farther up ahead. They had passed Ryder a while back but hadn't detoured to check it because the horses and trailer wheels they'd been following hadn't, either.

But that had just changed. Some of the captors had left the main group and crossed through the field, while the others—including the two trailers—continued up the road. Keo could tell the direction the split-off riders had gone by the trampled grass, still fresh under the scorching sun.

"What is it?" Yuli asked. He took the opportunity to grab his canteen out of his pack and took a drink.

"They split up," Keo said. "Trailers kept going, but some of the riders left the group."

"Why did they split up?"

"I don't know."

Yuli glanced up at the endless gray asphalt ahead of them.

"You still think Marie and Edna's in one of those trailers Roger saw?"

"Yes," Keo said.

"What if they took them out? Maybe they're on one of the horses that split from the main group?"

"Maybe."

What Yuli said was a possibility, but Keo thought it was unlikely. Whoever they were, Lara's abductors wouldn't give the women horses now—either their own mounts or force them to ride double with someone else. That was more trouble than it was worth. The women were easier to control if they were kept in one of the trailers.

"But you don't think so," Yuli said when Keo didn't add anything.

"No."

"So we should keep going." He put his canteen away and wiped at the sweat dripping down his face. "Right?"

"No," Keo said.

"Why not?"

He nodded at the horse tracks that had cut through the field. "We'll follow them."

"But you said Marie and Edna are still on the road with the trailers."

"And we're never going to catch up to them. Not on foot. But the ones that split up? They have something we want."

"Guns?"

"Horses."

"That was my second guess."

"Come on," Keo said, and jogged off the road and into the field.

It was easy to follow the riders—all he had to do was keep

the trampled grass in sight. There was no reason for Lara's abductors to cover their tracks. They hadn't done it when they had left the village, and they had no reason to start now. Besides, after what Ophelia had told him (*"I'm sorry, Bob. We couldn't do anything. They had guns."*), Keo didn't think the assholes had any fears of reprisal.

Yuli trailed behind, but he was still back there. Keo didn't have to glance back to confirm; all he had to do was listen to the Mexican's haggard breathing. There wasn't much in front of them except for some hills in the distance. As for the town of Silver Hills, it was farther up the road and to their left—maybe another kilometer or two—

The *crack!* of a gunshot.

Keo stopped on a dime and went down on one knee.

Yuli, running behind and slightly to his right, ran right past him, realized what had happened, and jumped face-first into the grass.

Damn, that's gotta hurt, Keo thought as Yuli groaned and slowly raised himself up from the ground, when there was a second *crack!*

Yuli disappeared back into the grass. Keo didn't bother to seek cover, because he had already judged that both shots had come from the other side of the two looming mounds in front of them. They weren't the targets; someone else was.

Yuli picked himself up again, but this time remained on his hands and knees as he crawled backward until he was along-side Keo.

"Who's shooting at us?" Yuli asked.

"No one," Keo said. "They're coming from the other side of those hills."

Yuli glanced forward, then slowly picked himself up until

he was kneeling. He swiped at clumps of dirt clinging to his shirt's front. "Jesus, I thought someone was shooting at us."

"You'll be fine," Keo said, and got up and continued jogging toward the hills, even as he heard the *pop-pop-pop-pop* of more gunfire ringing out.

Four shots, one after another. The first two had been single shots fired from a high-powered rifle. Probably a bolt-action similar to the one Yuli was carrying. These new bursts were coming from a semi-automatic. Possibly an AR like the one Keo had ditched.

He didn't slow down when he picked up Yuli's labored breathing finally catching up to him. It took five minutes of constant running to get from where they'd first heard the shots to when they finally reached the base of one of the hills. The incline wasn't steep enough that Keo needed to sling the MP9 and use his hands to climb; he was able to go up at a diagonal angle with the summit quickly arriving in front of him. He slid to the ground to lower his profile when he was finally at the top.

After the first two rifle shots and the returning fire, there'd been no more shooting. Either whatever had happened had run its course or the shooters were taking their time, looking for better shots.

Either/or was good for Keo. He just wanted a horse right now, and any horse would do. Once he got his hands on that, he'd be able to cut into the three-hour lead Lara's abductors had on him.

Yuli was out of breath when he dropped to his knees next to Keo. They were both dripping with sweat, and Keo swore the sun was harsher up here. The mound was tall enough for him to easily view the valley spread out on the other side, flanked by a wall of trees on his right and the rooftops of Silver Hills on his left. The town was much closer than he had guessed earlier. Of course, being this high up had greatly increased his perspective, so maybe it wasn't that close—

Sudden movement from the field below and in front of him, as a big brown horse appeared out of the carpet of grass.

Where did that come from?

Keo hadn't seen the animal when he scanned the area seconds ago. He didn't even know horses could hide that well, but apparently this one could. And it wasn't alone. There was a man clinging to the saddle, one hand gripping the reins while the other clutched to the horn. Horse and rider had, literally, just popped up out of the grass.

The horse was a big brown chestnut, and it let out a furious whinny as it found its footing and took off, heading left in the direction of Silver Hills. Keo couldn't make out the rider's face from his position, but he had noticed how smoothly the man was holding on while riding as low as possible, clearly hoping to avoid being picked off. The rider was wearing some kind of tactical vest, and a rifle was slapping against his back.

"They were even heavier armed than you two," Roger had said. *"MOLLEs, packs, and I think one of them even had a 249 SAW, but I could be wrong. Definitely a squad weapon of some type, though."*

The horse was fast, and the rider clearly knew what he was doing. If there was a shooter out there—and there had to be, otherwise there would be no reason for the man to be hiding in the grass until now—the sudden reappearance had caught them by surprise, too, because no one had fired a shot yet.

Three seconds since the man popped up.

Four seconds...

"Where do you think he's going?" Yuli asked as they watch the chestnut streaking across the base of the hill below them.

"No idea," Keo said. "I don't think he knows, either. Probably just trying to get out of here before—"

The *crack!* of a rifle shot echoed.

Or not, Keo thought, as the rider looked like he was about to fall off the saddle but somehow managed to hold on anyway. But he was now leaning more heavily along the side, so the shot hadn't missed completely.

Keo waited to hear the finishing shot, but it didn't come. The shooter would have seen that he'd hit his target, even if the man continued to cling on for dear life. There was only one shot left for the sniper: the horse. All he'd have to do was drop the animal to stop the escape. As fast as the chestnut was moving, it was a big target. Much bigger than the man.

Except there wasn't another shot, and the rider slowly got smaller as he got farther away. Keo watched the man the entire time, waiting for him to fall out of the saddle, but he never did, despite the fact Keo was sure he'd been shot.

Dammit. I need that horse!

The horse and its wounded rider continued to fade as they headed toward Silver Hills in the distance.

Keo started to get up when Yuli reached over and grabbed his arm. "What are you doing?"

"I need that horse," Keo said, and jerked his hand free.

"Wait—" Yuli said but never finished, before another *crack!* rang out and the ground in front of Keo exploded in a burst of brown cloud.

Keo jumped back down on his stomach and chest, eating a mouthful of dirt at the same time.

A mouthful of dirt's better than a bullet in the head, pal!

Another *crack!* and another puff of dust appeared in the air, this time about five feet on the other side of the sloping hill.

Missed again, sucker!

But even as he thought that, Keo scrambled backward as fast as he could. Yuli did the same next to him, until they were both back safely on the other side. A bullet could go through a lot of things, but a mound of earth wasn't one of them.

"*Now* they're shooting at us, right?" Yuli asked.

"That's a good guess," Keo said.

The Mexican had unslung his rifle and was slowly lifting his head to get a look over the hill. Keo grabbed him by the collar of his shirt and pulled him back.

"Stay down," Keo said.

"I can't see him," Yuli said.

"Good. That means he can't see us, either."

"Why's he shooting at us?"

"Probably because he doesn't know we're not friends of the guy he's trying to kill. Perfectly logical."

"It is?"

"I'd do the same in his shoes."

Keo sat up and spat out some dirt.

"You okay?" Yuli asked.

"Never been better," Keo said, and wiped dirt clinging to his palms on the slanted hill he was sitting on.

"So what are we going to do now?"

"I need that horse."

"The one that got away?"

"Yeah."

"How are we going to get it?"

"The rider's making a beeline for Silver Hills," Keo said as he got up. "He's wounded. He won't get far."

Keo began skipping down the slope.

"Wait for me!" Yuli shouted from behind him.

Keo reached the bottom and turned right and began running alongside the base of the hill. Yuli caught up to him a moment later.

"Keep up," Keo said.

"I'm keeping up, I'm keeping up," Yuli said.

As they ran, Keo thought about what he was going to do with Yuli once they found the horse. Sure, they could ride double, but that would slow the animal down. Keo couldn't afford that. He needed speed on his side. He needed a lot of speed.

But he kept that to himself...for now.

SIX

Silver Hills was at least four times the size of Ryder, which was one reason Keo and the others had spent more time inside it. The place was spread out, with the bulk of the commercial properties concentrated in the very center. The residential areas were on the north side, with Keo and Yuli entering from the south.

They had lost track of the horse as soon as the animal left the grassy field behind and started moving across concrete. Fortunately, while the animal's trail died, its rider's didn't. All Keo had to do was follow the small drops of blood as they wound their way through back alleys and sidewalks and across city streets.

Like Ryder and every other city near the Texas-Mexico border, Silver Hills was a ghost town and had been since The Purge. The buildings were empty, and nothing worked. Anything worth taking had either rotted away or been taken. The bleached-white bones of dead ghouls showed up every now and then, but they were rare, and the ones that could still be found almost two years after The Walk Out had been thoroughly worked over by animals.

The place hadn't changed very much since the last time Keo was here, about two months ago. Small towns like this weren't supposed to change after The Purge; they were more like museums now, frozen in time—reminding passersby of what used to be. The big cities, on the other hand, were another story.

The only sounds Keo could pick up were the wind howling through the alleyways; not that the occasional breeze coming in from the fields beyond the city limits did anything to lessen the heat threatening to drown him with every step he took. Yuli wasn't doing any better, but at least they had some shade now, thanks to the abundant rooftops around them. Walking was also a lot better than running, and Keo's legs, already sore from all the jogging he'd done up to this point, were jelly. He kept waiting for the aches to numb over, but it hadn't gotten there yet.

Any minute now...

So they followed the small drips of blood from the edge of the city all the way to its center. The horse and its rider had weaved through shops and apartments and warehouses without stopping. Keo knew they hadn't stopped, because the drops of blood never widened into a puddle, which would have happened if they'd paused to let the man bleed at the same spot for any length of time.

Was the rider afraid the sniper would follow him into Silver Hills to finish the job? It was possible. Keo had only spotted one man escaping the valley—so where was the other one? Or other two? He knew for a fact that more than one horse had left the road and cut across the field earlier.

So where were the rest?

"Where do you think he's going?" Yuli asked after a while. Keo was surprised it had taken the young Mexican this long to finally give voice to what must have been going through his head for some time now.

"I don't know," Keo said. "There's nothing up there but abandoned businesses. Empty stores and apartments, and not much else."

"What's on the other side?"

"Silver Hills's residential area." Keo stopped and pointed at a big, bulbous object in the distance. "That's the water tower."

"You think he's headed there? I don't mean the water tower. I mean the homes?"

Keo shook his head. "I don't know. He might be dead, for all we know."

"You think he's dead?"

I thought that was what "for all we know" meant? Keo thought but said, "I dunno. We'll find out soon enough."

The drops of blood became rarer as they traced them past storefronts that stood still, though time would tell for how much longer. The brick-and-mortar structures would last for a while, but the ones with metal would eventually rust under the southern Texas rain. And with no one to fix leaking rooftops, the interiors would become—

Keo stopped, and Yuli bumped into him from behind.

"What is it?" Yuli said. He had unslung his rifle and was gripping it in front of him, ready for action.

Keo looked toward the mouth of the alley they had been

walking through. Sunlight glinted off the harsh concrete in the street beyond, and trash fluttered across the opening. The sidewalk on the other side was empty except for a bench and a garbage bin. A tree, long dried out and a shell of its former self, barely moved against a weak wind.

He could make out businesses, including a Mark's—some kind of meat market with murals of a man in a big apron painted on the tinted windows. The rest belonged to a phone store (cleverly called Cell it Here), a dress shop (Muriel's Shop, which wasn't so clever), and a two-story gray building with a sign that read Pick It (the best of the three names). The last one featured a large acoustic guitar and a pair of hands, cut off at the wrists, stringing it with a pick.

Keo glanced up at the second floor of the music store for a few seconds. Half of a window looked back at him, the visible part of the glass tinted black. He resisted the urge to move forward to get a better look at it, because the first thought that popped into his head when he saw it was:

Now, that's a perfect sniper's nest if I ever saw one.

Another step or two, and he would get an eyeful of the window—and vice versa.

And there was the blood. Or lack of. The droplets had disappeared completely halfway through the alley, which had prompted him to stop in the first place.

"Why did we stop?" Yuli asked.

"The blood," Keo said.

"It's gone," Yuli said.

"Yeah."

"What do you think happened?"

"I don't know."

"Maybe there's more out there," Yuli said, and walked past Keo toward the sidewalk.

Keo grab his arm and pulled him back. "Not yet."

Yuli let himself be yanked back. He waited for Keo to continue, and when he didn't, the young Mexican said, "What is it? What's wrong?"

Keo didn't answer him. He squinted at the bright sunlight just outside the alley opening. They had spent the entire morning running and were well into midday, with the sun at its peak. The heat, coupled with the light, gave Keo bad vibes. Or maybe it was just all the sweat dripping down his face and sticking his clothes to his skin like a second layer causing him to overreact.

He wiped his perspiration-covered hands on his pants legs before returning them to the MP9. Keo stayed where he was and hadn't moved any closer toward the exit. He could see parts of the sidewalk and buildings across the street just fine from here. To get a better look at what was around him—including the rest of that second-floor window—would require committing to exiting the alley.

"Keo?" Yuli said after a while. "Why are we just standing around? He could be getting away right now."

"I don't think he went anywhere," Keo said.

"How do you know that? He could have stopped the bleeding."

"Maybe." Keo shook his head. "But I think he knows someone's been following him, and he's waiting to get a shot at whoever that is."

"More guessing?"

"That's all I got."

And a hell of a bad vibe, he thought but didn't add.

"So, you could be wrong," Yuli said.

"Could, yeah," Keo said.

"The other possibility is that he's lying out there on the sidewalk. And if he is, what about the horse? It could be getting away right now."

Yuli made a good point. Keo really was just guessing here. Maybe he was being overly paranoid.

"I think we should find out," Yuli said.

Keo looked over at him. "It's your funeral."

"Mine—?" Yuli said. Then, understanding what Keo was trying to say, "Oh."

Yuli glanced over at the bright streets beyond the alley opening and squinted. The young man looked like he was trying to psych himself up. Keo wasn't sure if Yuli was waiting for him to talk him out of it or not. If he were hoping Keo would intervene, he would have been disappointed. Keo needed to know, too, and if it meant not having to risk his own hide...

Hey, he offered.

"Well?" Keo said.

Yuli gave him a forced grin. "Cover me, okay?"

"Sure thing, Yuli."

"Okay." He looked back toward the street but didn't move. Then, "Okay, okay."

"Okay," Keo said.

"Okay, okay," Yuli said again.

Those last two *Okays* were clearly for his own benefit. It seemed to work, because Yuli took one hesitant step, then another one, toward the opening.

After the third step, he moved with more confidence, until

he was leaning against the brick wall almost at the corner, and peeked out.

"I don't see—" Yuli started to say when the *pop!* of a gunshot rang out and a chunk of the brick in front of his face sprayed the alley.

Keo lunged forward and grabbed Yuli by the arm even as the man stumbled back, having dropped his rifle. The younger man was reaching for his face while howling in pain. He was also shouting something in Spanish, but Keo had no idea what.

You dumbass, Keo thought as he dragged Yuli forcefully farther back into the alley with him. The young man struggled against his grip, but Keo held on.

There was only the one gunshot, and it was still echoing across the dead city when Keo got Yuli to safety, depositing him on the filthy floor. Keo reached for his bag and the water inside it but thought better of it and unzipped Yuli's pack and took out the Mexican's canteen instead.

Hey, it was his stupid idea, so it might as well be his water, too.

The bullet had missed Yuli, but only by inches. The round had instead shattered the piece of brick he was leaning against, sending a shower of concrete mist directly into his face. His eyes were red when he opened them, his mouth forming a big O as he tried to stretch out every inch of skin to get rid of the sting. Keo tilted Yuli's head and poured water down on his face. He wasted just enough to clear out the layer of gray and saved the rest.

"Relax, relax," Keo said. "You have shit in your eyes, but that's it. The bullet missed. You hear me? The bullet missed."

Yuli blinked rapidly back at him, his mouth opening and

closing like a fish learning to breathe out of the water. "*Madre de dios,* that was close. That was too close."

Keo glanced back at the street, then got up and went over to retrieve Yuli's rifle. He brought it over to the former journalism student. Yuli took it almost reluctantly, still blinking his eyes wide to help with the stinging. Both his eyes were bloodshot, and Keo couldn't tell how much of the water dripping down his cheeks was from the canteen and how much were tears.

"You think that was him?" Yuli asked. "The rider?"

"Maybe," Keo said. "Only one way to find out."

"How?" Then, when Keo didn't answer, "Aw, man. Can you do it this time?"

Keo grinned. "I'm not going to do what you just did. I'm going to do something else."

"Like what?"

"Like run across the street."

"Are you being serious right now?"

"The fastest route to a target is a straight line."

"What's the safest?"

"That's going around the street, then outflanking him. Go into the back of that two-story building he just shot at you from."

"You know where he shot at me from? 'Cause I didn't see shit."

"It's the gray one. Second floor, above the guitar store."

"You saw him?"

"No, but it's the most obvious location. There are no windows on the first floor, just the door, and he wouldn't be behind that. Also, the round came at you from a high angle."

"Which means he was high up at the time," Yuli said.

Keo nodded. "My guess is the horse is inside that building with him."

"You really think so?"

"Horses are smart. And they've been hiding indoors since The Purge. Also, the rider kept himself on the saddle all the way here; he's not going to let that chestnut go now."

"What's a chestnut?"

"The horse. It's chestnut-colored."

"Oh." Yuli seemed to have gotten control of his facial tics and swiped at his face with his hands to clear out the lingering dust. "So how are we going to do this?"

"You sure you're ready?"

"As ready as I'm ever going to be. Like you said, we don't have a lot of time. Those assholes are getting farther and farther away with Marie and Edna as we speak."

"Lara," Keo said.

"Who's that?"

"Lara. Edna's real name. It's Lara."

"Wait. So she's not really Edna, either?"

Keo smiled. It still amazed him that Yuli thought his real name was Bob. George had known right away it was made-up, and so had Ben and the others. But, like Yuli had said, no one had been nosy enough to ask for the truth. He guessed, when all was said and done, everyone at the village was running from something, and they (rightfully) just assumed Keo and Lara were as well. In many ways, the village was a second chance for everyone.

"Her real name's Lara," Keo said. He stood up and looked toward the streets outside the alley before turning back to Yuli as the young Mexican struggled to get back up on his feet. "I need you to give me some covering fire."

"How?"

"You saw the window on the second floor of the gray building while you were leaning out there?"

"Barely..."

"How many were there? Two?"

Yuli nodded. "Yeah. I saw two."

"Okay. I need you to punch out the glass on the one the shooter is hiding behind. That will be the one on the left."

"How do you know that? I didn't see where the shot came from..."

"It's where I would be if I was waiting for someone to poke their head out of this alley."

"What if he moved over to the other one?"

"He's not going to. That left-side window is still the best perch for him."

Yuli nodded, though he didn't look entirely convinced.

"Don't shoot yet until you can confirm it's the right window," Keo said. "When you do, take out the glass."

"But he'll have to start shooting at you first for me to confirm," Yuli said.

"Yeah, I know."

The younger man blinked at Keo, his red eyes squinting painfully. "You don't look scared."

"Don't I?"

"Not even a little bit."

"Trust me, I'm scared. I'm just very good at hiding it."

Keo walked back toward the opening, with Yuli following closely behind. He didn't expose himself to the left-side window, but he leaned against the wall and looked past the streets and toward the phone store, then Pick It next door. There was no alleyway between the two buildings across the street, so Keo didn't have to worry about anyone popping out of there. The windows into Cell it Here were broken, and the interior, along with its counter and discarded phones, very visible against the bright sunlight. No one in there, either.

Of course, it wasn't Cell it Here that Keo was worried about. It was the second floor of Pick It. He had no doubts that the shooter was still up there, waiting for a second chance behind that first window. The man wouldn't abandon it to watch the first floor. Not with that perfect sniper's nest up there.

"Are you really going to do this?" Yuli asked.

Keo looked back at him. "I just need you to take a couple of shots at the window he's hiding behind."

"The left one."

"Probably. If you don't see him shoot, just shoot the left one anyway. Make sure you hit the glass panes. Give him some falling hardware to think about."

"Okay," Yuli said, and gripped his rifle tighter.

Keo stared at the young man for a moment. Yuli wasn't a killer. The Mexican had always done his part around the village like everyone else, and he was competent enough. You didn't have to be an expert at anything, really, to get by. Keo would know—the only expertise he had was killing people, and he hadn't had to do that once in all the time he was "retired."

"Okay, okay," Yuli said again, more to himself than Keo. "We can do this. We can do this."

"Yeah, we can," Keo said. He smiled, hoping that would reassure Yuli. "Don't expose yourself until I do. I should be halfway across the street by the time he sees me and almost on the other side when he takes his shot. That means you have to be looking out by the time I'm halfway across. And you know what that means, right?"

"I'll have to expose myself again."

"Uh huh."

Yuli nodded and pursed his lips. "Okay, okay..."

"Okay?"

"Okay, okay."

Keo smiled. "Okay, kid. Okay."

They moved closer to the sidewalk. Keo shrugged off his bag and dropped it, then also took out the Ka-Bar and laid it down. He removed everything else from him except for one spare magazine for the MP9 that he left in a pouch around his waist. He also kept the Glock in the hip holster and its fully loaded mag. You never knew when you'd need a backup piece. The MP9 was a good weapon, especially in close quarters, but you rarely went wrong with keeping a pistol around.

Just in case.

Keo glanced back at Yuli and found the other man looking expectantly back at him, sweat dripping down his face. Keo's own face was probably similarly wet, but he hadn't bothered to wipe it down in the last few minutes. What was the point? It'd just get covered again.

"You ready?" Keo asked.

"Yeah," Yuli said. "No. Yes. *Yes.*"

Keo grinned. "Which one is it?"

"Yes," Yuli said. Then, again, "Yes."

"All right, then. I'll take that as a yes."

Keo turned around and looked out at the street beyond the mouth of the alley. He still had two meters between him and the sidewalk. The walkway itself was forty-eight inches, give or take. The two-lane street after that was approximately three meters each, so six total for both lanes. All in all, just a shade under ten meters to get from one side of the street to the other.

It wasn't exactly a long-distance run, but it would be a very short one if he couldn't cross it before the shooter got a bead on him. If he had to put a number on it, Keo would peg his chances of success at seventy-thirty, as long as Yuli did his part. That, unfortunately, was a pretty big if, and would require Yuli to get over almost being shot in the face just a few minutes ago.

But it was doable.

It was very doable.

God, he hoped it was doable.

"Are you going soon?" Yuli asked.

"Hold your horses," Keo said. He opened one of his pouches and took out the spare magazine for the MP9 and thumbed loose the top round. "On my count."

"Count of what?" Yuli asked. "I mean, what are you counting down to?"

"Five."

"Five. Right. Got it."

You sure? Keo wanted to ask but didn't.

Instead, he slung the MP9 and pulled the straps tight against his body to keep it from moving around back there before pinching the bullet between two fingers on his left hand. He took one step, then another toward the mouth of the alley before leaning slightly forward, and with just enough force to get it into the street but not moving *too* fast or going *too* far beyond the shooter's peripheral vision, he let the bullet go with a swinging toss.

The round bounced once and ricocheted back into the air.

Then it landed a second time and skipped right back up, sunlight glinting off its brass casing.

On the third bounce, Keo sprinted out of the alley while a voice in the back of his mind shouted, *You're putting your life in the hands of a former journalism student. Do you know how crazy that is? That's just bonkers, pal! Pure bonkers!*

The single *pop!* of a gunshot, followed split seconds later by the *pop-pop-pop!* of someone taking full advantage of a semiautomatic rifle, filled the empty streets of Silver Hills.

SEVEN

Five meters...

You're going to die.

Ten...

You're so going to die.

Fifteen...

Here it comes!

The first shot he'd been waiting for finally came, striking the white divider line between the two lanes. The bullet dug an instant crater and flicked small chunks of concrete into the air, some of them pelting Keo's legs.

He sidestepped slightly to the left, hoping it would force the shooter to waste a precious half-second or two (or more, if he were *really* lucky) to adjust.

All the while, his mind shouted, *Don't stop! Don't stop! Go, go, go!*

And he didn't stop. Not even for a heartbeat. Aside from the brief sidestep, he pushed on forward.

Seventeen meters..

Eighteen...

The *crack!* from behind him (*Yuli! About damn time!*) echoed along with the sound of glass breaking in front of him.

Keo glanced up briefly, catching glimmers of sunlight dancing off sheets of falling windowpanes coming down from the left-side window on the second floor of the gray building. Yuli's shot had hit high. Keo couldn't make out a figure anywhere up there, but no doubt the man was reacting to all that falling glass. Or, at least, Keo hoped he was, because if he wasn't, then this was going to be a short run.

The shards of glass were still falling when he jumped onto the curb and lunged forward, sticking out both hands to keep from colliding with a section of the wall that made up the front part of Pick It. The *clink-clink-clink* of broken glass against the sidewalk behind him, pieces of it bouncing in his direction, but not enough for Keo to be worried. He was too busy unslinging the MP9 and scooting past a peeling poster featuring celebrities wielding their Fender guitars on his way to the door. Fortunately he didn't have to worry about windows on the first floor, because there were none.

Keo stopped at the door and tossed a quick look across the street, back toward the alleyway. Yuli, peeking out briefly, flashed him the *Okay* with one hand. Keo mirrored it, before sucking in a deep, relieved breath, and faced the door.

The elongated shadow of the large Pick It sign fell over Keo and most of the sidewalk, providing a nice shade from the searing heat. The doorframe was black matte solid steel along the sides and tinted glass in the middle. There was a handle and a security keyhole on top of it. As long as the door was unlocked, opening it was a simple matter of grabbing the handle and pulling.

Gee, that's all?

As long as there wasn't someone waiting inside to shoot him, anyway. But that was doubtful if there was just one shooter; he wouldn't have the time—and Keo wasn't about to give him that time—to hustle down to the first floor before Keo could get inside. And besides, hustling back and forth between floors wasn't something a guy who had been shot could pull off.

No. The bigger threat was if the man had boobytrapped the entrance with something like, say, a grenade. Or punji sticks. Okay, so the punji sticks were a bit out there, but the guy could definitely have rigged a grenade to blow as soon as someone opened the door. All he'd need was the skill and resources. Keo could see himself doing something like that if he couldn't watch an entire floor but did have some grenades on hand. The only thing extra he'd need would be some rope. Or string.

All those possibilities took five seconds between when Keo reached the sidewalk and reached for the handle, and by the sixth second, he had pulled the door open and lunged inside, hoping for the best but expecting the worst.

Store, don't blow me up now!

It didn't, but he almost killed himself anyway by losing his balance on the slick linoleum tiles as he entered the place. Both legs came out from underneath him, and Keo fell down on his ass, all of his concentration spent keeping the MP9 in front of him the entire time, telling himself, *Don't lose the gun! Don't lose the gun!*

He didn't lose the Bugger & Thomet, thank God, and was scrambling back to his feet when he felt someone watching him. Keo froze halfway up from the floor and stared back at two big black eyes.

A horse.

Not just any horse, but the same one the sniper had been riding. The big brown chestnut.

The animal stood behind the counter at the far end of the shop, racks of guitars lining the wall behind him. Despite the absence of windows on the first floor and the tinted front door behind Keo, the bright sun provided plenty of natural light for Keo to make out more guitars on the walls and shelves that flanked him. Some had fallen to the floor, where they looked as if they'd stayed for years now, unmoving.

Keo finished picking himself up, moving slowly so the horse wasn't spooked. The animal—Keo couldn't quite tell the breed—continued to watch him back with something that almost looked like...amusement? It was certainly not scared of him, that was for sure. It still had the saddle on its back, the reins dragging on the floor. No supply bags, but Keo could make out spots of blood along the animal's flanks. Not the horse's, because it didn't look injured, but rather its currently missing rider.

Well, the man wasn't really missing. He was somewhere above Keo, with a semiautomatic rifle.

Yeah, about that guy...

Keo wasn't sure how long he stared across the lobby of Pick Me at the animal, and vice versa, but eventually the horse got bored with him first and went back to doing what it had been up to before he burst into the place. Whatever that was, it was behind the counter and out of Keo's view.

He turned and focused on the hallway to the left of the counter. He moved toward it, submachine gun leading the way. He slowed down his breathing, very aware of the *crunch-crunch* as his boots stepped on debris scattered across the floor. Not too loudly, but they might as well be thunder to his ears. He resisted the temptation to look down to see what he was stepping on.

Keo slid against the wall next to the back hallway entrance, peeking in quickly—not even half a heartbeat—before pulling behind cover again. He'd seen very little, not helped by the dark ambiance in the narrow passageway. He had been able to make out a flight of stairs that went up, before turning right and doubling back and upward. At the end of that would be the second floor, and Mr. Sniper.

A rustling of movement as the horse looked up from whatever it was doing next to the cash register to gaze at him. Keo narrowed his eyes back at the animal. He'd met and bonded with a few horses over the years, and what Keo had found was that every horse had its own personality. Most of them were used to human presence, even strangers with guns.

About five seconds later, the animal must have decided Keo wasn't worth spending too much attention on and dipped its head out of view behind the counter once again. Keo made a mental note to find out what it was doing back there that seemed to require so much of its time.

But not yet. Not just yet.

After the first shot out in the street, the sniper hadn't gotten off another one. That was thanks to Yuli, who also hadn't fired again. So two shots in all had gotten Keo from one side of the street to the other. He had to admit, it was a lot easier than he'd expected. Maybe the horse's owner was worse off than Keo had assumed. The man was shot, then had to endure a rough ride to Silver Hills. If luck was really on Keo's side, Yuli might have actually killed the guy, either with his return fire or from all that falling glass.

You should be so lucky, pal.

He had to find out, one way or another. The only other option was to grab the horse and take it while the shooter was still upstairs. It wouldn't be too hard to keep himself and the animal hidden from the second floor windows once they were outside.

Yeah, he could do that, but he wasn't going to. He needed more than just the horse. He needed to know who the rider was—and more importantly, who his friends were that still had Lara. Keo hated going up against an enemy he didn't know a lick about, except that, according to the ex-vet Roger, he was dealing with people who had been *"through the shit."*

Keo leaned around the corner and glanced in at the stairs again. It was a straight shot up eight of the generously-spaced steps before the curve at the end. Eight more after that to the second floor. Doable, unless the shooter had realized where Keo was and was waiting to shoot the first head that popped up the stairs.

Oh, who are you kidding? He's definitely waiting for you up there. He'd have to be a total moron not to know what you're trying to do.

Keo sighed. It was a good point. He liked it when he made good points, and this was definitely one of them.

The shooter knew he was already inside Pick It. The man would also now know that the only way up was the stairs. So all he had to do was lie in wait with that AR or whatever he was using. A semiautomatic rifle with half a magazine was more than plenty to shoot Keo dead into next week.

So why didn't he just grab the horse and exit Silver Hills?

Keo looked across the open hallway entrance at the chestnut. He could only see its white mane as it busied itself with whatever was on the floor behind the counter, either oblivious to Keo's nearness or...just not interested in what was going on.

The horse. Just take the horse. All he had to do was leave with the horse and not risk going up there and getting shot. Because that was exactly what was going to happen. And he really, really didn't want to get shot.

Oh, goddammit, Keo thought just before he pushed off the wall and darted into the dark corridor and up the stairs.

He tried to make his steps light, but it was difficult and the sound of his boots pounding against the creaking stairs was like exploding grenades. Maybe just like the grenade that was waiting for him upstairs.

Or the sniper with his rifle...

He got halfway up the stairs, the MP9 in front of him, forefinger against the trigger the entire time. He was ready and expecting the first shot to come at any second—

Any second now!

—even as he rounded the end of the stairs and swiveled right almost a full 180-degrees to reveal the double-back section—

Any second now!

—and saw...eight more evenly-spaced steps leading to the above floor.

But there was no one squatting or standing or lying in wait for him. If there were, they would have fired and he would be dead. Or wounded. Or wounded briefly before getting shot again, and *then* dead.

Either way, he was expecting the worst and didn't get it.

There was no one up there.

Or, at least, no one that he could see.

Keo's heartbeat was in his throat when he took the rest of the steps, rising, rising higher up the stairs to the second floor.

Bright sunlight flooded the room, coming through the two windows in the back. One was closed, its panes tinted black, while the other featured a top portion that had been blown out by Yuli's shot.

And there, sitting on the floor between the two windows, his back against the wall, was a man wearing black clothes, staring back at Keo. The man's right hand was holding an AR-15 rifle, and he was trying to raise it, fighting desperately to lift it and point it at Keo and shoot him. But he couldn't do it; he was either too weak or—

No buts. The man just couldn't do it.

Keo climbed the final two steps and hurried across the wide-open floor. Pick It's first floor seemed even more crowded now that he was up here. There were some shelves on one side, boxes on the floor next to them, but nothing that looked as if the owner had really made much use of the other half of his building.

Slick, tiled flooring squeaked under Keo's rubber soles as he moved to the man on the other side. Dark hazel eyes followed Keo's every movement, sweat dripping down an already-slicked forehead and nose and chin. Keo saw the desire in those hazel eyes to shoot him as he approached, but the man was too weak to put his wants into action.

Lucky for me. Really, really lucky for me.

Keo grabbed the AR by the barrel and yanked it easily out of the man's grip, then unholstered a SIG Sauer and put that behind his waist. The sniper had taken off his MOLLE, and it lay nearby; the vest was covered in blood and dirt, but mostly blood.

There was glass all over the floor next to the window that Yuli had shot out. Shards *crunched* under Keo's boots as he looked outside and waved, before shouting, "All clear!"

He spotted Yuli leaning out from the alley across the street. "You okay?" the young man shouted back.

"All clear!" Keo said again.

Yuli waved back.

Keo walked over to the sniper. The man looked like death warmed over, his face ghostly pale, and he hadn't moved very much—or seemed capable of even doing so—since Keo first spotted him. He had no trouble watching Keo's every move with his eyes, though.

"It's a good thing looks can't actually kill, huh?" Keo said as he crouched in front of the sniper.

He was young—mid-twenties, possibly—with short, dark-black hair. He'd been shot in the side and might have bled out if he hadn't stanched the bleeding with a square compression gauze. He'd gotten to the wound just in time, but it had taken a lot out of him. So much so that Keo was sure now that, even had he wanted to, the shooter wouldn't have been able to run downstairs to cover the first floor.

Keo stared at the shooter, and the man stared right back at him. He might have been hurt and near death—enough that he hadn't even been able to ambush Keo as he came up the stairs —but there was still a lot of defiance in those eyes.

"You don't look so hot, pal," Keo said. "I bet you could use this." He opened one of his pouches and took out a syrette—a small tube with a hypodermic needle attached to one end. He held it up for the man to see. "You're going to die. I can't help you with that. You did good fixing up the wound, but you and me both know it's just a temporary bandage. The only thing I can do for you is give you some of this morphine to help get through it."

The man's eyes went to the syrette, then to Keo, before returning to the small tube. He didn't say anything, either because he couldn't or he didn't want to. Keo hoped it wasn't the latter; he could work with the former, but if the shooter was intent on taking his secrets to the grave, then Keo was out of luck—and he'd risked his hide coming up here for nothing.

"You can have it," Keo said. "It'll help with the pain. You'll still die—nothing I can do about that—but it won't be as bad."

The shooter's eyes zeroed in on Keo's. "What do you want?" he asked. His voice was so soft that Keo had to strain to hear him.

"Your friends. The ones that are still out there. Who are they?"

"My friends..."

"Yeah, that's what I said. Who are they?"

"My friends. They're my friends."

Keo grunted. He wasn't sure if the almost-dead guy was messing with him or if that was the only answer he thought mattered. Either way, Keo didn't waste time asking the same question. He had the feeling he was quickly running out of that: time.

"All right, your friends," Keo said. "You guys have a leader?"

"Yeah," the man said.

"What's his name?"

"Owen."

Now we're getting somewhere.

He said, "Owen was the one who decided to kidnap the doctor from the village?"

The wounded man nodded. Barely.

"Why?" Keo asked.

"His brother. Jackie."

Keo thought about everything he'd known so far about the abductors. Mostly, he replayed what Ophelia had told him.

"They showed up after you and George left, looking for a doctor. Someone told them we had one in the village."

"Jackie's the one that's hurt?" Keo asked. "He's the one who needed a doctor?"

There was no answer this time, but not because the man didn't feel like responding. Keo noticed the light starting to slowly fade from the shooter's eyes.

"Shit," Keo said, and pulled the cover off the syrette's needle and jammed it into the man's thigh.

Not yet, pal. I can't let you go just yet. I could have taken your horse and run off, but I didn't, because I need what you got. I need information.

He tossed the syrette and tapped the man on the cheeks to wake him up. "Hey, what's your name? Tell me your name." When the man didn't respond, Keo tapped harder. "Come on, wake up. What's your name? Tell me your name."

"Ronald," the man said as he opened his eyes back up.

"Ronald," Keo said. "Your name's Ronald?"

A slight nod as Ronald tried to keep his eyes open.

"Tell me about Owen, Ronald," Keo said. "Where is he taking the women?"

Ronald blinked back at him but didn't answer.

Keo snapped his fingers in front of the man's face to get his attention. "Ronald. Pay attention. Hey, Ronald. Where are your friends going? Where is Owen taking the women? Ronald. Ronald!"

Ronald forced his eyes back open. Barely. "I need another one."

Another one? Keo thought, before understanding. Ronald was asking for more morphine.

Keo took another syrette out of his pouch. It was his last one. "Tell me about Owen. Where's he going with the women? With the doctor?"

"Owen?" Ronald said, as if he had never heard of the name before.

"Yes. Owen. Where is he going?"

"I need that," Ronald said.

"Tell me about Owen."

Ronald pointed at the syrette. Or pointed as much as he could. He barely managed to lift his hand and couldn't quite straighten out his forefinger. "I need that. It still hurts too much."

"Tell me about Owen," Keo said. He took the cover off the needle. "Who is he? Where's he going?"

"You don't want to..." Ronald said.

"What?"

"You don't want to..."

"I don't want to what?" Then, when Ronald didn't answer, "Ronald. Wake up. Stay with me. Tell me about Owen. Where's he going?"

He began tapping the man's cheeks until he opened his eyes back up.

"Owen," Keo said. "Tell me about Owen."

"Owen," Ronald said. Or whispered.

"Yeah, Owen. Tell me about him."

"You..."

"Me? What about me?"

Ronald closed his eyes back up. Keo slapped him on the cheek and pried his eyelids open.

"Ronald," Keo said. "Stay with me a little longer. I need you to tell me where Owen's going with the women."

"...fuck with him," Ronald said, and his eyelids struggled to close back up against Keo's fingers, but Keo wouldn't let them.

"Fuck with who? Owen? I don't want to fuck with Owen?"

"He'll kill you," Ronald said. "He'll fucking kill you and piss down your throat."

"Is that right?" Keo said, but Ronald didn't answer him, because he couldn't.

Keo was still forcing his eyes open, but it didn't matter anymore. The light had gone out in Ronald's eyes, and the man had stopped breathing.

"Shit," Keo said out loud to the empty room.

He sighed, let go of Ronald, and put the syrette back into his pouch. He never had any intentions of giving it to the man anyway. You never knew when some morphine would come in handy—

"Damn, that was cold-blooded," a voice said from behind him.

Keo snapped up to his feet, spun around, and pointed the MP9 at—

Yuli.

But it wasn't just Yuli staring back at Keo. There was a second man standing behind the young Mexican, holding a shotgun.

EIGHT

"Tell me the truth. You were never going to give him that second morphine shot, were you?" the man with the shotgun asked, his eyes just barely visible over Yuli's right shoulder. "Well. Were you?"

"No," Keo said.

Keo didn't need the red dot scope on top of the MP9 to see he was in serious shit. Or Yuli was, anyway. Keo wasn't in any danger at the moment, not with the stranger's shotgun pointed at Yuli somewhere between the young man's shoulder blades. One pull of the trigger, and Keo was going to be able to see through the hole that had magically appeared in Yuli's chest and at the man who had just killed him.

"Slick," the man with the shotgun said. "Heard you getting all that information out of him while me and your compadre here were sneaking sneaky-like up the stairs. I couldn't have done it better myself. Well, maybe a little better."

"How so?" Keo said.

"For one, I wouldn't have let him die."

"I guess I'm just not that good at interrogations. Had to take the class twice and barely passed the second time."

The man flashed Keo a crooked grin. He was slightly shorter than Yuli—though not by much—which helped him to hide behind the Mexican. Keo could tell the man was slightly bending his knees to achieve a lower profile, peeking out occasionally to keep an eye on Keo.

They stood across from one another on each side of the room—close enough to see that things weren't going to end very well if one of them started shooting. The only positive Keo could see was that the shotgun's barrel wasn't pointed anywhere in his vicinity. If the man fired, he'd have to reload, which would give Keo the prime opportunity to take him out. The problem, of course, was Yuli standing between them.

Right now, Mr. Shotgun was counting on Keo trying everything possible to keep Yuli from getting dead.

Was he right? Keo wasn't entirely sure. He liked Yuli, and they'd always been on good terms back at the village. Lara was also friendly with Yuli's wife, Marie, but it wasn't like they were besties. That was Ophelia, George's significant other. And if Keo were pushed, he would probably say George was his.

The man with the shotgun chuckled, and Keo said, "What's so funny?"

"I can see what's going through that mind of yours," the man said.

"Oh yeah? What's that?"

"You're trying to decide if it's worth keeping this guy alive."

Yuli's entire body stiffened at the remark, and his eyes, still red from almost getting shot in the face by Ronald earlier, widened noticeably.

"Don't listen to him," Keo said to Yuli. "I'm not going to let him shoot you."

"Yeah, don't listen to me," the man said. "I'm just the guy with the shotgun, that's all."

Sweat poured down Yuli's face and dripped from his chin, creating puddles around his boots. "I'm sorry," he said.

"For what?" Keo said.

"He snuck up behind me in the alley. I didn't hear him until it was too late."

"It's okay. Everything's good."

"I'm sorry," Yuli said again.

"Everything's good," Keo said again.

He refocused on the hostage taker. Short blond hair matted to his forehead with sweat, the rest of his face covered in a generous coating of dirt and dust. He was armed with the shotgun but had a rifle slung over his back, the long barrel of the bolt-action sticking out from behind one broad shoulder. He was wearing a tactical backpack and cargo pants and boots, along with a short-sleeve T-shirt. The term "good ol' boy" came to mind when Keo first spotted the guy, and the way he talked had only confirmed it.

"Nah, everything's not good," Mr. Shotgun was saying. "But I'm willing to come to an agreement, seeing how things have shaped up."

"What does that mean?" Keo asked.

The man gave a slight nod toward Ronald, behind Keo. "I wanted him. Had my own set of questions for the fellow."

Keo paused for a moment, letting this new information process.

Then: "You were the one in the valley that shot him when he was riding away."

"That's me. And you two were on the hill."

"That's right."

"Almost got you."

"Almost only counts in grenades and horseshoes, pal."

"Never played horseshoes. Played with grenades plenty of times, though."

"I find that hard to believe."

"That I never played horseshoes or that I played with grenades?"

"Either/or."

"That makes no sense."

"Sure, it does."

"Nah, it doesn't."

"Whatever," Keo said. Then, "Dead guy back there wasn't alone in the fields."

"No, he wasn't. He had a partner."

"Just one?"

"Just one."

"What happened to him? I didn't see a body."

"It's out there. Got him first."

Keo narrowed his eyes at the blond. "Who are you, exactly?"

Yuli's captor narrowed his own eyes back at Keo. "Who are *you*?"

"Keo."

"What did you just call me?"

"My name. It's Keo."

"Oh." Then, "What kind of name is Keo?"

"Ronald was taken. What's yours?"

The man snickered. "Clever. You use that line a lot?"

"Whenever I get the chance."

"Sounds like you've had practice." Then, "You can call me Bunker."

"Is that because you live in one?"

"That's my name, smart guy."

"What kind of name is Bunker?"

"Keo was taken," the guy who called himself Bunker said.

Keo smirked.

Bunker snorted.

"You gonna kill him or what?" Keo asked.

"You want me to?" Bunker said.

"No, no, don't do that," Yuli said. "Don't kill me. Please."

"I won't, if your buddy over there puts down his weapon," Bunker said.

"You put your weapon down first," Keo said.

"Not gonna happen."

Keo sighed. "You heard me interrogating Ronald?"

"Badly," Bunker said.

"Answer the question."

"Yeah, I heard. What of it?"

"Then you know I'm not your enemy. He and his pals took a couple friends of ours. Two women. We're trying to get them back."

"Yeah, they have a bad habit of doing that," Bunker said. "Taking things that don't belong to them, I mean."

"They did the same to you," Keo said. It wasn't a question.

"That they did."

"So, back to my original thesis. We're not enemies. You agree?"

"That depends..."

"On what?"

"What are you gonna do when you catch up to that dead guy's buddies?"

"Shoot them. Then shoot them some more. Basically, keep shooting them until they die."

Bunker chuckled. "That's your big plan? Catch them and shoot them?"

"What can I say? I'm a big picture kinda guy."

"Yeah, I can see that."

"So?"

"So, what?"

"Are we good, or are we good?"

"Are those my only two choices?"

"You need more?"

"Let me think about it for a sec."

Bunker gazed back at Keo. He hadn't moved even a little bit since their back and forth began. Keo recognized a man capable of pulling the trigger on a shotgun shoved into the back of another human being when he saw one. Bunker could do that, and more.

And I can use a guy like that, Keo thought, looking at the two men in front of him. What he wouldn't give to switch Yuli with his captor. The thought made him feel a little guilty—just a little—but he got over it quickly.

This was about Lara, and if he had to ditch Yuli somewhere along the road in order to get her back...

"Well?" Keo said.

"What?" Yuli said.

"Not you. The other guy."

"Yeah, okay," Bunker said.

"Okay?"

"Okay," Bunker repeated, before lowering the shotgun and taking a step away from Yuli. "Your turn."

Keo lowered the MP9.

Yuli stumbled forward, gasping for breath like a drowning man. "Jesus, what's going on? What's going on?"

You almost got shot dead by a shotgun at close range, that's what, Keo thought, but he didn't think Yuli needed to hear that right now, so he said instead, "Everything's fine. Everything's good..."

"His name's Ronald?" Bunker asked.

"That's what he said," Keo said.

"Doesn't look like a Ronald."

"What does he look like?"

"Maybe a Clark. Or a Mark. Or possibly a Stark."

"Stark?"

Bunker shrugged. "Something with an a-r-k at the end."

"Why does it have to be something with an a-r-k at the end?"

"Why not?"

"Yeah, okay," Keo said, and looked back at Ronald.

Or Ronald's dead body. He was still just sitting against the wall, his head lolled slightly to one side as if he were taking a nap. They had gone through his corpse, but there wasn't much to find. His MOLLE had a spare magazine for the AR and one for his SIG Sauer sidearm, but that was about it. Yuli sat on the stairs behind Keo and Bunker, going through Ronald's backpack.

"So, what did he and his buddies take from you?" Keo asked Bunker.

"Horses," Bunker said.

"Horses? As in plural?"

"Yeah. Seven."

"You had seven horses?"

"I have more than that, but they were just able to take seven of them."

Keo thought about his reaction to finding out that Ronald's buddy Owen and the others were moving on possibly a dozen horses, with more pulling two utility trailers. He'd wondered where they had gotten their hands on so many of the animals. Now he had a part of that answer: They had some already, but they'd taken the rest from Bunker.

"I have a ranch north from here, near the shoreline," Bunker said. "One day this douche meister and his buddies showed up and decided they wanted what I had. Well, of course I said no. One thing led to another, and we're exchanging gunfire. Long story shorter, they absconded with seven of my horses. Horses that I took a lot of time to find and break and then raise. Needless to say, I am not a happy rancher."

"So what, you've been following them ever since?"

"Pretty much. Ran across them earlier today."

"They spotted you?"

"More like I showed myself and got them to chase me. I was hoping for all of them, but the head honcho, Owen, sent just two of his buddies. I killed one of them in the valley out yonder and nipped this fellow."

"What happened to the second guy's horse?"

"It's waiting for me in the valley. One of mine."

"And the one downstairs?"

Bunker shook his head. "Not one of mine. You can have it."

Keo gave him a surprised look.

"What?" Bunker said. "I don't take what's not mine. That's not how I was raised, end of the world or not."

"Well, thanks."

"No need to thank me. Finders keepers. And you killed its owner, so now it's yours to take care of."

"Noted."

They looked back at Ronald.

"So, they took your woman?" Bunker asked.

"Yeah," Keo said. He nodded over his shoulder. "His, too."

Bunker glanced back at Yuli, still rifling through Ronald's bag across the room from them. "Figured that one out for myself. He doesn't look like the chase them-down-and-kill-'em-all type, though."

Keo smiled. "And I do?"

"I'm pretty sure you didn't get that big, nasty scar on your face shaving."

The scar along the left side of Keo's face tingled. It always did that when someone mentioned it. "This was courtesy of a guy named Pollard."

"What happened to him?"

"I buried him."

"I'm sure he had it coming."

Keo shrugged. "Eh."

Bunker chuckled. Then he reached over and turned Ronald's head until it was straight and staring at them. When he let go, the head flopped right back over.

"Two down, eleven to go," Bunker said.

"Eleven to go?" Keo said.

"There's thirteen of them."

"Someone told me twelve."

"Well, someone told you wrong. There was fifteen, but I cut that number down during our tête-à-tête."

"I don't think exchanging gunfire over horses is what *tête-à-tête* means."

"That's not what Mr. Webster says," Bunker said, standing up.

Keo did, too, but not before picking up Ronald's AR and the MOLLE from the floor. There was blood on both items, but he couldn't care less. Especially when it came to the vest, which he could use to store extra magazines and supplies.

"So, what now?" he said to Bunker.

"Same thing I've been doing," Bunker said. "Track them down, and take my horses back."

"They're just horses. You can always find more out there."

"Yeah, you can. But I found and raised the ones they took. And I want them back. If a man's just gonna let any ol' body take his stuff from him, he's got no right to call himself a man."

"Your poppa taught you that?"

"My momma," Bunker said. He looked back at Yuli, and in a slightly lower voice, "I don't think your friend there likes dead bodies."

"Nobody likes dead bodies," Keo said. He walked over to Yuli. "Find anything worth keeping?"

Yuli glanced up at him. He'd laid out a bunch of supplies, including a small first-aid kit, a half-empty bottle of water, some changes of clothes, and five beaten up red apples that looked a bit smaller than the ones Keo was used to seeing in this part of Texas.

"Just these," Yuli said. He looked back at Ronald. "What did he tell you about Marie and Edna? I mean, Lara?"

"The guy who took them's name is Owen," Keo said. "That's about it."

"Did he say where they were going?"

"He didn't get around to it."

"Should have given him the second morphine," Bunker said.

"Yeah, yeah," Keo said. Then, to Bunker, "The bad guys have wounded comrades. You wouldn't happen to know anything about that, would you?"

"Possibly."

"Let's hear it."

"The night they came to steal my horses, I nipped three of them while they were being all criminal-like, but the fourth guy got away. Jackie, Owen's little brother. I swore I got him, too. Looks like I might have, but he survived." Then, "Which one of the ladies is a doctor?"

"Mine," Keo said.

"Doctors are rare out here."

Lara's rarer, Keo thought.

He said to Yuli, "Let's go."

Yuli stood up. "We're still chasing them, right?"

"You're damn right," Keo said. Then, to Bunker, "How many horses do you have, not counting the one downstairs that's not yours?"

"Two," Bunker said. He grinned at Yuli. "Looks like you're not going to have to walk after all."

"Walk?" Yuli said. "Why would I be walking?"

"Obviously, because this guy was going to take the horse downstairs and leave you behind. That's the only way he could catch up to Owen and Jackie faster." He turned that same grin in Keo's direction. "Am I right, or am I right?"

"Not even close," Keo said, but he thought, *Damn, this guy knows me too well.*

Before Yuli could suspect that maybe Bunker was close to the truth, Keo quickly added, "Come on. We're wasting daylight."

Keo went down the stairs first, carrying Ronald's blood-soaked vest and not-quite-as-bloody rifle. With eleven more guys out there, a semi-automatic AR, even one without burst fire capability, was going to come in handy. Besides, he had a horse to help carry the extra weight now.

Yuli and Bunker followed behind him, and Keo heard Bunker saying to Yuli, "You ever killed anyone before?"

"No," Yuli said.

"Ever tried to kill anyone before?"

"What do you mean?"

"It means what it means. Did you ever try to kill anyone before?"

Yuli didn't answer. Maybe he was thinking about the answer, or maybe he was stumped. Keo didn't glance back to be sure which one it was.

"Leave him alone, Bunker," Keo said.

"I'm just trying to get to know you boys," Bunker said. "Seeing we're gonna be partners and all."

"Save it for the sleepover. Right now, we're wasting time."

Keo found his duffel bag downstairs resting on the counter, along with Yuli's rifle and backpack. They grabbed their things, Yuli transferring the supplies from Ronald's bag over to his. The Ka-Bar he'd left in the alley was already in the bag.

The chestnut horse was still on the first floor, now licking at some covers of Blu-ray movies for some reason. Keo leaned over the counter to get a look at the floor. More specifically, to see what the horse had been so preoccupied with earlier. There was nothing down there—

Except for an almost-gone apple core next to the wall.

I guess he likes apples. Really, really likes apples.

He went over to join Yuli and Bunker, the two men watching the horse as it licked a copy of *RoboCop.* The special edition version.

"That's a good movie," Bunker was saying to Yuli.

"The sequels were pretty good, too," Yuli said.

"The sequels were trash, and anyone who likes them don't have taste in movies."

"Stop busting his balls, Bunker," Keo said. Then, to Yuli, "Give me one of those apples."

"An apple?" Yuli said.

"Yeah," Keo said, looking over at the horse.

Yuli took one of the fruits out of his bag and handed it over. Keo walked to the chestnut. The animal turned its head toward him even before he got close.

Keo smiled. "You like apples, Deux?"

"What did he just call that horse?" Keo heard Bunker saying behind him.

Keo ignored them and concentrated on the horse. The chestnut stared at him warily for a second before looking down at the apple, then back up at Keo. But whatever suspicion it had eventually faded, and the animal walked over and let out a cautionary snicker.

"Yeah, you like apples," Keo said.

He held the beaten and battered fruit out, and the horse took it into its mouth and began chewing. Keo put one hand on the chestnut's mane and rubbed it down gently. When the animal didn't become irritated, Keo picked up the reins from the floor.

"He likes you," Yuli said.

"That's not like; that's pure bribery at its finest," Bunker said.

"Hey, whatever works," Keo said, and thought, *And whatever gets me to Lara faster.*

NINE

Bunker had ridden his horse, a brown and white spotted Paint breed, into Silver Hills, dragging along the Quarter Horse that he had taken off Ronald's partner. The rancher had left both animals a block away while he snuck up on Yuli. They headed over there now, with Keo walking the chestnut by the reins. According to Bunker, Ronald's mount was a Cleveland Bay.

"Is that because it's originally from Cleveland?" Yuli had asked.

"If you're talking about Cleveland, Yorkshire, back in Jolly Ol' England, then yessirree," Bunker had said.

That had drawn a blank look from Yuli. Keo hadn't known that, either, but his knowledge of horses was relatively new. The last—and only real—horse he'd had for longer than a few days was Horse, which wasn't like any other horse, of course. In honor of that one, Keo had named the chestnut Deux, the sequel.

"You calling it Deux?" Bunker asked him now as they walked through the empty city.

"What's wrong with Deux?" Keo said.

"It's a stupid name for a horse."

"Oh, yeah? Then what do you call yours?"

"Lucille. The Quarter Horse that I just retrieved is Galahad."

"And those are better names?"

"Of course," Bunker said, as if it were the most obvious thing in the world.

Keo thought Bunker was a strange guy—he was in his early thirties, not that much older than Yuli or that much younger than Keo—but he acted as if he'd been around for at least a generation before either one of them. And yet, he also talked like a teenager at times and had the mannerisms of one, even though anyone with eyes could see he was well past his teenage years.

But Keo didn't mind any of those eccentricities as long as Bunker did his part. Keo hadn't really had time to consider what he was going up against when he thought Owen's crew only numbered a dozen (*Really? "Only?" A dozen is a lot, pal.*); he'd been too busy running to catch up. Now that he had a moment, it dawned on him that he was chasing after heavily-armed bad guys who, according to Roger, had been *"through the shit,"* which was just another way of saying Owen's gang wasn't just going to line up in single file for Keo to shoot them one by one.

Nothing can ever be that simple, can it? Sheesh.

So now he had an extra gun in Bunker. Counting Yuli, that was a gun and a half to wield against Owen's forces. The Mexican had done well shooting out Ronald's window earlier—that had taken some guts after almost getting shot in the face—but Keo didn't have any illusions that the former journalism student would be rock steady in a full-blown gunfight.

Bunker, on the other hand, was a different story. The man had chased Owen all the way down here after the thieves had taken his horses. And he'd known exactly how many he was going to have to contend with from the very beginning, but he'd done it anyway. To look and listen to him, Keo would think the guy was on vacation and having the time of his life. Maybe that was true. Keo knew plenty of guys who thrived in combat, who felt most alive when bullets were flying over their heads. Some people had accused him of being one of them, but that couldn't be further from the truth. Keo didn't like it; he just did it well, that's all. There was a difference.

Or, at least, that's what he told himself.

They finally reached Bunker's horses, Lucille and Gala-had. The animals were waiting in the big lobby of an office building near the edge of the city, tucked away from view and eating apples scattered on the floor. Deux, walking beside Keo, sniffed the air and let out a soft whinny when he noticed the fruits.

"Oh, come on, you just ate," Keo said.

Bunker picked up the reins on Lucille, the Paint horse, and handed the brown one's to Yuli. "You know how to ride, right?"

"I've ridden horses before," Yuli said.

"Yeah, but do you know to *ride?*"

"What's the difference?"

"Not a lot, until you fall out of the saddle."

"I won't fall out of the saddle."

"Let's hope not. When I shot Galahad's thieving previous rider, he just kept on going. He'll probably do the same to you if you fall off."

"Thanks for the warning."

"You're welcome," Bunker said, and walked Lucille out of the building.

Keo followed with Deux, with Yuli bringing Galahad behind them. The sun was still high when they stepped back outside, but there was a noticeable drop in temperature. Not much, but noticeable. Keo's watch confirmed the time.

4:11 p.m.

He'd wasted too many precious hours in Silver Hills, and every second and every minute that passed meant Owen was getting farther away with Lara.

"You said Owen sent Ronald and the other one after you?" Keo asked Bunker.

The rancher nodded. "Yeah. What about it?"

"I'm wondering if Owen will slow down and wait for Ronald and the other one to catch back up to the group."

"Your guess is as good as mine. He didn't seem to care about the three I nipped back at my ranch."

"They didn't try to take you out after the confrontation?"

"Nope."

"Probably because of Jackie."

"That's what I figured, too. He cares about his kid brother. Not so much about the others."

He cared enough to kidnap Lara to save this Jackie asshole's life. That's the last mistake he's going to make.

They had reached almost the end of town, with the open field in front of them, when they climbed into their saddles. Deux turned his head to give Keo a look when he settled in on top of him, as if to say, *So you're riding me now, is that it?*

Keo patted the animal on its withers. "Let's see how fast you can run, boy. I once had a horse—he was like no other horse, that horse—who could run pretty well. What do you say? Wanna show me what you got?"

"Horses can't talk," Bunker said, adjusting his bags around his own mount's saddle horn. "FYI."

Keo rubbed down Deux's mane and leaned to whisper to the animal, "Don't listen to him. I know you're just playing dumb."

Deux raised his head and snickered.

"Did it just...answer you?" Yuli asked. He was on top of Galahad, and while he wasn't completely out of place on top of the Quarter Horse, he didn't look entirely comfortable, either.

"Of course not," Bunker said. "Horses are smart, but they're not *that* smart."

Bunker rode on ahead, guiding his painted mount back toward the highway. Keo followed, with Yuli behind him, and it didn't take long before all three of them broke off into a gallop to make up for lost time.

The state highway (it had a number, but Keo hadn't bothered to commit it to memory, and signs were far and few for whatever reason) was just as endless and empty as the last time he was on it. The only difference now was that he could travel faster, and that was what he did.

Keo rode Deux on the right side of the two-lane road, while Bunker kept to himself on the left. Yuli had elected to travel with Keo, the two of them keeping off the shoulder and the hard asphalt to lessen the burden on their mounts' unshod hooves.

By 4:50 p.m. they had made great progress, but there were still no signs of Owen and his crew. Keo's hope that the man might have lingered and waited for Ronald and his partner to catch up to them was for naught. Owen had continued on after siccing two of his men on Bunker, which furthered Bunker's theory that Owen really didn't give a whole lot of shits about his men. *If* they were his men and not just a bunch of guys who had fallen in with him. Either way, the man didn't seem all that concerned about the welfare of his group.

Well, except for Jackie, the little brother. Owen seemed to care a hell of a lot about that one. It was a vulnerability that Keo wrote down and hid away in his cabinet of mental notes in case he needed to exploit it in the future.

"What's up ahead?" Bunker asked around 5:00 p.m.

"You don't know?" Keo said.

"Not my part of the country. This is all Injun territory to me, chief."

"Harlingen's coming up in about fifty more kilometers if we keep on this road. There's a dozen or so small towns before then."

"Kilometers?" Bunker smirked. "What are you, European all of a sudden?"

"Thirty miles or so, if it makes you feel better."

"Yes, it does. You're in 'Murica, fella. Act like it." Then, "What's the next town up?"

Keo didn't answer right away. He sifted through his memory, remembering all the places he and Lara had passed—and more all the ones they had avoided—after that whole mess at Darby Bay.

He finally said, "Norman. About two more klicks up ahead. We should be seeing it now."

"What's that in American?"

"One-point-three miles, give or take."

Ahead of them was a gradual incline in the road, like a hump sticking out of the asphalt. It wasn't unusual; this part of the countryside was filled with similar rises and troughs to accommodate the oftentimes sloping land.

It was past five, but the sun was still being a brutal bitch, making Keo's clothes stick to his skin again after the reprieve of Silver Hills's rooftop shades. The addition of Ronald's blood-soaked vest didn't help keep him any drier. He'd been out of the blistering heat for so long that he had forgotten how hot it was out here. That was, until he was back under the harsh, cloudless sky. The almost mirage-like flickering in the air from the sun made him rethink the MOLLE. It was useful, but he'd be damned if it wasn't also suffocating.

"Is it me, or is it hotter out here than before?" Yuli asked as he pulled up beside Keo.

"It's your imagination," Keo said.

"You sure?" He took out a rag and wiped his face with it. "God, it's hot."

"It's not going to get any less hot the more you talk about it," Keo said as beads of his own sweat stung his eyes.

"Sorry," Yuli said, and put the rag back into his pocket. Or he was doing just that when *he fell off his saddle?*

What the fuck?

Keo reacted by pulling on Deux's reins. It was a hard move, and the horse fought against it, struggling underneath Keo even as he spun it all the way around to get a look at Yuli.

And it was that response by both him and the horse, he would realize later, that saved Keo's life.

But he didn't know that at the time. He did, though, feel

something hard and fast and subsonic *zipping* past his face, its heat trail nearly singeing his left cheek. He recognized it for what it was instantly—a bullet, fired from a suppressed weapon, nearly taking his head off!

He jumped off Deux, eating a fistful of dirt and grass as he collided with the solid earth and rolled away even as he felt but not heard more gunshots.

Zip-zip-zip! as they struck the ground where he'd initially landed, kicking up small clouds of dirt into the scorching-hot air.

Keo kept rolling, grunting when the sharp ends of the submachine gun strapped behind him dug into the exposed parts of his back. Fortunately, the vest took the brunt of the stabbings, and he was able to keep rolling, getting as far away from the side of the road as possible while staying low. Thank God for all the knee-high grass around him, providing natural camouflage against the shooter.

Sniper! It's a sniper!

After at least a dozen—but it could have been twenty or more; it wasn't like he was counting—full rolls, Keo came to a stop and turned himself over until he was facing the direction where the shots had come from.

Up ahead, in front of them, where that hump in the road was waiting.

Fucker was lying in wait the whole time! Shit!

Keo glanced back, trying to find Yuli's body in all the grass. He hadn't seen where Yuli was shot, but it had to have been a good one, because the Mexican had gone down and was staying down. And he wasn't making any sounds at all.

"Keo!" a voice shouted.

Bunker, from somewhere across the road. Keo had been wondering what had happened to the rancher.

"Yeah!" Keo shouted back.

"You okay?" Bunker asked.

"Yeah! You?"

"He almost had me. But like you said, *almost* only counts in horseshoes and grenades!"

"Let's hope he doesn't have grenades!" Keo shouted.

The shooter hadn't fired again after his initial barrage, which was a sign he didn't have a bead on Keo's location. That allowed Keo to lie still, confident that he was safe where he currently lay, flat against the ground on his chest, his head slightly tilted to make sure no one was rushing him.

There was no one out there. At least, no one charging his position.

He concentrated on the hill in the road. It was a good 200, maybe 250 meters in front of him. Way too far to throw a grenade but plenty close enough for a rifle. At the same time, far enough that Keo hadn't heard the gunshots. Suppressors could lower a weapon's decibel by a lot, but it wasn't completely silent like in the movies. Keo would know, having spent more than half of his "working life" running around with a suppressed MP5SD.

And all that meant...what?

Not much, except that Yuli was dead. Or dying. Either way, the man hadn't said a word since Keo saw him falling off his saddle out of the corner of his eyes. He knew now that Yuli hadn't fallen but had been, literally, shot out of his saddle.

Just to be sure, Keo called out, "Yuli!"

There was no answer, and the only sound was Keo's voice echoing for a second or two before fading completely.

He tried again: "Yuli! Can you hear me? Yuli!"

Echoes, then silence.

Five seconds...

Ten...

"Yuli!" Keo shouted again.

"I think he's gone, man," Bunker said.

"You saw him go down?"

"I saw where he fell, yeah."

"And?"

"And nothing. He's not getting back up."

"Shit," Keo said under his breath, wondering what he was going to tell Marie when he finally caught up with her.

Maybe you should worry about getting out of this first, pal.

That was the real problem, and one he couldn't see any way out of. At least, not anytime soon. There was a sniper out there, and he had already taken out Yuli. The three of them had been moving pretty fast on their horses when Yuli got hit. Keo would have been Casualty No. 2 if he hadn't pulled on Deux and spun the horse around suddenly—

Deux. Where was the horse?

Keo raised his head farther up from the ground—but not *too* high!—to get a better look around him.

There. The Cleveland Bay was enjoying some grass near the shoulder of the road, as if nothing had happened. The horse was close enough to Keo that he could hear the chestnut chewing, but too far to think he could climb into the saddle and take off. Not that Keo was entertaining any such thoughts, anyway. The sniper had already shot Yuli while he was moving. Keo presenting himself to the man now—standing up, climbing into the saddle, then starting to ride off—would be akin to serving himself up on a silver platter to get shot.

Yeah, that's not gonna work. Not gonna work at all.

Yuli's horse, Galahad, had wandered slightly ahead after losing its rider but hadn't gone very far. Bunker's painted Lucille was on the other side of the asphalt, standing with its head high in the sun as if it was trying to figure out what to eat for dinner. All three animals hadn't gone anywhere, which didn't surprise Keo. Violence was nothing new to these horses. They had, after all, survived The Purge.

"You see him?" Keo shouted.

"Shooter?" Bunker shouted back.

No, the Fairy Godmother, Keo thought but said, "Yeah. He's gotta be on the hump up the road."

"I figured as much," Bunker said. "You got a shot?"

"A shot? I can't even see the fucker!"

Besides, Keo only had the submachine gun on him, and the weapon wasn't exactly known for its long-distance ability. He'd need a rifle to even come close to nailing a target from 200 to 250 meters away. The AR he had taken from Ronald was strapped to the side of Deux's saddle at the moment.

Yuli's rifle.

The dead (?) man was carrying the bolt-action with the big scope on him when he had dropped off his horse. And he was still back there, somewhere.

Keo turned his body around slowly, keeping his chest pressed against the hot dirt. He crawled over, using the chestnut's easily visible tall frame to mark the shoulder of the road without having to raise his head up too high and risk getting it shot off. Yuli would be right about there—

The Cleveland Bay lifted its head and turned toward him.

Oh...

Keo stared back at it for a second, until he realized it was a dumb thing to do.

...*shit!*

Zip! as a bullet struck the ground in front of Keo's face, barely missing his head by a few inches.

Shit, shit, shit!

Keo quickly rolled away.

Dammit, Deux, you gave me away!

Zip-zip! as two more rounds landed, each one striking the ground far from the first shot—the shooter trying to cover as much field as possible. Keo didn't think the man could see him, but he had definitely spotted Deux turning and staring and figured out that the horse was doing it for a reason.

You almost got me killed, you stupid horse! Keo thought, and wanted to laugh out loud, but of course he didn't.

He stopped rolling when the third round hit and a fourth vanished in the wrong direction. He turned over onto his back and let out a relieved sigh, even as the sun continued to bake him in its brightness.

The sun...

It wasn't going to last forever. Sooner or later, night would fall, and then—what? Either the shooter would pick up and take off, giving this up for a miss, or he wouldn't go anywhere.

Which option was more likely?

Keo didn't have a clue. He didn't know what kind of man he was dealing with. The guy was definitely patient, because he had been lying in the middle of the road, under the scorching sun, for God knows how long. Minutes? Hours? Probably hours. Then, when he couldn't locate a shot, he'd gone quiet and waited.

Patient motherfucker is patient.

Keo wasn't too worried about nightfall, anyway. He'd gotten through it too many times before, and night these days weren't like the night of The Purge year or even the immediate ones after that. Of course, Keo had been pretty sure there was nothing to fear about the night, until Merrick showed up. That blue-eyed ghoul had brought an army with it. A big enough horde of bloodsuckers that they'd almost toppled Lara's Black Tide in one night. Almost.

How many more black eyes were still out there right now, waiting for sundown? They hadn't had a lot of ghoul problems at the village. None, in fact. The seawater nearby was Kryptonite to the creatures, just as silver and sunlight were lethal. It was one of the main reasons the village had been such a good spot to spend the rest of their lives and why they'd found similar survivor hubs up and down the beach. Back at the village, he could forget about the dangers of the world.

Keo couldn't ignore those same things out here with the dead cities and wild fields—

Pek-pek! coming from nearby.

Bullets, striking the ground, but not anywhere close to his position.

"Bunker?" Keo called out.

"Yeah!" Bunker shouted back.

"What happened?"

"I wanted to check if Marky Mark out there could see me!"

Marky Mark? Keo thought.

He said, "So what's the verdict?"

"Yeah, he can definitely still see me!" Bunker said.

Keo had to grin at that. Despite their dire situation, Bunker still maintained a sense of humor about the whole thing. Then again, the man had been stalking Owen's group despite knowing the odds against him. That meant he either had a little death wish about him or—well, that was probably it.

"Who's Marky Mark?" Keo asked.

"You know, the rapper turned actor?" Bunker said.

"That doesn't help at all."

"He starred in a movie about a sniper."

"This guy Marky Mark?"

"What, you never saw it?"

"I don't watch a lot of movies."

"Oh, you're missing out. It's a great—"

Pek-pek-pek! coming from the other side of the highway, interrupting Bunker in mid-sentence.

A few seconds later, Bunker grunted out, "Shit!"

"What happened?" Keo asked.

"Asshole saw sunlight reflecting off my optic while I was looking to see if I could find him first. Spoiler: He won."

"Might wanna be careful with that."

"Yeah, yeah," Bunker said. Then, "You got any ideas?"

"No," Keo said.

"None?"

"None."

"Well, you're useless."

"You're not doing so good yourself."

"Touché," Bunker said.

Keo had rolled back onto his stomach. He peered forward now, through the drooping stalks of grass in front of him. There wasn't nearly enough wind to keep him cool even this low to the ground, but at least he was somewhat shielded from the full force of the sun. He didn't bother unslinging the MP9 to try to get a shot. He was much too far away. Besides that, what had just happened to Bunker was still fresh on his mind.

Yeah, don't wanna do that.

So what could he do? He couldn't very well just lie here all day and all night, waiting for the sniper to make his move. As far as he could tell, best case was to outlast the sniper. Sooner or later, the guy would get tired or bored, and he would leave.

Worst case? The shooter had enough supplies to last for days.

Keo did, too, but they were currently dangling off Deux's saddle. He could see himself crawling over and retrieving them —slowly and carefully; very, very carefully—but being able to know exactly where the horse was was also a negative. If he could see the chestnut, then so could the sniper. The man was, no doubt, keeping one eye on the horses at all times while trying to locate them among all the grass. He would notice if Keo got close enough to grab the supply bag. Hell, he'd been smart enough to almost deduce Keo's location just from Deux staring at Keo earlier.

So where did that leave Keo? Somewhere between a rock and a hard—

"Bob?" a voice said from nearby. It was soft, barely audible, and in great pain. "Bob, Jesus. Bob? Bob? I think I've been shot..."

Bob? Keo thought.

Then: *Oh, shit.*

The voice was Yuli's. He was still alive!

TEN

"Bob? Bob, are you there? Bob, I can't see you..."

Fuck.

Yuli was still alive.

Fuck, fuck.

That was going to complicate matters.

Fuck, fuck, fuck.

A lot.

"Bob?"

And he was calling Keo by Keo's made-up name. Which meant...what? That he was delirious, probably. Getting shot could do that to you, especially if you'd never been shot before. Keo wished he had that problem.

Among a million other things.

"I can't see, Bob. I can't see..."

"Your friend still alive?" Bunker called out. He sounded incredulous.

"Yeah, sounds like it," Keo shouted back.

"Damn. Thought he was dead."

"Me too."

"Bob?" Yuli again. His voice was weak, taking a lot of effort. "Where are you? I can't see..."

"Stay where you are, Yuli," Keo said.

"Bob?"

"Yeah, it's me. Bob."

"I thought you said your name was Keo?" Bunker called.

"It is," Keo said.

"So why did he just call you Bob!"

"It's a long story. Now, would you shut the hell up so I can keep him alive?"

Bunker shut the hell up, allowing Keo to search for and find Yuli somewhere to his left, near the shoulder of the state highway. He couldn't see the wounded man, which was also probably the only reason the sniper hadn't finished him off yet. As with Keo and Bunker, the shooter couldn't see Yuli unless he did something stupid like try to get up, which thank God he hadn't done yet.

"Yuli, stay down," Keo said. "Don't try to move."

"Bob?" Yuli said. "Are you there?"

"Yeah, yeah, it's me. I'm nearby. Did you hear me? Don't get up."

"Where are you? I can't see."

"Can you see anything at all?"

"No..."

Great. More complications. Just what I needed.

"Listen to my voice, and do what I say," Keo said. "I want you to lie perfectly still and don't move. Don't even try to lift your head. There's a sniper out there, and he's going to kill you if he sees you moving. Do you understand?"

Yuli didn't respond.

"Yuli, *do you understand?*" Keo said.

"Yes," Yuli finally said. "But I can't see, Bob. I can't see."

That was a new one. Keo had witnessed men suffer all kinds of injuries, including some psychosomatic ones, from being shot, but he didn't recall anyone ever losing their vision. Either that, or Yuli was just imagining that he couldn't see. People who had never been shot before usually had some very weird reactions post-impact. If, that is, they survived.

"Bob?" Yuli was saying. He sounded even weaker than before. "Are you still there?"

"Yeah, I'm still here," Keo said. "Where are you hit?"

"I don't know..."

"You really can't see?"

"No. Why can't I see? I don't know why I can't see anything, Bob."

"It's okay," Keo said. "Just lie back. It's okay. Bunker and I are still here. We'll handle this."

"Who is 'we,' white man?" Bunker said, before cackling to himself.

Not the time, Bunker, Keo thought.

But he concentrated on Yuli. "Don't move. Don't raise your head. Just lie there for now."

"Okay, Bob," Yuli said. "Okay..."

Yuli sounded coherent enough that there was a good chance he could survive his wound. That, unfortunately, only made things more complicated for Keo. Before, when he thought Yuli was dead, Keo only had to worry about keeping himself alive. (Bunker could take care of his own damn self.) It was something he was very good at—staying alive—and he was sure he could get through this, too, even if he didn't know how he was going to do it exactly.

But Yuli had to still be alive.

Nothing's going right today, goddammit.

It wouldn't have been too hard for Keo to crawl to Yuli. If the sniper couldn't locate any of them in the tall weeds, he wouldn't be able to do so when Keo made his move over to the wounded man. The problem was what to do after he got there. Yuli didn't sound in tip-top shape, but he also didn't give Keo the impression he was at death's door, either.

Of course, if he were…

God, I'm such a prick, Keo thought, wondering what Lara would say if she found out the kind of things going through his mind right now while a friend (Well, more of an acquaintance, really.) was lying nearby, probably bleeding to death.

Then again, he didn't actually *have* to tell Lara. All she would have to know was that he had initially left the village with Yuli, but somewhere along the way the other man got shot and killed. There would be no need to elaborate on the details, especially to Marie.

Marie…

She was a nice kid. A beautiful girl who was probably going to give birth to a beautiful bouncing baby boy or girl. She was sweet and kind and was always smiling. That was the thing about her that Keo noticed right away—she was always smiling. He'd never met a more happy human being in his life. When she learned she was pregnant, that smile had turned into a big, bright sun, like the one trying to bake him right now.

"Sorry, Marie, but I had to let your husband bleed out in the grass. Yeah, I could have saved him—or tried to—but I just, you know, didn't want to risk it. I mean, can you blame me?"

Yeah, she could blame him.

So could Lara.

If he told them what happened.

If he was too dumb to keep all of this to himself.

If he could look Lara in the eyes and lie...

Shit.

He could spin a web of half-truths to a lot of people with a straight face and never feel an iota of guilt about it. He'd had practice. His world before The Purge required it most of the time.

But it wasn't that world anymore. This was another world. This was one where he had a woman and a nice place by the beach and...

Lara. He wouldn't be able to lie to Lara. It didn't matter how hard he tried to convince himself otherwise, he knew that when the time came to look her in the eyes and tell her how Yuli died out here, under this relentlessly hot sun...

Fuck my life, Keo thought, before he called out, "Yo, Bunker!"

"Yeah?" Bunker shouted back.

"I got a plan!"

"I'm listening."

"How good are you with that rifle?"

"You know back at the valley, when you were standing on top of that hill?"

"What about it?"

"I could have taken your head off, but I fired warning shots instead."

"Bullshit. You missed."

"No bullshit about it, buddy. Only reason I didn't pop you was because I wasn't sure who you were, and I don't like to go around shooting innocent civvies. Besides, I didn't recall a Chinese guy being part of Owen's crew."

"You saw all of their faces?"

"I've been stalking the thievin' scumbags for a while now. What do you think?"

"So you saw my face in that scope of yours," Keo said.

"That's right."

"Which means—"

"I can hit the shooter if I can see him."

"Okay," Keo said.

"Okay what?" Bunker said.

"I'm going to draw his fire. When I do, you shoot him."

"He's using a suppressor. Or didn't you notice we haven't been able to hear the gunshots every time he tried to take our heads off?"

"A suppressor, but not a *flash* suppressor. There'll still be some muzzle flashes."

"At this range? You're reaching, buddy. I'll be lucky if I can see anything at all, much less something worth shooting."

"We know where he is—on top of that hump. That's a limited area. There'll be something for you to see when he opens up."

"I'll need time."

"That's what I'm going to give you. Time. Five seconds. Maybe ten."

Bunker laughed. "You're crazy. Crazy Bob. That's what I'm going to call you from now on."

"Yeah, yeah," Keo said. "You better make the shot."

"I'm not promising shit, Crazy Bob."

"Fuck," Keo whispered to himself. Then, louder, "On the count of five!"

"Got it!" Then, not even a second later, "Wait, wait."

"What is it now?"

"Is that one to five, or five to one?"

"Five to one. Who the hell would count *up* from one to five?"

"Hey, I just wanna be sure, that's all."

"Are you sure now?"

"Pretty sure."

"You better be sure! It's going to be my skin on the line out there."

"Yeah, yeah, I'm sure."

"On the count of five. You set?"

"Just do it, already!"

"Five!" Keo shouted.

He reached down and tightened the straps of the MP9 against his body. The last thing he wanted when he popped up was to have the submachine gun dangling off him. Even worse if he somehow tripped over it. Now, that would have been embarrassing. Not to mention deadly, for him.

"Four!"

He wondered if Yuli had heard Keo's back-and-forth with Bunker. Probably. He'd seemed pretty aware of what was happening, if blinded—literally, in this case—to his surroundings. But then again, he'd also called Keo "Bob" more than once. For all Keo knew, the man had completely lost his mind.

"Three!"

Keo placed his palms flat against the hot earth and went parallel against the ground, the noses of his boots pushing down as well. He thought about how many times he had done something stupid like this for a woman. He could count them on one hand, and more than a few of them had been for the same one. Lara. After everything he had been through, everything he had done, it always came back to Lara.

"Two!"

He sucked in a deep breath and glanced up at the sun. It was still bright up there, despite it being almost five-thirty, with evening creeping up on them. That meant the sniper would have no trouble whatsoever seeing him when he popped up. It was probably going to help that Keo was wearing the all-black vest he'd taken from Ronald.

Maybe I should ditch it...

"One!" he shouted and thought, *Too late!*

His legs shot forward, bending at the knees, even as he pushed simultaneously down and drove himself upward. Basically the second half of a burpee, but without the tossing his arms up over his head part.

He was on his feet a split second later and running away from the road. The farther he could get from the asphalt, and Bunker on the side, the more opportunity he could give the rancher the time to locate—

The first bullet *zipped!* past Keo's head, so close that Keo swore he could feel the unnatural heat as the round missed by mere inches.

Goddammit! Already?

"Bunker!" Keo shouted. "He's shooting at me!"

He didn't hear anything back from Bunker, but he needed the man to know so he could start looking.

Keo kept running, putting more distance between him and the highway. By now, Bunker would be searching with his rifle, looking through that scope of his for a target...

How much longer? One second? Five seconds?

Zip-zip! as two more rounds nearly took Keo's head off. He ducked his head down slightly to make himself less of a target but never eased up. He was almost at top speed now and getting faster still—

Pek! as a round kicked up dust in front of him.

Keo reflexively hopped over the cloud of dirt, thought, *What the hell are you doing? You're just making yourself a better target!*

But it was too late. He was already in the air.

He landed—still alive, thank God!—and continued on, arms swinging wildly at his sides, his breath hammering through his lungs—

Something hit him in the back while he was in mid-stride, and Keo spun, instinctively slowing down at the same time.

What are you doing? Don't slow down, you idiot! Don't slow—

What felt like a hammer struck the front of his chest, so hard that Keo lost his balance, stumbled, and began to fall.

He was halfway down to the ground when he heard the sudden *crack!* of a single rifle shot. It was so loud that Keo's ears were still ringing as he slammed into the hard earth and gasped for breath.

Dumbass down! Dumbass down!

He blinked rapidly up at the sun, trying to decide if he was already dead or just wounded—and if it was the latter, how badly. He could still see, so he wasn't suffering from Yuli Disease just yet. There was some pain, but it was more shock than anything as Keo looked down at this chest.

The MOLLE was made of nylon mesh—tougher than most fabrics—but it wasn't bulletproof. That would have made the vest too heavy for what Keo needed it for, which was carrying spare magazines and supplies.

His eyes widened, zeroing in on what looked like a crushed

bullet sticking out of one of the smaller pouches along the vest, close to where Keo's kidney would have been.

What the hell?

He reached down and pulled open the Velcro flap over the pouch and took out its contents. It was a knife. A tiny one —barely four inches of blade—with a dull gray handle. There was a small crater the size of a penny in the middle. Titanium. It had to be titanium. Nothing else would have been able to stop a bullet moving at 2,500 feet a second. An inch and a half farther to the right or left, and he'd be bleeding out right now.

Jesus. That was close.

Jesus Christ.

Keo sighed and lay back down before he realized how quiet it had gotten around him all of a sudden. He didn't immediately raise his head or try to get back up. There were still some jolts of pain coming from the spot where the bullet had slammed the knife against his body, but a little pain was better than sitting up and taking a bullet to the face.

"Hey, Crazy Bob!" someone shouted. *Bunker.* "You still alive out there? If so, you can come up for air now! I got 'em!"

Thank God, Keo thought, sitting up.

Bunker was all the way across the field from him—at least a good fifty meters, maybe even more—and had already walked quite a distance up the road. He was searching for Keo among the grass before finally spotting him. The rancher waved, a big, dumb grin on his face. Or Keo thought it was a big, dumb grin. He couldn't quite see it all the way out here.

Damn, he'd gotten pretty far before the sniper could manage to knock him off his feet. Keo guessed he was a lot faster than he thought. But then, there was nothing quite like literally running for your life to help dig deep for speed you didn't know you even had.

He waved back at Bunker, then followed the man as he turned and began jogging up the highway toward the hump in the road. Bunker was out there in the open for at least twenty seconds while Keo watched, and that was more than enough time to convince Keo that the rancher had gotten the shooter.

Keo stood up and ripped off the MOLLE and turned it around. There was a straight line near the center of the vest, as if someone had slashed at the nylon mesh fabric with a knife. That wasn't too far from the truth, he guessed. A bullet had done that. The same one that had spun him earlier.

He put the vest back on and walked the long distance over to the highway. He was still surprised at how far he'd run, mostly because he didn't remember going that fast.

Yuli was lying a few yards from the shoulder of the road, just deep enough in the grass that the sniper hadn't been able to spot him and finish the job. The reason why he was telling Keo he couldn't see probably had something to do with all the blood that caked the side of his face.

Keo pulled off Yuli's backpack and took out the first-aid kit.

"Bob?" Yuli said. His eyes were wide open, but the way he was staring up at the sun told Keo he really couldn't see anything. "Is that you?"

"It's me," Keo said. "Relax. I'm going to fix you up."

"I can't see, Bob. Why can't I see?"

"I don't know, Yuli. Let me fix up you for now, and we'll figure it out later."

"I can't see. I can't see..."

The shot that had knocked Yuli off his horse had struck him along the right temple. Keo could make out the large, ugly gash and could see white bone underneath all the red wetness. The bullet had ricocheted off Yuli's skull but hadn't penetrated, which was good. What wasn't so good was that it had managed to do a lot of damage anyway. Keo wasn't too worried about all the blood—that was one of those "it looks worse than it really is" things—but the lack of vision, on the other hand...

He's really blind. How do I fix that?

He didn't, that was how. Keo wasn't a doctor. He wasn't even a failed medical student. He knew enough to wipe the blood off Yuli's face and treat the wound so it wouldn't get infected before covering it up with a square of gauze. Beyond that, he was out of ideas.

Yuli grimaced and moaned as Keo worked, but he never stopped blinking, trying desperately to see, and failing.

"How is he?" Bunker asked.

Keo glanced over. The blond rancher had returned with a new rifle—some kind of AR with a collapsible tripod under the barrel for steadying shots. The big scope on top was almost as large as Bunker's, but the magazine gave Owen's sniper more rounds to play with.

"You got him?" Keo asked.

"He's deader than dead," Bunker said.

"Was he alone?"

"Unless you count the horse he's got nailed to the ground back there. Gasper."

"Gasper?"

"The horse. It's one of mine."

"So what does that make? Three down?"

"Three ass clowns down, ten more to go. Five more horses to take back." He nodded at Yuli, who Keo had laid back on the ground to wrap some gauze around his head and over his eyes. "How is he?"

Keo shook his head, and Bunker mouthed, *He's really blind?*

"I think so," Keo said.

"Damn," Bunker said.

Keo stood up and tried to think about what he was going to do with a former journalism student who couldn't even shoot now. Yuli's usefulness had been questionable before, but now...

"Shit," Keo said.

"You can say that again," Bunker said.

"Shit," Keo said.

ELEVEN

"What are you gonna do about him?" Bunker asked.

"I don't know," Keo said.

"He's blind."

"Yeah, I can see that."

"Was that a joke?"

Keo sighed. "No."

"I don't believe you. I think that was a joke."

"It wasn't."

"I still don't believe you. That was definitely a joke. And at your buddy's expense, no less."

"Whatever, Bunker."

Keo glanced back at Yuli, standing on the highway and looking around. Well, he wasn't really "looking," because he still couldn't see anything. Keo knew that because Yuli hadn't said a word about the gauze bandages covering his eyes. He knew they were there; they just didn't make any difference to his vision. But at least Yuli was on his feet again, which was better than thirty minutes ago. Not by much, but better.

He really is blind. Now what?

"You can always take him back to that village of yours," Bunker was saying.

They were talking in a slightly low voice, so Yuli couldn't hear, while they got the horses ready. The sniper's stolen mount, Gasper, was another big Cleveland Bay. The animal was chewing grass nearby alongside Yuli's horse, Galahad. Keo had swapped Ronald's AR with the sniper's—it was a better weapon by every stretch of the imagination—and was cinching it to Deux's saddle.

"Can't do that," Keo said. "I'm already too far behind. Silver Hills, now this. I can't afford to go backward."

"You're not actually thinking of bringing him along, are you?" Bunker said. "The guy can't even see. Let's face it, the only reason you kept him around in the first place was because he's another gun. He's not even that anymore."

Keo didn't reply right away. Bunker wasn't telling him anything he didn't already know and hadn't thought to himself over and over. The problem was that Keo didn't have a lot of choices right now. He couldn't very well just cut Yuli loose, but he also couldn't waste the time to take him back home.

Besides, there was no guarantee the village was even still back there. For all Keo knew, it could have already burned down to the ground. That was very likely, given how forceful the fire had been when he last glimpsed the place.

So what were his other options?

Options? You're being overly optimistic, pal. There are no "options." Maybe there's one option, but face it, even that's stretching.

"Shit, you really are going to take him with you, aren't you?" Bunker said, chuckling.

"I haven't decided yet," Keo said.

"Just remember, he's your responsibility. I'm just telling you that right now."

Keo picked up Deux's reins and walked to Galahad grazing nearby, collecting the horse and heading back to Yuli.

The young Mexican must have heard his footsteps, because he turned to "look" in Keo's direction. "Are we going now?"

"Yes," Keo said.

"I still can't see, Keo." He paused, then, "I called you Bob before, didn't I?"

"Yeah."

"Sorry."

"Don't worry about it. Bob, Keo—it's all the same. Just don't call me late for dinner."

"Dinner? Are we eating?"

Keo pursed a smile. "No. Not yet."

"Oh," Yuli said, and Keo thought he looked a bit disappointed. "I heard you talking to Bunker earlier..."

Dammit, Keo thought. *I guess we weren't being as quiet as we thought.*

He said, "I can't afford to take you back to the village, Yuli. I don't have that luxury right now."

"And I don't want you to," Yuli said. "I'm not going back until we rescue Marie and Edna anyway. I mean, Lara. That's what we're going to do, right?"

"That's the plan." Keo held Galahad's reins toward Yuli—for a brief second, before realizing the man couldn't see. "Give me your hand."

Yuli held out both hands, and Keo placed the reins into one of them.

"Can you feel Galahad?" Keo asked.

Yuli nodded as the Quarter Horse nuzzled against him. Yuli groped with his fingers, found the saddle, then the horn.

"Stirrup," Keo said, guiding Yuli's boot. Then, when Yuli found it, "On three. One, two, three."

Yuli managed to land in the saddle without falling or even struggling too much. He leaned down and patted Galahad on his mane. "Good boy, good boy."

Keo watched the Mexican in silence while trying to convince himself that this was better than the alternative.

He wasn't entirely successful.

Bunker rode his painted horse over while leading Gasper by the reins. The rancher tapped his watch. "We're losing daylight. Hour, maybe less, before nightfall."

Keo glanced up and blinked at the darkening skies.

"You said there was a place nearby?" Bunker asked.

Keo nodded. "Norman. Two more klicks, give or take."

"We can make it easily, then."

"You afraid of the dark, Bunker?"

"Aren't you?"

"I've been out here before."

"So have I, but I try not to push my luck." He glanced around. "So Norman, then."

"That's not where I'm going," Keo said. "Owen had a three-hour head start on me when today started. That was before Silver Hills. Now, after tacking on this little mess, he's probably widened his lead to half a day. I know for a fact he'll hunker down for nightfall. So I'm not going to. That way, I can make up for lost time."

"You wanna ride out here at night?" Bunker asked. Keo wasn't sure if he sounded incredulous or impressed.

"I need to make up time," Keo said. "You're free to head for Norman. And take Yuli with you."

"No way. I'm not going anywhere but after Marie," Yuli said.

Keo ignored him and said to Bunker, "How much do you want to get the rest of your horses back?"

"A lot, but I'm not suicidal," Bunker said. He grinned. "You, on the other hand, don't seem to have that problem."

"You coming with me or not?"

"One more day or seven more days, don't make much of a difference to me. I'm getting back what's mine. Eventually. So there's absolutely no reason for me to take on more risks than necessary."

"Fine," Keo said, swinging into Deux's saddle. "That means you're taking Yuli with you."

"The hell I am," Bunker said.

"The hell he is," Yuli said.

Again, Keo ignored Yuli and concentrated on Bunker. "You can do that, or you can leave a blind man out here by himself. It's up to you."

Bunker narrowed his eyes at Keo. "You're bluffing."

"Bob—Keo—" Yuli said.

"Catch up to me in the morning," Keo said to Bunker. "Chances are they'll stick close to the highway even if they stray, but I'm sure a capable fellow like yourself can pick up their tracks again."

Bunker smirked. "You're not going anywhere."

"Yes, I am."

"I call bullshit."

Keo grinned at him. "See you when I see you, Bunker."

Bunker's eyes widened as Keo rode past him. "No fucking way..."

"Keo?" Yuli said. Then, when Keo didn't respond, he called out, "Keo! Keo! Dammit, Keo!"

Keo spurred Deux on, picking up more speed.

From behind him, he heard Bunker shouting, "You motherfucker!"

Keo grinned and kept going.

Soon, Deux was moving at a fast gallop, and they were up and over the hump in the road where Owen's sniper had lain in wait. Keo looked down briefly at the body as they passed. The man's head rested on one cheek, his face turned in Keo's direction. Keo couldn't tell what the man looked like because the center of his face was gone, blown away by Bunker's bullet.

One more asshole down, but still way too many to go.

Keo looked forward, enjoying the wind against his face. The free-flowing air helped to combat the stifling heat but it didn't stop him from hearing Yuli, back there somewhere, shouting his name...

He came up to Norman faster than expected. The highway split up, with a section leading toward the city on the right and the rest curving left. Keo stayed on the main road, guiding Deux farther northwest.

There was nothing but open country in front of him, which was to say it was the same thing he'd been looking at since he left the village this morning. With Norman in the background, there would be a lot of kilometers left before Harlingen, with a couple of smaller towns between here and there. Now all he had to do was figure out if Owen would risk going into a big city like Harlingen or if he would choose one of the smaller ones to bed down for the night. Keo was betting on the latter. No one went into big cities these days unless they were suicidal. There were things worse than ghouls in those places.

The problem for Keo was that the tracks he'd been following had been disappearing little by little since Silver Hills. The trailers had been on the road for so long that whatever clumps of dirt they had built up had fallen away. There were the occasional horse hooves along the shoulders, but even they were becoming increasingly rare. It didn't help that he was losing sunlight. Sooner or later, the trails would vanish completely, leaving Keo to guess where to proceed next. It was too bad he never got Ronald to tell him where Owen was headed.

Maybe I should have given him that second shot of morphine after all.

Shoulda, woulda, coulda, pal.

What were the chances Owen would abandon the state highway completely? The rough and uneven terrain would be no trouble for horses, but Owen's crew was pulling two trailers with them. The vehicles had large tires that could take a lot of pounding, but the people riding inside them might not be able to. Keo was thinking about Jackie. If Owen was willing to grab Lara to save his little brother, he wouldn't subject the wounded man to further unnecessary injuries unless he absolutely had to.

So what qualified as "absolutely had to?"

Owen didn't know about Keo. Or, at least, Keo didn't think the man knew about him. But Owen knew plenty about

Bunker, and he had already wasted three men trying to take the rancher out. Would having Bunker on his tail be enough to make Owen leave the road in an effort to shake off the rancher?

Maybe.

What was that Ronald had said to Keo about Owen?

"He'll kill you. He'll fucking kill you and piss down your throat."

Now, that was one hell of a statement. Keo had met plenty of dangerous guys—some bad, some good, but most in-between —but none of them had made him afraid. It helped, of course, that he'd been at this for a while now, and he usually shot first.

But the way Ronald had said it... The man had definitely believed what he was saying. Did that make any difference?

Maybe, again.

Ultimately, how dangerous of a man Owen was made no real difference. If he had his way, Keo would shoot first and from a distance. In the back. There was absolutely nothing wrong with taking out an opponent from behind. Keo had a lot of scruples—more than he would like to admit, frankly—but sneaking up and killing someone when they couldn't see him coming was not one of them.

We'll see who pisses down whose throat.

Ronald's words were still reverberating around Keo's head as he pushed Deux up the highway, keeping the animal to the side, where its unshod hooves wouldn't be punished by the hard pavement. The world was already starting to darken noticeably around him, even though the sun stayed out longer during the Texas summers.

Not that he was worried about riding in the dark. He'd done it before, once with a blue-eyed ghoul and a legion of its black eyes chasing him. So the idea of doing it again, but this

time with only the occasional undead to deal with, didn't even
register as a possible deterrent. That attitude, he was hoping,
was something Owen wouldn't share. They had ten people in
their party, according to Bunker—not including Lara and
Marie—and wouldn't necessarily be able to take on as much
risk as Keo.

That was his hope, anyway.

So there was a very good chance Keo could make up a lot
of time before sundown—

He pulled up on Deux and turned the horse around with
one hand, while the other moved the MP9 from behind him to
in front of him, his finger flicking off the safety a second later.
He had seen it out of the corner of one eye—a large, dark smear
on the shoulder of the road.

He climbed off the horse and scanned his immediate area,
but there was nothing out there but more open country and
the never-ending highway stretching in both directions. He
kept one hand on the Cleveland Bay's reins, the other on the
submachine gun, as he retraced their steps.

It was definitely blood. Dark and black because it had been
out here for a while, almost completely dry under the setting
sun.

A buzzing sound, followed by tiny—but multiple—movements attracted his attention, and Keo glanced into the thick
carpet of grass alongside the road. There was a cloud of flies
out there, flitting over a black object lying among the weeds.

No, not an object. A *body*.

If not for the blood, he might have ridden right past it.

Keo looked over at the horse. "Stay here."

Deux gave him a bored look before wandering off to chew
on some grass.

Keo walked into the field, sweeping the countryside around him a few more times for possible ambushes. After the incident with the sniper, he was a little wary of all the emptiness out there. All the *supposed* emptiness.

As he neared the corpse, something scurried away, the grass moving with its retreat. When he got closer, another "something" else raced off. Apparently, the man had attracted more than just Keo's attention. The presence of animals put his mind at ease, though; if the critters were already picking on the corpse, then there was less chance it was booby trapped. Keo didn't think it was, anyway, but there was little point in not taking every precaution right now. It wasn't just his life on the line, after all.

The dead man was lying on his stomach, and Keo used the toe of his boot to turn it over onto its back. It wasn't anyone he'd seen before—short brown hair and dark black eyes, but the most notable thing about the man was his nose. It had been broken recently, and dry blood caked a large part of his face. The jaw was frozen in place—wide open, like he was trying to swallow something—and the body was stiff. All those things told Keo the man had died more than two hours ago, for rigor mortis to have set in.

And the smell...

Keo took out a rag and put it over his mouth and nostrils as he crouched next to the dead man to get a better look at the destroyed face. The nose was shattered at the bridge, and because his mouth was so wide open, Keo could see a couple of missing teeth. Recently, too, judging by the blood clots along the gaps. Someone had taken the poor bastard out with a blow to the face. Could a fist do that? Maybe if the attacker was strong enough...or knew what he was doing.

Whoever had tossed the dead man out here had done a very thorough job of taking everything that could identify him, leaving behind just his clothes. He could have been anyone, including a member of Owen's crew.

Could Keo be that lucky? Was this one of Owen's gang? He had no clue. The man could have been anyone. Keo knew only one thing for certain: the body wouldn't have lasted very long out here. Either the animals would finish it off, or something else would come along at night—

He glimpsed it just underneath the man's short-sleeve shirt, on his left arm. Keo took out the Ka-Bar and used the point to slide the sleeve up until it revealed a tattoo. It wasn't very big—maybe only twenty millimeters in diameter—and Keo might have missed it completely if he hadn't been leaning in for a closer look.

He'd seen it before: It was a scaly creature—some kind of reptile, maybe a dragon or a snake—rendered entirely in flat black ink, eating its own tail.

An ouroboros.

The image brought back some memories, most of them not very good. Of course, there were a thousand reasons why the dead man would have such a tattoo that had nothing to do with Keo's past. Ink was in vogue before The Purge, especially with guys who thought of themselves as tougher than most.

Keo stood up and was putting the Ka-Bar away when he glimpsed something else—something he wouldn't have seen if he hadn't pushed the shirtsleeve up slightly. He quickly crouched back down and pulled the sleeve all the way up to the shoulder blade this time.

"Hunh," Keo said.

Someone had carved letters into the dead man's flesh,

using almost the entire width of his shoulder. Except it was hard to make out what had been "written" because of all the caked blood.

Keo used the rag to wipe at the dirt and blood. Slowly, the letters began to reveal themselves. They were small and hard to read, and someone had put them there with a blunt object and hadn't done a very good job of it as a result. Or maybe they didn't have enough time to make the whole thing legible. Not all the letters appeared finished, and they bled—literally, in this case—into one another. It might have looked like someone was just torturing the poor guy by cutting random strips into his skin if not for the fact that Keo could make out some of the words.

He couldn't read everything in one go, but once he determined what some of the letters were, he could begin to string them together into a sentence.

They read:

"BOBCHERRYPO"

Keo read it again:

"BOBCHERRYPO"

What the hell was "bobcherrypo?"

The name of a town, maybe? Or someone's name? Neither seemed very likely. Who would name their kids bobcherry—

"Bob," Keo said out loud. "B-o-b is Bob."

He grinned.

"Goddamn. B-o-b is *Bob*." Then, his smile widening, "Lara?"

He wiped at more of the blood with the rag, hoping that would reveal more letters, but they didn't. He turned the dead man over to check the back of his shoulder, but there was nothing extra back there, either.

Keo stared at the letters that were there, trying to make sense of them. Was this Lara? Was this dead man part of Owen's crew, after all, and somehow—some way—his girl had managed to carve a message on the body for Keo to find? If the man was already dead, and she had just enough time...

"Cherrypo?" Keo said out loud. "What the hell is Cherrypo?"

But he was certain the first part—*b-o-b*—was Lara talking to him. The rest was her trying to communicate something else.

What was she trying to say? What was Cherrypo?

Of that sentence (if that was even what it was), the *Cherry* part was obvious.

Cherry. Like the fruit.

So what was the *p-o*?

He squinted at the letters, now with a new perspective.

He imagined Lara being in a rush when she carved the letters with something blunt, possibly scissors. That would explain why she hadn't been able to "write" everything down as clearly as possible. She didn't even have time to space out the words to make it easier for him. Which meant *Cherrypo* could be anything. The first part might not even have been *Cherry*, because she'd used all capital letters.

Che? Cher? Cherryp?

The only *Che* he knew was Che Guevara, but that didn't make any sense.

What would, then? What would Lara risk—*if* this was even Lara—to tell him?

Something important, something vital to saving her and Marie. That was the only explanation. She would know Keo would come after her. The *Bob* was the tipoff.

It had to be Lara. It *had* to be.

God, he hoped this was Lara...

And if it was, what was she trying to tell him, knowing that he would be chasing her abductors? Because if anyone knew Keo wouldn't just give up on getting her back, it would be Lara.

But the letters didn't make any sense.

Cherrypo? What the hell is Cherry—

"It has to be where they're taking you," Keo said out loud. "You would try to tell me where they're taking you."

Keo got up and ran back to the horse. Deux lifted his head in curiosity as Keo grabbed the bag from the saddle. He rummaged through it and pulled out the map of Texas. He scanned it, limiting his area of interest to the southeast, where he was at the moment, before expanding out—

There.

Keo chuckled. "Goddamn, woman, this is why I love you," he said out loud, his forefinger resting on a very specific part of the map.

Cherry Point Lake.

TWELVE

"You should let me go."

"You're needed here."

"He's going to die. I can't help you with that. I'm not a miracle worker."

"You're better than anyone here."

"I can't save him. The best I can do is make him comfortable."

"And that's what you'll do."

"You don't understand what I'm trying to tell you..."

"Oh, I think I do."

"No, you don't."

"So tell me what I don't understand."

"There will be consequences to taking me. That's what I'm trying to get through to you. This won't go unanswered."

"And what would those consequences be?"

"My man. He'll come after me."

"I saw a lot of men back in the village. None of them did anything when I took you."

"He wasn't there at the time."

"No?"

"No. He was fishing."

"Fishing, huh?"

"That's right. He fishes in the morning with a friend. But he'll find out what happened soon enough. And when he does, he'll come after me. You really, really don't want that."

"You seem certain."

"That's because I am."

Owen stared back at her. He wasn't impressed. Or moved. The man didn't seem capable of any emotion other than calmness. But she had a feeling even that emotion was a front, a mirage to hide the storm raging behind it. This was a dangerous man. A very, very dangerous man.

"You should let me go," Lara said.

"You're talking about one man," Owen said. "What can one man do?"

"Whatever it takes to get me back."

"You mean that much to him?"

"Yes."

"Are you his property?"

"I'm his woman."

"That's not very politically correct of you," Owen said. There should have been a smirk to go along with that comeback, but Lara didn't think the man remembered how to do even that.

"*Politically correct* went out with the old world," Lara said. "This is just the reality of things now. I'm his, and he's mine. And he'll come after the people who took me from him. That should scare you."

"I've killed a lot of men." There was no bravado in that

statement; it was simply, she saw, fact. "What makes him so special?"

"If you don't let me and Marie go, now, you'll find out. And I promise you, you won't like it."

"Maybe you're overestimating him."

"I'm not." Lara smiled. It was, she realized, the first time she'd smiled since this morning. "I'm really not. You should let us go while you still can. If you do that, I'll tell him to drop this. I'll tell him not to come after you."

"And he'll listen?"

"He'll listen to me."

"You mean that much to him?"

"I'm everything to him."

"So he would die for you."

"Yes."

"And would you die for him?"

"Yes," she answered without hesitation.

"You should pray I don't make you prove that," Owen said. "Because if my brother dies, your life won't mean anything to me."

"You've made that perfectly clear."

"Just so there's no misunderstanding."

"There isn't."

"Good."

He picked up a branch and poked at the empty fire pit. There were some old rocks inside, but the last time anyone had started a fire was months ago.

When he didn't say anything else for a while, Lara said, "You really should take this offer. You might not get another chance after tonight. It'll be too late by morning."

"Because he's coming after us. Your man."

"That's right."

"And he's good."

"Yes. He's very good. He doesn't like to admit it, but this was what he was born to do. He hasn't done it for a long time now, because of me. Because he loves me, and he would do anything for me. He would even hide the real him. But you've ruined that illusion by taking me, and he's not going to stop until he gets me back."

Owen tossed the branch and picked up his canteen. He unscrewed the top and offered it to her.

She ignored it and kept her eyes focused on him. Lara had been reading her captors ever since they took her and Marie from the village. She had been eavesdropping on everything they said to one another when they didn't think she was listening. Every order Owen gave, every disagreement among the group, was potential information she could use to further an escape.

As soon as Owen stepped into the clinic and asked which one of them—her or Marie, who was there for her morning checkup—was the doctor, Lara knew she was dealing with very dangerous men with little to lose. She also quickly understood that they were being led by a man who had to be even more dangerous in order to keep the rest in check. A man who would do anything to save the one person he cared about more than anything in the world.

For the next half hour, Lara had kept Jackie alive, reversing all the damage the traveling and bad field medicine had done to his body. Owen had stood nearby, like a silent gargoyle, never straying too far from his little brother. When she was done, she knew it was a mistake—keeping Jackie alive—because now she had become too useful. Owen knew she wouldn't leave with him—not voluntarily, anyway—and that was where Marie had come in.

A gunshot, a terse threat, and the words, "Come with us or she dies," was all it had taken for Lara to leave the village with them. Ophelia was the first to notice that Lara and Marie were being put into one of the trailers, but she couldn't do anything to stop it. Lara had locked eyes with the other woman and shook her head to let her know not to even try. George's wife would have just gotten hurt, and Lara already had a pregnant Marie to worry about.

"You shoot anyone, and you can forget about me going with you," she had said to Owen.

While they were being pulled away from the village, the flames were already engulfing the clinic and spreading fast. Owen said it was an accident, but Lara didn't believe him. It didn't look like an accident to her. If anything, it looked more like a distraction to keep the men in the village busy while Owen left with her and Marie.

In the hours after the abduction, Lara thought about Keo and how long it would take him to find out what had happened, then pursue. Because she knew he would do just that. He was her man, after all, and she was his woman. She was glad he hadn't been at the village at the time; as good as Keo was, she didn't like his chances against Owen and his men, even if one of them was a half-dead Jackie.

Now, as she stared across the dark fire pit at Owen as he picked at a bag of MRE with a spork, she thought, *Be careful, Keo. These are dangerous men. And they're being led by a viper. Hurry up and find me, but be careful. Be very, very careful.*

"You should eat," Owen said, looking up at her.

"I'm not hungry," Lara said.

"Suit yourself." Owen nodded at the trailer parked nearby. "What about her?"

"Leland already gave her something."

"Take this anyway. You'll be hungry later."

Owen opened one of their supply bags and tossed her an MRE. She caught it. It wasn't like the U.S. Army ones she and Keo had taken from the truck after Darby Bay, but commercial versions of the same products. These had *XMRE* on them, and the packages were more aesthetically pleasing than the ones she was used to.

"You should let us go," she said.

"You already said that," Owen said as he went back to eating. "More than once. And it's getting tiresome."

"This is going to end badly for you. When it does, I want you to know that I tried to convince you to take the easy road out. That I gave you every opportunity in the world."

"I appreciate that," he said, with all the sincerity of a venomous reptile.

He fixed her with a cold, hard stare that told her the conversation was over. For a man in his forties, Owen was lean and muscular, and she had no trouble picturing him dominating—physically and emotionally—everyone he came across. That included his men—or the ones that were still around, anyway.

She knew for a fact that three were missing. A fourth, Granger, had died when he rebelled loudly, then later tried to sneak off with supplies. Walter, Owen's right-hand man, had caught him, and Owen had supplied the punishment. Lara didn't see the fight, but she could hear it. The sound of breaking bones, the grunts of pain. Later, they brought

Granger's bloodied body over to her and told her to keep him alive.

Lara had tried to save the man, but she knew it was a lost cause as soon as she saw the damage Owen had inflicted with just his fists. When no one was watching, she had taken the surgical shears and did her best to carve a message for Keo. It was difficult and messy, and she hadn't been able to write everything with Owen's men constantly hovering around. The only reason she wasn't discovered was because Granger was already so bloody. Still, she'd almost been caught once or twice.

Now, as she sat across from Owen in a dark campground that no one had used for months, or possibly years, she thought about Keo. He was out there. She was sure of it. Night was starting to fall around them, and soon it would be pitch-dark all across the South Texas countryside. She pictured Keo alone, stumbling across the puddles of Granger's blood on the side of the road, then the body itself in the weeds.

Cherry Point, Keo. They're taking me to Cherry Point Lake.

But what if it was too dark and he couldn't see the blood on the shoulder of the road or the body they'd tossed into the field? Or what if he wasn't even on the same road they had taken? What if Keo wasn't even chasing after her?

No, she didn't believe that last one. The first two were possibilities, but the third?

No, she didn't believe it for a second. Keo would come after her whether he was alone or not. She didn't have any doubts about that whatsoever.

Not one single shred of doubt.

Be careful, Keo. They're dangerous. They're very, very dangerous.

After she made her intentions clear she wasn't interested in eating with him, Owen sent her back to the trailer. Leland, one of his men, walked her across the campground. Leland was a hulking man with biceps twice the size of her two arms put together. He was imposing, and walking alongside him made her feel like a child.

"You should eat that. It's pretty good," the big man said, nodding at the MRE bag in her hand.

"I'm not hungry," Lara said.

"You should eat it anyway. We won't get to Cherry Point until tomorrow. You'll be starving by then."

"I'll give it to Marie." *She needs it more than I do, since she's eating for two now*, Lara almost said but stopped in time. She added instead, "Thanks."

"For what?" Leland asked.

"Being concerned."

"I wasn't. I was just being friendly."

"Sure you were."

Leland grunted. It sounded like something a bear would make. "I'll bring you some more food later for you two if you're still hungry."

"Thanks."

"Sure."

Lara noted where Owen's men were as she was led back to her "prison." Besides Leland and Owen, still back there at the fire pit, eating by himself, there were two more standing guard at the edge of the clearing. Another one kept an eye on the horses tied together in a picket line nearby, and a fourth sat on top of his horse looking off at the fading sunlight on the horizon. There were others that she couldn't locate but was sure were out there somewhere, scattered along the perimeter.

That was one of the first things she noticed about Owen and his men. They were organized, and with the exception of Granger's ill-fated rebellion, willing followers. They had all the looks and feel of an ex-army unit; or at least, men that had been fighting together for some time now. That realization made her wonder where they had come from, or who they had been fighting for, before all of this. She didn't ask, because she didn't want Owen to know how much she'd already deduced about them. In her experience, the more men saw you as a helpless female, the easier it was to defeat them.

"Stop it," Leland said, surprising her.

She looked over and up at him. "Stop what?"

"You're thinking about it," the big man said.

"I don't know what you're talking about."

"Uh huh," Leland said.

When they reached the trailer, he stopped and turned to face her. It was darkening, but she could see the look in Leland's eyes and was amazed that in a group of hardened men, the biggest among them was the softest.

"Just keep doing what you're already doing with Jackie until we get to Cherry Point," Leland said. He had, she noticed, lowered his voice slightly, as if he were afraid the others might overhear. "After that, everything will be fine."

She stared back at him, trying to give nothing away. She wondered if he actually believed what he'd just said to her.

"I'm not going to do anything," Lara said. "How could I? Look around you."

Leland narrowed his eyes. He clearly didn't believe her. "Just hang on, okay? I'll make sure nothing happens to you two. That's my job."

"Your job, or your order?"

"Same difference."

"No, it's not, Leland. It's not."

He sighed and glanced in Owen's direction before looking back at her. "Just play it cool. It'll work out in the end. I promise."

"Okay, Leland," Lara said, and forced herself to smile at him.

It must have been convincing, because he smiled back, nodded, and said, "I'll bring some more food over later."

"Thanks," Lara said, and climbed into the trailer.

Marie had come back from the bathroom break they'd allowed her earlier when Leland had come to fetch Lara. The young woman was sitting on the covered floor, already eating from her own bag of MRE when Lara climbed inside.

"This is almost as good as the ones you brought to the village," Marie said. She was a small girl and looked even smaller in the cramped space.

Leland had taken up his post outside, his huge shadow looming against the thick white tarp that covered the trailer, making it look like a wagon from the Old West. The five-by-nine vehicle was pulled by two horses and had four wheels to stabilize it, so when Lara and Marie moved around it barely wobbled. If she weren't being held hostage and forced to treat a half-dead man, Lara wouldn't have minded riding around in the thing.

"You doing okay?" Lara asked.

Marie looked up from her MRE and nodded. She had some spaghetti sauce under her chin, and the trailer smelled of food. For some reason, Lara still wasn't hungry, and she tossed the bag Owen had given her into a corner.

"I forgot how hard it was to go to the bathroom when someone's watching you," Marie said.

"Did they try anything?" Lara asked.

"No."

"Good."

Lara sat down across from Marie. The floor was covered with a thick blanket to make the ride more comfortable, and it was. The "ceiling" above them was held up by metal rods welded outside the vehicle, allowing the two of them to move around without worrying about bumping their heads against the dust-covered tarp all the time. It still happened, especially in the beginning, but they'd grown accustomed to walking around bent just slightly over. The trailers had been used for something else—maybe ferrying supplies—but had been repurposed to transport people.

"How are you?" Lara asked, making sure Marie saw where she was looking at the same time—the other woman's stomach.

Marie glanced quickly toward Leland's shadowed form before looking back at her. She rubbed her stomach with one hand and pursed a smile. There wasn't a baby bump yet; she had a few weeks to go before she would show. Lara was hoping their ordeal would be over by then; she didn't want to think about caring for an obviously pregnant girl in the midst of these men.

"Everything will be okay," Lara said. "We'll *all* be okay. I promise."

Marie nodded again and went back to eating. She was a pretty girl, with the kind of smile that could steal any man's heart. Yuli was lucky to have her, and Lara thought he knew it, too. It was just Marie's bad luck to be at the clinic when Owen and his people showed up.

This morning was still fresh in Lara's mind. She'd spent most of her free time waiting for Marie to show up, thinking about that talk with Keo the night before. The one about the two of them having a baby. She had regretted bringing it up, because she could see how uncomfortable it made him. In so many ways, she agreed with what he'd said, that this wasn't the kind of world you wanted to bring a child into if you had the choice.

Now, sitting in a cramped trailer while men with guns and the bad will to use them at an instant's notice decided their fates, she realized just how right Keo was.

Lara sneaked a look over at Leland's large shadow before locking eyes with Marie. Then, in a low voice, "Remember, stay as close to me as possible at all times, okay? Don't let any of them take you away without me or Leland knowing where you're going. If I'm not around, and Leland's busy with something, make sure you're within sight of Owen at all times."

"Owen?" Marie whispered. "Why him? He's the reason we're here."

"Because he's not going to let anything happen to you. I made it clear that you're the only reason I'm here. But the others..." She shook her head. "They don't care if Jackie lives or dies, but Owen does. As far as I know, he's the only one who does."

Maybe Leland, too, she thought but couldn't be sure of that. And right now, she needed to be sure of everything.

"Stay close to me at all times whenever possible, okay?" Lara said.

Marie nodded. Her face had paled, and she looked more frightened now than when their nightmare had started this morning. Lara hated to bring up the subject, but she had no regrets. It had to be done. She had to make sure Marie understood the situation.

"One last thing," Lara said.

She leaned closer toward Marie, and the younger woman met her halfway.

"He'll find us," Lara whispered. "When he does, we have to be ready."

"Who?" Marie asked.

"Bob."

"Your Bob?"

Lara smiled. She always got a kick out of people calling Keo *Bob*, and she thought it was the same with him when people called her Edna.

"Yes," Lara said. "Bob will find us."

Marie gave her a puzzled look. "Who is he? Bob, I mean. Yuli and I talked about you guys sometimes. Mostly about Bob. That scar of his... We always wondered how he got it."

"You never asked him?"

Marie shook her head. "You know how it is. We don't ask people about them before they showed up. Everyone's starting over, so..."

Lara nodded, understanding. The lack of curiosity—or, at least, overtly—was one of the reasons she and Keo had stayed. The first few weeks had been uncomfortable as they tried to assimilate, but it was people like Marie, Ophelia, George, and Yuli that made the transition successful. It was also why, when no one stepped up to stop Owen from taking her and Marie, Lara didn't feel the anger toward them that she might have six months ago. The only thing resistance would have resulted in was unnecessary deaths. Owen was a killer—as were the men with him—and it would have taken just about everyone in the village to stop them. Lara didn't need or want that bloodbath on her hands.

Not anymore. Not in this new life.

"Edna?" Marie said. "Who is Bob? Why are you so sure he can help us?"

"Bob is..." Lara stopped and thought about it.

Should she tell Marie about their lives before the village? It was another lifetime now. How much did Lara want to tell this kind, young girl about the life she used to live? Leading men into battle, giving orders that cost so many people their lives, fighting for a cause that ended up in tears...

"Bob is a man who won't give up," Lara said, holding Marie's hand tightly in hers. "So we can't give up, either."

"You know something," Marie said.

Lara checked on Leland again. He hadn't moved from his post, as far as she could tell.

She turned back to Marie. "Jackie's going to die," she whispered. "There's nothing I can do about it. He was bad when they brought him to me, and he's only gotten worse. Right now, I'm barely keeping him alive. He's going to die, Marie—soon. Very soon. When that happens, Owen won't protect us anymore, because we won't be of any use to him."

Marie's face paled noticeably, even in the dark and cramped space of the trailer.

"You have to be ready for whatever happens between now and then," Lara whispered. "For both of you."

Marie put her hand on her stomach again and nodded. "I'll be ready."

Lara forced a smile and nodded, even as the thoughts *Don't screw this up. Do you hear me? Don't you screw this up* again, swirled around inside her head.

THIRTEEN

Jackie was going to die, and there was nothing Lara could do to prevent it. She could prolong it, which was what she'd already been doing, but the damage was too great. He'd been shot in the waist by a large caliber round from a rifle. If Lara had to guess, it probably happened when Owen and his group encountered this Bunker that Owen had previously sent two of his men after. Bunker, whoever he was, was a dangerous individual, because those two hadn't returned, and Owen had proceeded as if they were dead.

That incident had only added to the contentious relationship between Owen and Granger, the only member of Owen's gang who ever raised any vocal disagreements with Owen's leadership while Lara was around. Lara hadn't witnessed how it happened, but she'd seen the end results. Granger had looked...bad when they brought him to her.

But she was thinking about Jackie tonight. The young man was only twenty-five or so, which would mean he was a teenager before The Purge. Owen loved his brother. Lara could see that. Everything he was doing now was for Jackie, trying to wring out every last hour they had together. That was where she came in...for now. Lara had a feeling that Cherry Point was going to be the end of the line, one way or another.

But they weren't in Cherry Point Lake yet. Not until morning. Right now, Owen had set up camp off the main state highway in the abandoned campground. There was a stream nearby, the sound of running water the only thing Lara could hear other than the crickets in the fields around them.

Marie was snoring softly next to her. Lara was surprised the young woman could sleep at all after the conversation they'd had. Then again, Marie had been afraid the entire day, ever since they were taken from the village. Hours later, and everything must have caught up to her, because she was out just seconds after lying down and closing her eyes.

It wasn't as easy for Lara. She lay on her back, staring up at the unmoving white tarp above them. There was no wind outside, so nothing moved other than her chest, and Marie's next to her. The night helped with the heat, whereas in the day she felt like they were baking inside the trailer, her only relief whenever they made her go check on Jackie in the other vehicle.

She hadn't had to worry about all the dangerous things that could be lurking within the night for so long, that being out here again, far from the safety of the village and the seawater next to it, made her alarmed at every sound. She hadn't realized how good she had it until now.

And there was Keo. He'd saved her life after that mess in Darby Bay, and he was the reason she always felt so safe out here. His presence was like a wall around her, keeping all the bad things at bay. In the months after they arrived at the village, she'd become used to seeing him heading off with George in the mornings, but she could never deny the relief when he returned later in the day. After a while, she'd stopped noticing the night.

But Keo wasn't here now. He was out there, somewhere, looking for her. She was as certain of that as she'd ever been of anything in her life. He would come back to the village, see what had happened, and give chase. He would never just let someone take her without a fight.

That was why she loved him.

Lara smiled to herself. It had taken a long time to get used to that, to admit to herself that there could be someone after Will.

But there was. There was Keo.

He was out there right now, looking for her, so she had to be ready when he found her. She didn't know how, or when, but he *would* find her.

She thought about what she had told Marie, about Owen and his group no longer having any uses for them once Jackie finally succumbed to his wound. That hadn't been entirely true. The men would still have uses for them; it just wasn't going to be for anything they were going to like very much.

She shivered at the thought and turned to look at Marie, sleeping nearby on the thick bedding. There was a blanket, but neither one of them was using it. It was simply too hot, even with the darkness outside. Marie lay on her side, breathing softly, both hands wrapped around her stomach. It would be weeks before her belly started to show. Not that Lara had any illusions the reveal of Marie's pregnancy would stop the men outside from doing what they wanted to do to the pretty girl.

All of the men outside, with perhaps the exception of Leland.

She glanced toward the back of the wagon. It wasn't Leland outside but his night replacement. Leland, though, wouldn't have wandered off too far. His job was to watch her and Marie, to keep them from escaping, but Lara thought that was only half of it. The other half was to keep the other men away from them.

In another time, another place, Lara thought she could make friends with someone like Leland. He wasn't any different from the hundreds of men that had gone through Black Tide's ranks. Because of that, she thought there was a decent chance she could get him on her side. All she had to do was work on him.

That was the problem.

Time.

She was running up against time. She needed—

Her thoughts cut off in mid-sentence.

What just happened?

She didn't move, didn't even dare breathe, and just listened to...

...nothing.

It was dead silent outside, because the crickets had stopped making noise. If not for Marie snoring lightly next to her, Lara might have believed the entire world had simply ceased to exist suddenly.

She sat up as slowly as possible, but the tires underneath them creaked against her sudden movement anyway, and Lara cringed. She glanced over at Marie, but the young woman remained asleep, oblivious to Lara's movements and the silence outside.

Why is it so quiet outside?

Leland's replacement was sitting on the flat bumper at the back of the trailer, his silhouetted form leaning slightly to one side, probably because he was half-asleep.

Lara looked to her left, but there was just a sheet of white tarp. The fabric, designed for long-term storage against the elements, did a tremendous job of keeping cold out, but it also maintained a steady humidity inside the trailer. And it was thick, which made it difficult to see through.

The campground was nestled inside a small group of trees about, as far as she could tell, two or so miles from the highway they had been traveling on all day. Owen had decided—smartly, she thought—that the potential risks out here were better than the potential dangers lying in wait in a big city like Harlingen.

Doing her best not to wake Marie, Lara crawled toward the back, the trailer shifting slightly under her. It was more than enough for her guard to notice, and the figure stood up and turned around. She saw the long barrel of a shotgun in his hands casting a warp silhouette against the tarp as he did so.

"What are you doing in there?" her guard asked.

Lara pulled the plastic material to one side and looked out at the man. He'd introduced himself as Portman earlier. He wasn't nearly as tall or big as Leland—but then, no one in the group was—but he was large enough that he didn't really need the gun to intimidate her. He was wearing a red Texas Rangers baseball cap and had week-old stubble. Thirties, but he looked older.

"Something's wrong," Lara said.

Portman cocked his head slightly, like he thought she was up to no good. "What are you talking about?"

"Can you hear it?" Lara asked him.

"Hear what?"

"Listen."

"I am."

"No, you're not," Lara whispered. *"Listen."*

He did—for real, this time—while his eyes remained fixed on her.

After a while, he said, "I don't hear shit."

"Exactly," Lara said. "The crickets. What happened to the crickets?"

That got the response she wanted. She wondered if he hadn't noticed because he was half-asleep out here or if he was just that thick. No, it was probably the former. She could make out grogginess in his eyes.

"What happened to the crickets, Portman?" Lara asked again.

Portman didn't answer. Instead, he turned around. Suddenly, Lara was no longer his priority as he clutched and unclutched the shotgun and squinted his eyes at their surroundings.

Lara leaned out just far enough to see what was out there.

The campground was filled with sleeping bodies, not that she could tell one apart from another. Three, maybe four lay on top of their sleeping bags around the unlit fire pit, their snoring the only sounds Lara could make out against the suddenly (*too*) still night. Two more figures were deep asleep next to the horses on the other side of the clearing. That made five, which meant there were two others out there that she couldn't see, not counting Portman in front of her, or Jackie in his own trailer.

Her guard turned back around. "Get back inside."

"Wake the others up," Lara said.

"I'm not waking anyone up," Portman said. "Get back—"

It came out of nowhere, leaping onto Portman's back, spindly limbs grappling around his arms and legs. Portman screamed, and the shotgun fired, the *boom!* so loud that Lara's ears were still ringing when she fell backward reflexively and the tarp opening flopped back into place in front of her.

She couldn't see it, but she could hear Portman struggling, screaming, when another shotgun blast *boomed.* Lara continued stumbling backward, not sure what to do, grabbing the sides of the trailer to keep from falling over—

"Edna?" a voice said behind her.

She spun around to find a sleepy Marie sitting up on the bedding.

Marie was rubbing her eyes. "I thought I heard—"

The *bang-bang-bang!* of gunshots cut her off.

Lara whirled back around as muzzle flashes appeared all around her, silhouetted figures darting around desperately from one side of the campfire to the other. Someone screamed (Was that Portman? Lara couldn't be sure.), and someone else let out a slew of curses. Then someone opened fire with a semi-automatic rifle, and that was all Lara could hear for the next few seconds.

Marie screamed, and Lara turned to ask what had happened when she saw it. Even if she hadn't seen it first, crawling into the back of the trailer with them, she would have smelled it.

A ghoul.

It pulled itself through the tarp, eyes snapping from Lara to Marie and back again. Moonlight gleamed off its pruned black skin, equally dark, hollow eyes focusing on Marie. Lara didn't know why it was doing that, why it was concentrating so hard on the other woman instead of her, who was closer.

Then, a horrific possibility: Was it the baby? Could the creature sense the baby inside Marie?

"Get behind me!" Lara shouted.

The young woman was scrambling to do just that when the monster bounded across the trailer. Its eyes zeroed in on Marie, mouth opening wide to let thick, black liquid ooze from caverns of spiky yellow and brown teeth. At least it had teeth; she'd seen plenty of ghouls that were all pulpy black gums.

But it was the smell that got to Lara and wouldn't let go. It reeked, like melting vomit in a hot concrete sidewalk. The stench filled up the enclosed space of the trailer and clawed its way into her nostrils, trying to drown her in its unnatural filth.

"Edna!" Marie shouted.

"Stay behind me," Lara said. "Stay behind me!"

The gunfire outside hadn't stopped for even a second, which told her there were more ghouls out there. The muzzle flashes continued, as did the screams and cursing. The *boom!* of shotguns mixed with the *bang-bang* of pistols and the relentless *pop-pop-pop* of semiautomatic rifles.

Somewhere outside, she heard Owen's voice, shouting, "Silver bullets! Use your silver bullets!"

Wait. They weren't using silver bullets until now? Lara thought. Everyone knew to arm themselves with silver. If not bullets, then knives—or some kind of bladed weapon coated with the precious metal.

Everyone knew that.

So how did Owen and his men not—

The creature leapt at them, and Lara stopped thinking and kicked out at it with both feet, while simultaneously pushing down on the bedding with her palms. She caught it in the torso while it was in midair, the force of the collision sending shock-waves through her legs. But it also did what she had hoped, and the ghoul flopped backward and crashed to the floor.

Then it was scrambling, frantically twisting its painfully thin and frail bones until it was on its hands and knees. Its eyes zoomed in on her, mouth opening to let more spit fly free. What little light there was in the trailer gleamed off its domed hairless head.

She wished she had a weapon, but she didn't. Owen only gave her the medical bag to treat Jackie, but he always made sure Leland took it back, along with everything in it, when she was done. Besides the bedding that they slept on, there was absolutely nothing else inside the vehicle for her to use. They didn't even have canteens or bottles of water. All Lara had were her hands and feet and the thick blanket that they couldn't use anyway.

"Get back!" Lara shouted to Marie.

The pregnant woman scrambled even farther into the back of the trailer as Lara grabbed the pile of fabric she'd been sitting on. It was warm and filthy and big enough for a queen-size bed, and she had to snatch it with both hands as the ghoul raced at her on its hands and knees, clamoring forward like a human-sized insect.

She threw the blanket into its path, and the creature disappeared headfirst into it before crashing wildly to the floor just in front of her. Lara lunged at it, wrapping and tightening her arms around the thrashing figure before it could shake the fabric free. She didn't bother hitting or kicking it. She'd seen ghouls stay "alive" even after losing all of their limbs. Compared to that, a good, swift kick wasn't going to do a damn thing.

No, she couldn't kill this thing, and that was the only way she was going to stop it. So she held on even as it flung itself side to side, back and forth, trying to get loose from her grip, from the blanket that covered it. Thank God the black eyes didn't have the kind of strength that the blue-eyed ghouls did. If anything, they were even weaker than the average human being, the same tainted blood that made them so fast and nearly unkillable having also turned them weak.

The creature refused to stop moving, to stop fighting. All Lara could do was tighten her arms further around what she thought was its head and squeezed for all she was worth, pushing her entire weight down on its constantly slithering body in an attempt to pin it to the floor. If she couldn't kill it, maybe she could contain it.

Then Marie was there, jumping on the bottom half of the ghoul and grabbing its legs—or maybe that was its arms?—and pushing down with everything she had, too.

"Hold it down!" Lara yelled. "Don't let go! Don't let it go!"

Marie was now using her knees to help keep the creature from getting back up. And yet it continued to fight them, refusing to surrender for even a second. Did the black eyes ever get tired? Everything she'd seen, everything she'd heard, said they could fight forever. Or, at least, until the sun came up. But that wasn't going to be for a while. Not for a long—

"Goddamn, look at you two," a voice said behind her.

Lara glanced back just as Leland was climbing into the

trailer, the vehicle rocking noticeably underneath his massive weight.

In all the fighting and trying to keep the ghoul down, Lara hadn't realized that the shooting outside had stopped. She could hear calm voices and see shadows moving around out there now. She thought she could even make out Owen giving orders.

"Need a hand?" Leland asked.

"Get in here!" Lara said.

The big man grinned and crouched between her and Marie. He drew his knife—it was a large weapon, fit for a man his size—and said to them, "Hold it still, ladies."

"Just stab it already!" Lara shouted at him.

Leland chuckled, then did just that, driving the blade into the convulsing figure underneath the blanket. It stopped moving almost instantly, and when Leland pulled his knife out, black blood squirted from the hole in the fabric.

Lara finally let go, unfurling her legs from around the still creature. She lay down on the floor and stared up at the tarp above her, gasping for breath. She had to do it with just her mouth, because the creature's pungent stink was everywhere.

"You guys did good," Leland said. "Had me worried for a second."

"You took your time," Lara said.

"Sorry about that. We had our hands full, too."

"And now?"

"Not anymore."

Lara sat up and looked across at Marie at the back. Their eyes locked, the other woman's face covered in sweat. She, too, was trying to catch her breath using her mouth only.

Leland stood up, the trailer squeaking under him again. "You guys want me to leave this here?"

Lara shot him an annoyed look.

The big man laughed, then raised his hands in surrender. "Guess that's a no." He took a bright-red silk handkerchief out of his pocket and held it out to her. "Here you go, Doc."

"What's that for?" Lara said.

"You got ghoul blood on your face."

"Ugh."

She hadn't felt it earlier, but as soon as Leland mentioned it, suddenly she could and had to keep from gagging. She took the handkerchief gratefully and wiped at her cheeks and chin.

"Thanks," Lara said.

"That's what I'm here for," Leland said.

He picked up the blanketed ghoul as if it weighed nothing and carried it to the back, where he tossed it outside.

"Leland," Lara said. Then, when he turned around, she held out his handkerchief. "Thank you."

"You guys look like you need it more than me."

"Are you sure?"

"It's just a kerchief," he said with a chuckle before climbing outside. "Come on, get some fresh air."

Lara put the silk fabric away and turned to Marie. "Okay?"

Marie nodded. "You?"

"Let's get some air."

She climbed out of the trailer, then turned around to help Marie down.

The campground was littered with bodies. There had to be at least a dozen ghouls, their bullet-riddled corpses bleeding on the ground around her. Owen's men were going from emaciated figure to figure, stabbing them with their knives. She guessed they were just making sure the creatures wouldn't get back up. The whole area smelled like a landfill. Lara took Leland's handkerchief back out and put it over her mouth and nostrils to combat the stink.

The dead weren't all ghouls. One of the two men sleeping next to the horses was being covered up with his own sleeping bag, while another one sat on the ground nearby holding his hands against his neck.

It was Portman. A couple of men, including Walter, were crouched in front of him, trying to stop the bleeding. Portman's face, even in the semidarkness, was pale and slicked with dripping sweat.

Owen walked past her. He was coming from Jackie's trailer, where another man stood guard now. Judging by Owen's calm demeanor (When was the man *not* calm?), Jackie had gotten through the night just fine.

She watched Owen as he walked over to where Portman kneeled and exchanged a glance with Walter.

"What happened to him?" Marie whispered.

"He's been bitten," Lara whispered back.

"How do you know?"

"His face," she said. "It's all over his face. He knows it's over."

"God—" Marie was saying when Owen drew his sidearm and shot Portman in the head.

Portman flopped to the ground and lay still.

"Make sure he doesn't get back up," Owen said.

Walter nodded and drew his knife.

"Come on, we don't need to see this," Lara said to Marie, and led her back to the trailer.

Lara helped the pregnant young woman into their prison

before glancing back and found Owen looking across the campground at her.

They locked eyes, and Lara thought, *Dammit, Keo, where the hell are you? I really, really need you right now.*

So hurry up already, before I have to do this all by myself...

FOURTEEN

Gunfire.

The staccato of muzzle flash, like fireflies blinking in the darkness. He could see them without having to strain his eyes, but knowing the exact details was another matter. He knew some of it, though.

Ghouls, for one.

He'd found their tracks a few kilometers back in the form of trampled grass and they had led him across the open field toward a small stream. They were moving fast and didn't have a clue he was behind them, and didn't care about hiding their presence. At least, none of them turned around and attacked if they did. Or maybe a camp full of people was the better option.

Either way, he got within two hundred or so meters of the campground when the shooting began. There was just the *boom!* of a shotgun blast at first, but that quickly gave way to handguns and semiautomatic rifles. That must not have been very effective (*No silver bullets?*), because the gunfire stopped and was replaced by hand-to-hand fighting.

Silver-bladed weapons. Apparently, the campers weren't smart enough to carry silver bullets on them but were smart enough to have silver knives available.

One out of two ain't bad, I guess.

Keo couldn't see everything that happened. He didn't have field glasses on him and was stuck with the very stingy moonlight to eyeball everything with. Not that the fighting lasted for very long. That was one of the advantages of having silver on you at all times; ghouls went down like stones once you pricked them with the precious metal. The Ka-Bar in the sheath wedged behind Keo's back now was similarly coated. He'd been sure to ask George all about it the first time he saw the knife on the boat.

He couldn't tell who was who in the campgrounds or which figure was human and which was ghoul. It didn't help that the group hadn't lit any fires before they bedded down for the night; they were probably hoping not to attract attention.

Better luck next time, guys.

He was most worried about Lara. She was in that camp, too, along with those very heavily armed men led by Owen, a.k.a. Mr. Piss Down Your Throat. Keo thought there were fewer people when the fighting finally finished, but he couldn't be sure of the exact number. What he wouldn't give for a pair of night-vision binoculars...

After a lengthy period of staring, letting his eyes adjust to the darkness, Keo could finally make out the two trailers parked next to each other on one side of the camp. The horses that had been pulling them were corralled on the opposite side, and the animals had kicked up one hell of a ruckus when the ghouls attacked. But Owen's crew had managed to keep them from running off, and despite all the noise, there was no second wave of nightcrawlers.

That last part made him feel better. You never knew how many of the creatures were still out there right now. Six or seven months ago, he might have said "not many" with some measure of confidence, but that was before Merrick.

Not long after everything calmed down at the bad guy camp, there was the *bang!* of a single gunshot. It was so loud and unexpected that Keo reflexively tightened his grip around the MP9 and expected a bullet to land somewhere next to him.

But the shot hadn't been directed at him. He'd seen the muzzle flash from the campground, then nothing.

What was that about?

Keo stayed where he was, surrounded by a seemingly endless open field, and waited. Wilting knee-high grass circled him, ensuring that even if anyone in Owen's group had NVDs, they wouldn't be able to spot him. Or, at least, he hoped not. It would suck if he was exposed now, before he could even come up with a plan to save Lara.

A plan. That was what he needed.

So what was the plan?

He had no idea. He'd been lucky to stumble across the dead body at the side of the highway, and even luckier to notice Lara's message carved into the man's skin. (*Damn, Lara. Now that's hardcore, babe.*) If not for that little message in a bottle, he might have continued on toward Harlingen instead of leaving the road and taking a shortcut across the prairie to Cherry Point Lake. Ten or so kilometers left to go, according to the map he had in his pocket. Sticking to the highway would have taken an extra ten. Stumbling across the ghoul tracks, then the campground, had been a stroke of good luck.

He wondered if Owen knew of a better shortcut to Cherry Point Lake. Was there another, smaller road somewhere nearby? What the hell was in Cherry Point Lake, anyway? There was a town called Cherry Point, with a lake nearby.

Cherry Point Lake. Now that's a great name for a romantic getaway.

Of course there wasn't going to be anything romantic about this. Keo was pretty sure he was going to have to take out Mr. Piss Down Your Throat and his crew before he could get Lara back. After everything they had gone through to grab her —and Marie, but this was mostly about Lara—they weren't just going to hand her over to him because he asked nicely.

Not that he planned on asking, anyway.

Keo sat down on the hard ground and took a long look at the campground across the field from him. People were still moving around over there, but they were maintaining the blackout. That was impressive. He was expecting a flashlight or two—maybe light from a portable LED lantern—to make an appearance while Owen's people surveyed the damage. But no. Still as dark now as it'd been before all the shooting.

He watched shadowy men dragging bodies across the camp and toward the stream on the other side. Ghoul bodies, and maybe a bad guy or two. Keo could only hope for the latter. It would make his job easier if the creepy crawlers had managed to take out some of Owen's men for him.

After the sudden burst of violence, the night settled down as if nothing had happened, but Owen's crew was clearly now more on guard—not that they weren't before. Just more so, now. Keo could make out a couple of figures standing near the horses and a few more spreading out along the area to provide additional perimeter defense.

Looks like no one's getting any sleep tonight.

He was definitely looking at a group that had been together for a while. They'd fought like it, too, with no one running away from the camp during the attack. Civilians always ran; soldiers—or those who had been playing one for a while—knew that their best chance was always to maintain the group.

Keo wasn't going to be able to do anything for Lara tonight. The bad guys would be running high on adrenaline after the fight, and they would probably shoot first and forget about the questions if he so much as showed his head.

No, nothing else was going to happen tonight.

So he turned and crawled away. He stayed low, fully aware of how high the blades of grass around him were, and didn't rise up to his feet until he'd put another hundred or so meters between him and the sentries. His legs and back were aching by the time he stood upright and walked the rest of the way.

Deux was waiting for him next to the same tree Keo had left him at. Keo had tied the Cleveland Bay's reins to a branch to give it incentive to stay put while he went to take a look. Not that the animal couldn't have broken free if he'd wanted to.

"Good thing you didn't run off," Keo said. "Otherwise, I would have eaten this myself."

He took one of the small apples out of the backpack, and Deux gobbled it from his palm. He'd taken the fruits from Yuli before leaving the Mexican behind, since Keo didn't think the former journo student would need it anyway.

"What's with you and apples?" Keo asked, not that the horse answered.

He sat down against the tree and put the MP9 in his lap. Deux *crunched* the fruit next to him, taking his time with his dinner.

Keo glanced down at his watch. Almost midnight. There was nothing for him to do before sunup. He couldn't get to Lara, not with Owen's group on high alert after the ghoul attack. But he had found them, and that was the important takeaway. He had caught up to the bastards.

Now all he had to do was take Lara back from them.

To do that, though, he needed a plan. That was the tricky part.

"You got a plan?" Keo asked the horse.

Deux ignored him and continued enjoying his apple.

"I guess not," Keo said.

He closed his eyes, leaned back, and tried to get some rest. Morning would come soon enough, and he wanted to be fresh and ready for first daylight. If there were more ghouls out there, either he or Deux would be able to smell them before they got too close.

He hoped, at least.

He was back, more or less, at the same spot where he'd watched the campground chaos last night, except this time Lara's abductors were in the process of packing. Keo was still too far away to get a decent look at their faces, and any one of them could have been Mr. Piss Down Your Throat. Which was too bad, because Keo would have loved to end it here and now with one bullet.

Instead, Keo treated himself to one of Deux's apples while

he observed the campground. The fruit was a nice change of pace from the MREs he'd been eating all day yesterday, even if it was about a couple of days away from being full-on rotten.

As the camp woke up, Keo kept waiting for signs of Lara. It was common sense that she would be in one of the trailers, though which one was the question. Would they let her and Marie out to stretch their legs before proceeding to Cherry Point? That would probably depend—

Then there she was, climbing down from one of the parked trailers while a big bear of a man stood nearby, watching her. It was Lara. He could tell that by the color of her hair.

"Lara," Keo whispered softly.

He couldn't tell the shape she was in. Was she hurt? Had they harmed her between this morning and last night? He hated not knowing, and hated that he couldn't do anything about it but sit there and watch her guard walk her over to the second trailer.

Once there, the big man handed her something, and Lara climbed inside.

That's gotta be Jackie's trailer.

Keo didn't see any signs of Marie, so he assumed she was still back in the other vehicle. Keo didn't know why they'd taken the pregnant girl along with Lara, and he felt a little guilty for not giving her the same kind of priority as Lara. But he was just being honest with himself, and it did no good to manufacture the kind of feelings he had for Lara for Marie.

Lara didn't come out of the second trailer right away, leaving Keo to watch the rest of Owen's men busying them-selves in and around the clearing. A couple were leading a pair of horses over to the trailers and hitching them into place. Keo wondered how many of those animals were Bunker's—

Clump-clump-clump.

Keo relaxed his bent knees and slid to the ground, tall blades of grass covering him up almost instantly.

Clump-clump-clump.

Horse hooves pounding against the ground behind him, getting closer.

Clump-clump-clump.

From behind and slightly to the right of him, to be exact, which was the only reason the rider hadn't spotted him poking his head up from the field like a prairie dog surveying its domain earlier. The rider just hadn't been looking in the right direction.

Clump-clump-clump.

Keo slid the MP9 up to his chest and flicked off the safety. Two hundred meters or so from the campground, so if he had to use the weapon, he could reasonably expect it to go unnoticed. Maybe. Even with the suppressor, the submachine gun would still make *some* noise. And out here, in the wide open with nothing but a barely-there breeze making the grasses sway to swallow up the noise...

Clump-clump-clump.

He glimpsed a flash of dark fur as a horse passed by on his right side. He adjusted his head slightly to get a better look at the man in the saddle. The rider was wearing a MOLLE vest, his slung rifle thumping against his back. Thank God the guy wasn't looking around. If anything, he looked bored.

Clump-clump-clump.

The man was headed toward the campground, which was a pretty good indication he was one of Owen's men and had either been doing perimeter security or...whatever the hell he was doing out here. Not that it mattered.

Keep going. Just keep on going, pal.

Keo listened to the *clump-clump-clump* of unshod horse hooves fading, feeling a little better about his situation. How close had he come to being spotted? A bullet-to-the-back-of-the-head-before-he-even-realized-it close.

Lucky. You got real lucky, pal.

Better lucky than good, he thought to himself as he continued to listen to the horse moving past him.

Clump-clump-clump.

Clump-clump—

Oh, goddammit, Keo thought when he couldn't hear horse's feet pounding on the ground anymore. That meant the animal had stopped, and not too far away, too, because it had only been a few seconds since he saw the rider. Five seconds? Ten?

Keo slipped his forefinger into the MP9's trigger guard and took a breath.

Nothing to see here. Just keep going. Your boss is waiting.

He heard the *clump-clump* again...except this time they were coming *toward* him.

Keo sighed.

Sonofa...

He bolted up—and looked right into the large black eyes of a big thoroughbred with a white stripe running down its forehead, standing less than ten meters in front of him.

But it wasn't the horse that Keo lifted the MP9 and took aim at—it was the man on top of it.

The *pfft!* of the gunshot was *just a little too loud*, and even before the man had toppled off his saddle, Keo was already scrambling to his feet. The horse, spooked by the sudden burst of violence, whinnied and quickly backed away, but for some reason didn't run off.

Keo raced toward the man in the grass. He was rolling around, trying to simultaneously get up on his knees and reach for his sidearm. Keo kicked him in the face before he could achieve either objective, and the man flipped over and landed onto his back.

Keo crouched next to the man, the MP9 aimed at a freshly bloodied face. Keo's kick had broken the man's nose, and blood ran down into and around his mouth even as he struggled to breathe. His right hand was still moving toward his holstered pistol even while his eyes locked onto Keo's.

"Really?" Keo said.

The man's hand stopped moving, and Keo grabbed the gun— a Glock—and tossed it away into the weeds. He pulled the AR off the man's shoulder and sent it to join the pistol. The man had a big Ka-Bar knife in a sheath on his left hip—almost identical to the one Keo was carrying behind his back, judging by the handle.

"Do I have to tell you not to make a sound?" Keo asked.

The man shook his head, his eyes still glued to Keo's face.

"Good boy," Keo said.

He glanced up and over at the horse. The animal was nearby, chewing on some grass.

That horse is definitely used to gunplay.

Keo looked back down at the wounded man. Keo's bullet had struck him just under his left shoulder near the armpit. It wasn't a killing shot but had been enough to toss him off his horse. He was in pain as blood seeped out of the wound and spread around his short-sleeve shirt, running down his arm and dripping to the ground under him.

"You got a name?" Keo asked.

The man stared bullets. He was clearly in pain, but Keo couldn't tell if that was from the broken nose or the gunshot wound. Maybe a little of both, even if the guy was putting on a brave face. Not that Keo bought it. Keo's current victim was a lot older than his last one, Ronald. Thirties, with sandy blond hair and gray eyes.

"Well? Do you?" Keo said when the man didn't respond.

"Fredericks," the man finally said.

"See? That wasn't so—"

"Fredericks!" someone shouted from across the field.

Shit, Keo thought, just before that same someone continued shouting:

"Fredericks! Where the hell are you? We're about to leave! Get your ass back here now!"

Keo glanced up briefly toward the campground to make sure no one was on their way to their position when Fredericks decided to take advantage of the momentary distraction and lunged upward. The man was reaching for his knife at the same time and had gotten his fingers around the handle when Keo squeezed the trigger—

Pfft! as his shot struck Fredericks in the gut.

But instead of going back down, Fredericks kept coming, pulling out the knife—

Keo, crouching at the time, lost his balance when he tried to backtrack. His ass slammed into the earth, and Fredericks was instantly on top of him, blood from his nose and armpit flitting through the air and splashing Keo partially in the face. But Keo wasn't worried about Fredericks's blood at the moment. He was more concerned with the big Ka-Bar knife in the man's hand, cocking backward—

Keo, the MP9 still in his right hand, tilted the submachine gun slightly and pulled the trigger again. The 9mm round made contact underneath Frederick's jaw and exited out the top of his skull.

The man fell off Keo, his knife falling and spearing the ground a few inches from Keo's head with a solid and dangerous *thunk!*

"Goddammit," Keo whispered even as he scrambled back to his knees and immediately looked over the grass and toward the campground.

He could make out a man on horseback riding slowly in his direction. The man stopped suddenly, but not because he had changed his mind. He was waiting for a second rider from the camp to reach him.

Time to go!

Keo glanced over at Fredericks's horse, still grazing on some grass nearby. He did some quick calculations in his head.

There was no way he was going to make it back to Deux on foot before Owen's men caught up to him. He needed a ride of his own.

He snatched up the half-eaten apple he'd dropped when Fredericks surprised him and walked calmly over to where the thoroughbred was eating its breakfast. The horse looked up and turned toward him.

Keo grinned and slung the submachine gun, then pushed the weapon behind his back. He held up both hands, showing the apple in one of them to the horse. "Horsey wants an apple? Of course you do. A horse wouldn't be a horse if he didn't like apples. Am I right?"

Keo checked on the riders. They were still coming, but not as fast as they could be. The two men were clearly taking precautions. That was good for Keo. It gave him more time to make sure Fredericks's horse didn't kick him in the head when he tried to ride it.

He smiled at that horse now. "Hey, let's go for a ride. What do you say?"

The thoroughbred didn't respond. It didn't do much of anything but stare back at him. Then again, it also didn't turn and run off, and it made no shuffling motions with its legs to indicate hostility toward his continued presence.

Keo took all those things as a good sign and hoped he didn't read any of them wrong. The only thing worse than getting shot was getting kicked and then stomped by a big horse.

He held out the apple, and the horse walked over and took it out of his palm.

"That's a good horse," Keo said as he patted the animal down with one hand, the other picking up its reins. "And there's more where that came from. Well, two more, and I promised Deux at least one of them."

He did another quick check on the two approaching riders. They had picked up their pace since the last time he looked.

"Time to go," Keo said, and swung himself into the saddle.

The black horse shuffled its feet slightly but didn't try to buck him off. It was definitely used to riders and wasn't the least bit picky about who was doing the riding. That was all good news for Keo, who turned them around and took off.

He glanced back over his shoulder, past the two riders and at the campground.

See you soon, Owen. I'll be seeing you real soon, pal.

FIFTEEN

The problem with Jackie's wound was that the round had entered him in the side but didn't exit. The bullet struck near the top of his pelvic bone, leaving behind fragments of itself along with pieces of the impacted ilium. It had taken Lara over an hour of sweaty work to remove all she could, but she had no doubts she'd left plenty behind anyway despite her best efforts. She just didn't have the right equipment on hand, and having Owen and his men hovering over the clinic had only compounded the problem.

Caring for Jackie afterward had been just as difficult. It didn't help that Owen had been carrying his brother around with the bullet and bone fragments inside his body for days until they finally found her. She still didn't know how they knew about her in the first place. Most of her work on Jackie for the last twenty-four hours boiled down to keeping the dressing and area around the wound clean; that included putting him on a course of antibiotics to fight infection and a steady diet of meds to keep him from constant and agonizing pain. Jackie was unconscious more than he was awake, and he only occasionally opened his eyes when she checked on him.

He was awake this morning when Leland brought her out of her trailer and led her to Jackie's. He always looked older when he was conscious, but maybe that was just because she had a harder time pretending he was just another unwitting victim of Owen's, the way she and Marie were. He wasn't anywhere near wide awake, but he was aware.

"What happened?" he asked when he saw her. "I heard shooting."

"Shooting?" Lara said.

She went around the thick blanket that he lay on, a makeshift bed designed to keep him from jostling around as they moved. She was careful not to step on anything she wasn't supposed to. Lara was used to the heavy medicinal smell in the air, most of it locked in by the heavy tarp. She put down the medical bag next to Jackie.

"I heard shooting outside," Jackie said. He turned his head to look at the silhouetted figures moving around outside.

"That was last night," Lara said.

"Was it?"

"Yes."

"I thought it was this morning." He gave her a confused look. Then, "What happened?"

"There was a ghoul attack."

"Was anyone hurt?"

"Portman and another man," Lara said as she opened the bag and took out the roll of bandages.

"I liked Portman. Who was the other one?"

"I don't know his name."

"Too bad. I liked Portman."

"I'm sure he appreciates that."

Jackie gave her an odd look that she couldn't quite read. "What does that mean?"

She pursed a smile. "It means, I'm sure he appreciates that you liked him." Then, turning toward the back of the trailer, "Leland, I need the shears."

The big man pulled aside the tarp and handed her a pair of surgical scissors from a small pouch around his waist. It was the same pair she'd used to quickly carve the note into Granger's body for Keo—not that anyone else knew that piece of trivia except her. She did, though, remember Leland giving her a slightly suspicious look when she handed the shears back to him covered in blood.

"Hey, Leland," Jackie said.

"Hey, kid, how you doing?" Leland asked.

"Good. I'm good."

That's not true, Lara thought, and she guessed Leland knew it too as she took the scissors from him.

The big man chuckled, though it sounded a little more forced than usual. "Hang in there, sport. We're almost there."

"Don't worry about me, Leland," Jackie said, and smiled. "I'm fine and dandy back here."

"Right on," Leland said. He gave Lara a look that convinced her Leland was probably the only other person in the caravan that cared as much about Jackie as Owen. "I'll be right outside as usual, Doc."

"Okay," Lara said, and set about cutting strips of gauze to replace Jackie's old dressing.

"Why do you always have to ask for it?" Jackie asked, watching her closely. He was sweating again, and she took a moment to wipe his forehead with a towel.

"Because they don't want me to have a weapon," Lara said.

Again, that curious look, like he didn't quite understand what she was saying. "Why wouldn't they want you to have a weapon?"

Because your brother kidnapped me, and if I had a weapon, I might stab him in the eyes with it, Lara thought, but she said, "No reason. I have to change your dressing now. Are you in more pain than usual this morning?"

"Not more than usual..."

"What's the level of pain, from one to five?"

"Three, I think."

"That's not too bad."

"It's not?"

"Well, it's not five."

"That's good, I guess," Jackie said.

Lara pulled down the blanket and lifted his shirt when she heard someone shouting outside, "Fredericks!" very close to their trailer.

It was Walter, Owen's second-in-command.

Then, moments later, Walter shouted again, "Fredericks! Where the hell are you? We're about to leave! Get your ass back here now!"

"What's happening now?" Jackie asked.

"I don't know," Lara said.

She paused what she was doing to listen. Walter was close enough to the trailer that Lara could overhear him without trying very hard.

A second silhouetted figure appeared next to him. "What happened?" the newcomer asked. It was Owen.

"Fredericks," Walter said.

"Where?"

"Out there."

"All I see is a horse."

"That's his horse. He was on perimeter duty this morning. Saw him coming back; and now, just his horse."

"Joyner, get yourself over here!" Owen shouted. Then, quieter to Walter, "Find out what happened. And watch for traps."

"Will do," Walter said.

"What happened to Fredericks?" Jackie was asking her.

Lara looked back down at the young man. She wasn't surprised he hadn't heard the same conversation that she had. He was basically surviving on meds at the moment, but even that wasn't going to last for very long. If she needed more proof, all she had to do was stare at his wound. It was infected and had been long before Owen ever arrived at the village. It was a miracle he was even still alive at all.

But he's not going to stay that way for very long.

It took all her effort not to let that knowledge show on her face. "Probably nothing. He'll be fine," she said. Then, before he could ask anything else, "What's at Cherry Point?"

"Cherry Point?" Jackie said.

"That's where we're headed. Cherry Point."

"Wow, I haven't heard that name in a while..." Jackie seemed to drift off momentarily, maybe reliving some memories. Then, after a few seconds of silence, "We're still in Texas? I didn't know we were still in Texas."

"We are," Lara said. "So, what's at Cherry Point?"

"It's where Owen and me used to go when we were kids. There's a lake there. Cherry Point Lake. Our mom took us every summer. Or most every summer."

"Just your mom?"

"Our dad died when we were young."

"I'm sorry."

"He was in the service..."

"Which one?"

"U.S. Army all the way." A big grin. Or as big as Jackie could make it. "He was a Green Beret. That's why Owen joined up, because of him. He always wanted to be like Dad."

"Did he?"

"Huh?"

"Owen. Did he become a Green Beret like your dad?"

"No. He went into buds instead."

"What's buds?"

"You don't know what buds is?"

"I know what Budweiser is. Is that the same thing?"

He smiled at her. "No. It's not the same thing."

Lara glanced up at the side of the trailer as the others continued to move around. Leland was still at his post near the back. Her shadow, for all intents and purposes. He was also possibly her best chance to escape if Keo didn't come through or get here fast enough.

Leland was the key. She just wasn't quite sure how yet.

"What's your name?" Jackie was asking her.

Lara looked back down at the young man. "My name?"

"I don't think I ever asked you your name. Or if I did, I might have forgot. Did I forget?"

She smiled. "No, you didn't. It's Edna."

"Edna," Jackie said. "That's a nice name."

"Thanks."

"You're so pretty."

"Thanks again."

"Have you ever been to Cherry Point Lake, Edna?"

"No. I've never heard of it until now."

"It's nice."

"Is it?"

"Yes. Or it used to be."

"'Used to be?'"

"I don't know how it is now. You know, after..."

Lara nodded.

"But it's nice to go back," Jackie continued. Lara couldn't tell if he was even still talking to her anymore. "He's taking us back there because of me. Because it was my fault what happened."

"Because of what happened?" Lara asked.

"Me getting shot. It wouldn't have happened if I didn't try to steal those horses..."

Horses? Lara thought. She didn't know what he was talking about. It never occurred to her that Owen's men had stolen the horses they had. She'd always just assumed the animals were theirs, but she guessed it made sense. Owen didn't have a lot of qualms about taking her and Marie. Why would horses be any different?

"You tried to steal the horses?" she asked.

"Owen tried to negotiate with the guy, the rancher, but he wouldn't play ball," Jackie said. "Later that night, I came back with some guys and took them."

"Why did you do that?"

"We needed them. We had too many people, and most of us were walking, taking turns on the horses..."

"So you decided to steal them? Did Owen know what you were planning?"

Jackie shook his head. "He would have said no. But I knew we needed those horses, so... He was so mad." He sighed, looking off for a moment.

She waited for him to continue, but he didn't.

He said instead, as if he'd completely forgotten the previous topic, "So when did you join us, Edna? I must have been out more than I thought, 'cause I don't remember. Was it before or after that whole mess in Darby Bay?"

Lara's eyes widened at the mention of Darby Bay. She had finished up and was wiping the blood off her hands with a wet towel when he mentioned the port city.

Darby Bay. Jackie had said Darby Bay. Didn't he?

"Did you say Darby Bay?" she asked, just to be sure.

He nodded. Or moved his head in a slight nodding motion. "Were you there with us? Or did you join later? I can't remember. I have trouble remembering a lot of things these days. Is that normal after getting shot?"

Depends on where you were shot, she thought but said anyway, "Yes. It's perfectly normal." Then, before his mind could wander off again, "You and Owen were at Darby Bay? When was this?"

"I don't remember. It's been a while."

"Around six or seven months ago?"

"I think so." Then, smiling again, "I guess you weren't there with us, or you would know. So you had to join up later."

She nodded. "Yes. I joined you guys later."

There was no point in correcting him. Jackie was a dead man; it was just a matter of when. There was no curing him, no taking away the infection eating away at his pelvic region even now. He couldn't feel it because he couldn't feel much of anything below the waistline. If he were more alert and wasn't swimming in medication 24/7, he would have noticed the lack of sensation down there.

"What did you guys do at Darby Bay?" Lara asked.

"Fighting these guys, these...I don't remember," Jackie said. "Owen tried to keep me out of it, but I wouldn't let him. I fought right next to him." He seemed to almost beam with pride. "We were a pretty good team."

"Yeah, I bet you guys were."

"We were. It was pretty cool."

Jackie looked away, and Lara thought, *Sonofabitch. They're Mercerians. They were there, that night Gaby...*

Lara looked up when she heard the *clump-clump-clump* of horses returning to the campground. A figure walked past the trailer to meet two approaching riders. One of them was Walter, because she heard his voice first.

"He's dead," Walter said.

"Fredericks," the figure that had walked over to meet them said. Owen again.

"Yeah. Got two holes in him that his momma didn't bless him with when he was born," Walter said. "Saw the shooter. He took off on Fredericks's horse before we could reach him."

"Who was it?"

"I don't know. Couldn't make out his face."

"Bunker?"

"Maybe. Could be anyone."

Owen walked past them and looked out toward the open field. "Why didn't you go after him?"

"Like you said, could have been a trap," Walter said. "I decided to play it safe. If it's Bunker, he'll follow us to Cherry Point anyway. We can take care of him there, once and for all."

Owen didn't reply for a moment.

Finally, he turned around and walked away. "Let's finish up. I want to be on the move again as soon as possible."

"What about Fredericks's body?" the second rider asked.

"He's dead," Walter said. "He doesn't care what we do with his body."

"Man, that's cold."

"Not out here, it ain't."

Lara watched Owen's shadow as it slowly disappeared out of view.

"You done?" a voice asked from the back of the trailer.

Lara turned to Leland, looking in at her.

She nodded and put the scissors back into the medical bag before handing it over to him. "Marie and I need to use the stream to clean up."

"Can't it wait?"

"It can, if you want to tell Owen to stop for us when we're moving again."

Leland sighed. "Okay."

Lara looked back at Jackie. He hadn't drifted off, but if he even noticed she was still there, she couldn't read it on his face. For all she knew, the young man was already dreaming about Cherry Point Lake. Or maybe he was reliving his heroics in Darby Bay while fighting side by side with his brother.

Darby Bay.

That goddamn city was going to haunt her until the end of time.

Lara climbed out of the trailer, with Leland giving her a hand.

"How's he doing?" the big man asked.

"Same as yesterday," Lara said.

"That good, huh?"

"That good."

Leland paused for a second to look back in at the trailer, at Jackie inside. "He's a good kid. Too bad."

He let the tarp drop and led her across the campground to the other trailer parked nearby.

"He told me it was his fault that he got shot, because he tried to steal the horses," Lara said.

"He told you that?" Leland asked. He sounded surprised.

"Yes. Is it true?"

"Yeah." The big man looked across the clearing at Owen, packing his tactical bags next to the fire pit. "Owen was *pissed.*"

"You're telling me Owen was just going to accept this Bunker guy saying no to him?"

"Well, maybe not accept it, per se."

Lara narrowed her eyes at Leland and wondered if he knew what *per se* actually meant.

"Maybe he would have taken them anyway," Leland continued. "But, you know, in a better and less shitty way than how Jackie went about it."

Owen's men were still in the midst of packing, and the horses were being prepped for the day's ride. There were a lot of men in black constantly moving around her. Lara found it slightly disheartening that despite losing two men last night to the ghoul attack, there didn't seem to be any noticeable drop in the group's numbers. That was impossible, but it didn't *feel* so this morning.

The leader himself stood on one side of the clearing next to Walter, the two of them talking in quiet voices while looking at a map. There was still blood on the grass—human blood, because ghouls' evaporated with the sunlight. She could detect the lingering scent in the air—an odorous, stinging aroma.

Instead of climbing back into their trailer, Lara pulled aside the tarp. Marie, sitting nervously near the back, looked over.

"Let's go wash up before we leave," Lara said.

Marie nodded and hurried over.

"Five minutes," Leland said.

"We'll be done when we're done," Lara said.

He rolled his eyes at her. "You want us to leave you behind?"

"Gee, would you?"

The big man chuckled. "You know what I mean."

Lara helped Marie down, and they walked across the campground with two small hand towels on their shoulders. Leland followed closely behind, handing the medical bag over to another one of Owen's men along the way.

As they walked through the place, Lara felt eyes on her and looked over to see Owen, across the clearing, watching her back.

"Where are you taking them?" Owen called over to Leland.

"Ladies need to freshen up," Leland said.

"Don't let them stray out of your sight."

"Gotcha, boss."

"Peterson, go with them," Owen said.

A man Lara had seen before but never really paid much attention to jogged over to join them. He was thin and didn't look entirely comfortable wearing his vest, and appeared tiny next to the large and towering Leland.

Peterson and Leland walked them to the stream nearby,

maybe fifty yards from where the clearing ended. There was nothing in front of them but a lot of grass and open skies; there was also no such thing as privacy.

"I don't suppose I have to tell you not to run," Leland said.

"How are we going to outrun horses out here?" Lara asked him.

"I just want to make sure we understand one another."

"I'm not an idiot, Leland."

He grinned. "I know you're not. I just don't want you to do anything stupid."

"Meaning?"

He leaned in slightly toward her and Marie, maybe to make sure Peterson, who stood nearby, couldn't overhear. "Look. We'll be in Cherry Point soon. After that, things will change. I'm sure of it."

She gazed back at him and understood that he meant it. Leland believed that all of this was going to end up okay for her and Marie. He actually believed it. She wasn't sure if that was because he knew something she didn't, or if he was just that optimistic.

"Just be cool, okay?" Leland said.

"Okay," Lara said, nodding.

"Be cool," he said again, before looking over at Peterson. "Let's give the ladies some privacy."

The two men stayed behind while Lara and Marie walked on ahead of them. But while the two didn't follow, Lara did notice Peterson lingering a little too long on Marie. He didn't completely turn around until Leland nudged him with an elbow—hard enough that Peterson shot him an annoyed glance, before turning his back to her.

"Do you need to go?" Lara asked Marie, dropping her voice to almost a whisper.

The other woman nodded. "You?" she asked before looking past Lara at the two men behind her.

"You go first. I'll make sure they don't get any closer."

Marie gave her a pursed—but very nervous—smile and stepped into the cold stream. Lara looked away to give her some privacy, too. She didn't bother checking on Leland and Peterson behind her. She had the big man back there, and she trusted him (*Really? You actually trust him? Are you crazy?*) to keep Peterson's eyes elsewhere.

Instead, Lara scanned the Texas countryside. It was so wide open, with nothing that even looked like a tree for miles, that she didn't think they could get more than a hundred yards if they started running now before they were caught again. Even if they had a huge head start, which they didn't.

She knew that they had to escape—the sooner, the better—but this wasn't the time. If only Keo was really out there. Was it really him and not this Bunker person that had just killed Fredericks? Right now, she would settle for anyone who didn't like Owen and his men as much as she did, but things would be so much easier if it was Keo—

Sunlight glinted off something in the distance, directly in front of her.

What...?

Lara squinted, but she couldn't make out what was twinkling out there. Was it some kind of metal? Glass?

She shot a quick look behind her, but Leland and Peterson still had their backs turned. Marie, too, was busy cleaning herself in the stream with the small towel. Which left Lara as the only person to see the glinting object.

Was that on purpose? Was she looking at someone trying to get her attention, or just some shiny object that the sun happened to hit at the right angles?

Then, as if on cue, *a figure rose from the field of grass and waved to her.*

It was a man, she was sure of it, but he was too far away and she couldn't see his face or tell what he was wearing.

But he was *definitely waving at her.*

"Time's up," a voice called from behind her.

Lara looked back at Leland, her heart in her throat, but there wasn't anything on his face that gave her the impression he'd seen the same thing that she had. When she looked forward again, Lara saw that the figure was gone—as if it were never there.

But she knew better. It hadn't gone anywhere—it had only slipped back under all the carpet of grass in the field.

"Already?" Lara said back to Leland.

"Sorry, but boss wants us to move now," Leland said. He was walking back to her when he stopped and cocked his head slightly. "What's the matter?"

"Marie's not done yet," Lara said, before turning to check on Marie—but really, to hide her face from Leland so he couldn't read it.

The other woman was just now pulling her shirt back down.

"You guys will just have to finish at Cherry Point," Leland said from behind her. "Come on, we gotta head back."

Lara helped Marie up from the stream. If Marie saw what Lara had, there was nothing on her expression to indicate it.

I guess it was just me.

The question was: Was that on purpose?

They followed Leland back to Peterson, who was watching them curiously. No, not both of them—just Marie. The young woman noticed it, too, and she reached for, found, and squeezed Lara's hand.

Lara wanted to comfort her, but she was too busy thinking about the figure out there, probably still watching them right now. Whoever it was, they had allowed her to see them on purpose. And just her. Which meant...

Keo. That's you out there, isn't it?

It has to be you.

She smiled to herself and fought the instinct to look back one more time. It was hard. It was so, so hard, but she somehow managed it—if just barely.

Back at the campground, Owen had climbed onto his horse, as had the others. He looked across the clearing at her as she returned. His eyes this morning were just as cold and unforgiving as they'd been when he put a gun to Marie's head and gave her the ultimatum a day ago.

She stared back at him, without flinching, and thought, *My man's coming for you. I hope you're ready, asshole.*

SIXTEEN

Lara saw him. He could tell by her body language. It had been a little risky (*A little? Try a lot, pal.*) to stand up and expose himself like that, with those two guys standing behind her and even more of Owen's gang in the background. All it would have taken was for one pair of wrong eyeballs (or just one eyeball) to glance over at the wrong time, and he would have been caught with his pants down.

But no one who wasn't supposed to see him had, and it had been worth it to let her know that he was here. *If* she even knew it was him, that was. Keo wasn't too sure about that. He was close enough—a hundred meters, give or take, about the length of a football field—but he had the advantage of a wall of grass surrounding him, and she didn't. For all he knew, she could have thought he was a dog poking its head up to survey the area.

Keo hadn't expected to see her out there; it was pure luck that she and Marie were being allowed to use the stream nearby. After he was sure that Owen's men weren't going to chase him—they'd stopped at Fredericks's body and never pursued—Keo had picked up Deux and circled the area. He'd been fully prepared to whittle down more of Owen's numbers, and maybe his would-be targets knew that, too. Out here, with no hiding place, chasing a man with a gun was a dangerous business. Especially one that had already killed one of your own.

It took them another thirty minutes or so before the group was ready to move. Keo remained where he was, lying flat on his stomach, and watched them head off. He wished he had some binoculars to get a better look at all the men and take a solid head count, but the only one he could pick out from a distance was the large giant of a human being that always shadowed Lara.

And there was Lara. Her long blonde hair, tied in a ponytail, made her easily stand out. Marie, with her dark black hair, also stood out. It was impossible to miss the two women in that company of brutes.

Keo didn't get up until the group had moved on for at least ten minutes, and he couldn't see or hear them anymore. Just to make sure Mr. Piss Down Your Throat wasn't trying to lure him out, perhaps thinking Keo might not have completely taken off after the Fredericks's incident, Keo gave it another thirty minutes. Forty minutes, give or take, wasn't going to make much of a difference considering how slowly the caravan was traveling.

While he was watching them, Keo was able to confirm a couple of things.

First: The women were being kept in their own tarp-covered trailer, just as he had already guessed. They weren't being tied up, but there were always a couple of men in the immediate vicinity to keep a close eye on them. Man Bear in particular, but sometimes there was a second guard.

Two: Jackie, Owen's wounded brother, was in the other utility vehicle. Again, just as Keo had guessed. Keo had yet to lay eyes on the man, but it was a safe assumption. They wouldn't be moving Lara between trailers for no good reason.

And three: Owen had had more men with him than Keo was expecting. He had deducted Ronald and his partner at Silver Hills, the sniper on the road, the dead guy Lara had used to send him her message, and more recently, Fredericks. According to Bunker's claim of thirteen, Owen should have been down to six guns (not counting the invisible and not-able-bodied Jackie). But there was more than that out there.

At least nine. At least.

Your math sucks, Bunker.

Keo finally got up after about an hour and jogged across the field to where Deux and his new companion, Tres, stood waiting next to a dying group of trees. Keo had tied their reins up, but like before hadn't made it too tight, so if the horses wanted to break free they could have without injuring themselves. Fortunately, neither one had gone anywhere when he returned.

Keo walked over to the horses and climbed onto Deux. The Cleveland Bay was slightly smaller than Tres, Fredericks's former mount, but Keo was used to it after almost a full day with the animal. He liked to think the horse had become used to him in return, but maybe it was just all the apples Keo was feeding it.

Hey, whatever works.

He gave Tres a slap on the rump to send it off, before turning Deux around and taking off. He hadn't gotten very far when he heard footsteps and looked back. Tres was following closely behind.

"Where are you going?" Keo asked the thoroughbred.

The horse seemed to lift its head up and whinnied in response.

"Okay, but don't say I didn't try to let you go," Keo said.

He turned around and kept going.

When he looked back, Tres was still following. Keo grinned and continued on. He didn't try to lose the thoroughbred or discourage it. You never knew when you might need an extra horse, after all.

It wasn't hard to reacquire the kidnappers once he knew their general direction—west, toward the town of Cherry Point. Even if Keo didn't already have that knowledge in his back pocket, he could have still found the group by the obvious trail they left behind as they cut through the field of grass. They were moving slowly—for Jackie's benefit, no doubt—toward their eventual destination. After about half a kilometer of traveling on the uneven dirt ground, they finally rejoined a new stretch of country highway that would, according to Keo's map, take them into Cherry Point. There was a lake that shared the name just half a klick past the small Texas town.

Keo had no intentions of stopping Owen's gang on the road. The last thing he wanted was to put Lara and Marie in the middle of a gunfight. He was pretty sure the tarp that covered their trailer wasn't bulletproof, and the possibility of Lara getting hit by a stray bullet left him cold.

So he followed them from afar instead. There was no risk

of losing them, and he was wary of a possible ambush similar to the one that had almost cost him his life outside of Silver Hills. Now that Owen knew someone was out there—though Keo doubted the man knew it was him; he likely thought it was Bunker again who had killed Fredericks—it wouldn't be out of character for him to leave a man behind to take, literally, a shot. Owen had already shown a general lack of disregard for the men he'd lost.

But there was no ambush. Not yet, anyway. The possibility always remained at the forefront of Keo's mind, and he took every precaution as a result. After all, if he thought of it, then Mr. Piss Down Your Throat would have, too.

Keo was too close to Lara now and didn't want to do anything stupid that would jeopardize that. Sooner or later, Owen would reach his destination. Sooner or later, the opportunity for rescuing Lara would present itself, and when it did, Keo was going to grab it by the balls.

Right in the fucking balls.

The gang stopped twice in the middle of the road, and Lara was brought out of her trailer and led to Jackie's. Even from a distance, Keo knew that was her because of the blonde hair. It also helped that Bear Man was always next to her, dwarfing her much smaller size.

Keo watched from a hillside more than two hundred meters away. What he wouldn't give for a pair of binoculars. Still, the higher elevation did give him a decent view of the caravan, and if he ever felt tempted to take a shot at all those warm bodies milling about down there—

Behind me!

He rolled over onto his back, the MP9 swinging up to fire.

"Whoa there, Jackie Chan, friendly incoming," Bunker

said, standing at the bottom of the small hill less than twenty meters from Keo's position.

Jesus Christ. How had the man gotten so close without Keo hearing him until now?

Bunker must have seen the question on Keo's face, because he chuckled. "Pretty good, huh? Don't be so hard on yourself. I've snuck up on horses before. Compared to them, humans might as well have cotton balls wedged in their ears and up their noses."

Keo relaxed, though not completely. That was impossible now, given the fact that someone had just sneaked up to him and gotten so close they could have shot him a dozen times before he'd even realized they were back there. This time, he had been lucky; it was just Bunker. But what if it hadn't been?

"Goddammit, man, I almost shot you," Keo said.

"That's highly doubtful," Bunker said. "Besides, you have trigger finger discipline. I saw that the first time we met."

"Where the hell did you come from?" Keo asked, turning back around and onto his stomach. He looked out at the road to make sure no one had noticed the sudden flurry of activity on the hill nearby.

No one had. The group continued to mill about on the asphalt under the hot sun.

Footsteps, before Bunker plopped himself down to the ground on Keo's right. "What's the word, hummingbird?"

"Second time they've stopped to let Lara check in on the second trailer. I'm guessing the brother's in there."

"Good guess," Bunker said. "Who's Lara?"

"One of the two women Owen took."

"I thought their names were Edna and Marie?"

"Edna is Lara. Lara is Edna."

"You don't say."

"I do."

"Interesting." Bunker had produced a pair of binoculars and was looking through them. "I don't see her."

"She's still in the second trailer. On the right."

Bunker swiveled slightly. "What's she look like?"

Keo reached over for the glasses. "Give me that."

Bunker smirked but handed them over. "You breaks them, you buys them."

Keo ignored him and looked through the field glasses. He got his best look at the group yet. And he saw him right away: Owen. Mr. Piss Down Your Throat himself.

The distance was too great for Keo to get a good look at the face, but he didn't need to. He could tell just by the way the man stood among the others, hands on his hips, while looking around. Keo recognized a shepherd in the midst of his flock when he saw one.

Just to be sure, he said, "Tall, black hair. Standing in the middle of the road. Is that him? Owen?"

"Lemme see," Bunker said. He reached over and took the binoculars back, and peered through them for a moment. Then, "Can't be one hundred percent sure, but that looks like him. The big boss man. You know, I can take him out right now..."

"Don't even think about it."

"Give me one good reason I shouldn't end it now."

"Because you wouldn't end it now. See all those men down there? They're not black-eyed ghouls. They won't just stop moving if you chop off their leader's head. Besides, I don't need a gunfight out in the open with friendlies in the crossfire. I'll take them when the time is right. And right now isn't it."

"Sure is tempting, though..."

"Don't do shit, Bunker."

"Yeah, yeah," Bunker said, though Keo didn't quite believe him.

But the man hadn't reached for his rifle yet, so Keo was safe for now.

"By the way, how many do you see?" Keo asked.

Bunker didn't say anything for a moment as he scanned Owen's caravan a second time. Keo guessed he was counting.

Finally, "Nine, not counting whoever else is in the trailers," Bunker said. "Why?"

"You said Owen had twelve guys with him. Thirteen, counting Owen himself."

"Yeah. So?"

"If that's the case, there shouldn't still be nine heads down there, should there?"

"Hunh," Bunker said. He lowered the glasses. "Maybe I miscounted. It happens."

"Not what I wanted to hear."

"Yeah, well, life's full of disappointments, Jackie. Get used to it."

Keo smirked before glancing behind him. "Where's Yuli? Don't tell me you left him out there by himself."

"Don't get your panties into a bunch. He's waiting with the horses nearby."

"By himself?"

"He's blind, not stupid. He'll be fine. Besides, *you* left him behind first. What do you care?"

"I care plenty."

"Didn't seemed like it yesterday."

Keo didn't know why he was even arguing with Bunker; he

didn't know this guy from Adam. Besides, he had a feeling Bunker was just trying to get under his skin, and unfortunately for Keo, he was succeeding.

Keo said, "They're heading for a town called Cherry Point, not far from here."

"Cherry Point?" Bunker said.

"You've heard of it?"

"Spent some summers there horsing around. No pun intended."

"What pun?"

"You know what pun," Bunker said. "But yeah, I know Cherry Point. It's not far from here. Last time I was there, it was a ghost town. So why are they headed there?"

"How the hell should I know?"

"How *do* you know that's where they're headed, then?"

"Lara told me."

"Lara, who is also Edna. Who is also Lara."

"Exactly."

"And how did she do that, exactly?"

"We have a psychic link."

"You don't say."

"I do."

Bunker snorted. "Whatever." Then, "So what's your big plan to get my horses back? I'm still down five."

"Don't take this the wrong way, but I really don't give two shits about your horses."

"Ouch."

"But my plan is to follow them to Cherry Point."

"And then?"

"I don't know yet. I'll think of something."

"That's your big plan? You'll think of something...later?"

"It's too risky to engage them out here. They have the numbers—more than they should have."

Bunker grunted.

"Better to let them get to where they're going and let their guard down before we act," Keo finished.

Bunker peered through his binoculars again. Then, after a while, "I'm missing a horse down there."

"What horse?"

"One of my horses. I don't see her down there."

"You recognize all of your horses?"

"Of course I recognize all of my horses. Just like you probably recognize every one of your guns."

"My guns?"

"You look like a gun nut to me."

Keo smirked. "This horse. Is it a black thoroughbred?"

"That's her." Bunker put down his glasses and looked over at Keo. "Her name's Phyllis. Where is she?"

"She's with Deux, not far from here."

"She okay?"

"She's a horse."

"That doesn't answer the question."

"Yeah, she's okay," Keo said.

"Good," Bunker said. "That girl and me go a long way."

They continued to lie on the hill and watch Owen's group milling about on the road below. Bunker didn't say anything for a long time, and neither did Keo. The caravan didn't seem to be all that anxious to be on their way anytime soon, probably because they were almost at their destination now, and there was no hurry.

Ten minutes turned into fifteen, then twenty.

Finally, Lara climbed back out of the trailer, and Keo

quickly grabbed the binoculars from Bunker. The closest he'd seen her was back at the stream near the campground, but he hadn't really gotten a good look at her condition.

Now, as he zoomed in as much as possible, he breathed a sigh of relief that she looked to be in good health. He wouldn't have been able to tell bruises anyway from this far, even with maximum magnification, but she seemed to be moving fine on her own. He'd been with her long enough that he would have noticed any abnormal signs, and there were none.

"That's your woman? The blonde?" Bunker asked.

"Yeah."

"Is she hot? I'm squinting, but I can't really tell. She looks hot. Is she hot? *Muy guapo*, as your blind friend would say?"

"Shut up, Bunker."

"It's just a friendly question. Don't have a cow, man."

Keo followed Lara as the Bear Man led her back to the other trailer. She climbed up, but not before exchanging some words with Owen. The head honcho had walked over and said something to her. Keo didn't know Owen was about to talk and hadn't focused on him fast enough to read his lips, and Lara's back was turned to Keo, so he had no chance with her, either.

Then she was back in the trailer, and Owen signaled for the group to get ready to move again.

"They're moving," Keo said, handing the field glasses back to Bunker before getting up and sliding down the hill.

Bunker followed closely behind him.

"Where's Yuli?" Keo asked.

"I told you, he's around," Bunker said.

"He's okay?"

"You mean, is he still blind?"

"Yeah."

"He woke up this morning and walked right into a tree. Does that answer your question?"

Shit, Keo thought, but he said, "You shouldn't have brought him along. It's too dangerous for him out here in his condition."

"Hey, you're the one who left him behind. You shouldn't be talking."

Keo didn't bother continuing to argue with Bunker—he had a feeling he was never going to win anyway—and walked along the base of the hill, taking his time like before in order to allow Owen's group to put some distance between them.

"You said Cherry Point is a ghost town?" Keo asked.

"Last time I was there," Bunker said.

"When was that?"

"About two years ago."

"No one was using it during The Purge? A place with a nearby lake is gold."

"Apparently, no one got the memo."

"So where did you spend that year?"

"At my ranch."

"By yourself?"

"Had a few people come and go, but mostly it was just me. Besides, horses make for way better company than people, anyway."

"That explains your shitty bedside manner."

Bunker grunted. "People are shitty in general. But I'm less shitty than most."

"That's what every shitty guy says."

They didn't reach the tree where he'd left Deux and Tres —a.k.a. Phyllis—to graze until about five minutes later. The two horses looked up, and Phyllis actually let out a soft whinny at the sight of Bunker.

"Hey, that's my girl," Bunker said, and hurried over to the black mare.

Keo guessed Bunker wasn't lying—Phyllis really was his favorite, and from the looks of it, the feeling was mutual.

"How you doing, girl? Did they hurt you?" Bunker asked as he rubbed the mare down and leaned in to press his cheek against the horse's.

Keo let them have their little reunion and untied Deux's reins from a branch. "So you know where Cherry Point is, right?" he asked Bunker.

"Like the back of my very big and masculine hand," Bunker said.

"Good. I'll ride on ahead to keep a closer eye on Owen's gang. Head back to Yuli, and bring him along with you."

Bunker looked across Phyllis at Keo. "You know he's just going to get in the way, right? He's a liability. You and me, we could take Owen and his boys. Seven, eight, ten—doesn't really matter, if we play it right."

"Yuli's a friend," Keo said. "Besides, Lara would kill me if I left him out here."

"She can't kill you if he gets you killed first."

"That's not going to happen."

"You seem awfully sure about that."

"That's because I am." Keo swung into Deux's saddle. "Catch up to me and keep an eye out for another ambush along the way. They've already tried it once, and after this morning, they might try it again."

Before Keo could head off, Bunker said, "About Yuli's woman..."

"What about her?"

"Her name's Marie, right?"

"That's right."

"She good looking?"

Keo narrowed his eyes at the rancher.

"I mean, if something were to happen to Yuli, she'd need a new man to take care of her," Bunker continued. "And I'm single. So, so single."

"I'm going to pretend I didn't hear that," Keo said.

"It's just an observation."

"Don't even think about it."

"I'm just saying, out here, a man can get pretty lonely..."

Bunker grinned, but Keo shook his head and turned Deux around. He was pretty sure Bunker was just kidding, but it wasn't like he knew the guy well enough to be absolutely sure one way or another.

But that was a problem for another time. Right now, he needed to concentrate on what was ahead of him.

And right now, that was Cherry Point.

SEVENTEEN

Cherry Point wasn't much to look at. It was just another abandoned town in a country full of them. Lara had seen more than her share of those over the last six years as she traveled from one state to another, trying to create alliances out of the ashes of the old world. All that effort and so much blood and treasure, and for what?

Stop it. Stop thinking about that.

Focus on the now.

Lara looked over at Marie, kneeling next to her. The young woman was peering through the tarp at the back of the trailer as the small, nondescript town passed by around them. Lara couldn't help but think about Gaby. Not that the two women looked anything alike; they couldn't have been more different, in fact. Gaby was tall, where Marie was short; Gaby was a soldier, where Marie wasn't; and Gaby was...

Her friend.

No, she was more than that. Gaby was like a little sister. Months after Darby Bay, and Lara couldn't forget their final conversation. Gaby's sacrifice had been for nothing. She was still dead, and men like Owen still roamed the countryside doing whatever they pleased. Lara had spent too many years of her life trying to make a difference. Long, hard years. She'd denied herself of things that others took for granted. She'd denied herself someone to care for, and who cared for her in return.

"Do you miss it?" she remembered asking Keo one night. They'd only been at the village for a little while at the time.

"Miss what?" he'd said.

"You know what."

"I don't."

"Keo..."

"No," he'd answered. "I don't miss it."

"Are you lying right now?"

"No." Then, after a few seconds of silence, "Do I miss it? I don't think I do."

"You don't think, but you're not sure."

"I guess I'm not. I do know one thing for sure, though..."

"What's that?"

"I like this."

"This?"

"This. You and me. Here. This. I like this more than I've ever liked anything in my life."

She had smiled. How could she not, hearing the sincerity in his voice?

"I think you're too good for me," she had said.

He had laughed. "Too good for you, or too good to you?"

"Can it be both?"

"Maybe, but don't tell anyone," he had said. "I have a reputation, you know."

She smiled now, remembering that night.

"You okay?" Marie was asking her.

Lara glanced over. Had she drifted off? Probably.

She smiled back at the young woman. "I was just thinking..."

"About what?"

Keo, she thought, and almost said his name.

She said instead, "Bob."

"You miss him."

"I do."

"I can tell," Marie said, smiling back.

"What about you? Are you okay?" Lara had looked down at Marie's stomach when she asked that question.

Marie nodded and pursed her lips, saying everything without the need for words. She was okay, but she would never be really okay until they were free from Owen and his men.

"Where are we?" Marie asked, looking out of the trailer again. "Is this Cherry Point?"

"I think so," Lara said.

"It doesn't look like much."

"No, it doesn't."

They looked out at the rows of storefronts, apartment buildings, and abandoned cars along Cherry Point's main street. There were no signs of people, and all indications pointed to the place having been abandoned years ago and never resettled. She found that odd, especially since there was a lake nearby. Usually a town this small, with an established lake, was ideal for resettlement during and after The Purge.

And yet there was nothing as they approached the town, and nothing still as they rode through it. No one had poked their heads out of the windows and doors, and everything was coated with thick layers of dust. Even the few strands of newspapers in the streets and sidewalks were yellow and faded. Most of the buildings looked intact, and plenty of doors were left open, as if people simply forgot to close them. How long ago now had they been that way? Maybe years.

"It kind of looks a little bit like where Yuli and I came from," Marie said.

"Most towns look like this now," Lara said.

"What about the cities? I've heard stories about them. Are they true?"

"You want to stay away from them, yes."

"You've seen them?"

Lara nodded, thinking about all the places she'd been since taking over Black Tide. She'd left the southwest and gone north as far as New York. She'd even had conversations with Danny about going across the ocean to see firsthand what Europe and Asia and the rest of the world were like.

But that's not you anymore.

Concentrate on the now.

And right now, all she could hear were the unshod horse hooves around them and the occasional wind blowing through the alleys and open windows of Cherry Point. There was an eerie vibe to the place, as if every door hid a ghoul that could attack at any second. But it was daylight, so that wasn't possible.

"Is he still going to die? Jackie?" Marie was asking her.

Lara nodded. "It's just a matter of when. When that happens..."

"They won't need you anymore," Marie said.

Lara nodded. She was glad that Marie understood what Jackie's imminent death meant to both of them. The girl might not have been as worldly as Gaby, or as strong and as good a fighter, but Marie wasn't a dummy. She knew, just as well as Lara did, that the only reason no one had dared to touch them *yet* was because of Owen.

And once Owen didn't need them anymore...

Keo, where the hell are you?

She needed him in the worst way. She was certain he was on his way, if he wasn't already out there, watching her right now. Maybe waiting for his chance, just like she was. Would that be soon? Tonight? Tomorrow? Could she afford to wait?

Lara stared out at Leland, riding behind them. He was her backup plan. Of all of Owen's men, he was her best chance to make it out of here alive if Keo didn't get to them fast enough.

And all she had to do was figure out *how* she was going to make the big man help them...

If Keo was truly out there (*You're out there, Keo. I know you're out there.*), and he had any plans to rescue her, he didn't spring them in the next few hours. They had arrived in Cherry Point around one in the afternoon and didn't pass completely through the place until almost two-thirty. Thirty of those minutes were spent outside a clinic where Owen ordered a couple of his men to go inside; they came back later with a wheelchair that they put into Jackie's trailer. The men hadn't managed to get in and out without incident, because Lara heard gunshots from inside the building. But both men came out in one piece, so she guessed it wasn't that much of a problem after all.

When they finally reached the other side of town, the

group stopped in front of some railroad tracks and Owen rode over and past Lara's trailer. He didn't bother acknowledging her stare and instead grabbed the reins on the horses pulling Jackie's trailer and led them over the tracks.

Lara looked after him, with Leland sitting on his horse next to her.

"Where's he going?" Lara asked.

"The lake," Leland said. "That's why we're here in the first place."

"We're not going there, too?"

"Nope. It's a solo mission."

Not completely solo, Lara thought, because Owen had taken Jackie.

"It's where Owen and me used to go when we were kids," Jackie had told her. *"Our mom took us every summer. Or most every summer."*

He was talking about Cherry Point Lake, which rested on the other side of the train tracks somewhere. It was the only reason they were here, where a man once spent his summer vacations with his family. Everything that had happened to her —being abducted and dragged across Texas—was so Owen could relive childhood memories with his little brother one last time.

She wasn't sure if she felt for the man or hated him for it. A part of her had some sympathy (most of it, though, was for Jackie), but she couldn't get past the fact that all of this was of their own making. They'd done this. They'd stolen the horses and gotten shot because of it. Without that crime, they wouldn't have come looking for her, and she wouldn't be in Cherry Point now with a scared and pregnant young girl to look after.

And none of it was going to matter when Owen returned from the lake alone. Jackie was living on borrowed time, and it was running out quickly. Unfortunately that meant she, too, was running out of time...

"Is he coming back?" Marie was asking. The young woman was also looking after Owen as he got smaller in front of them.

"Yeah, he's coming back," Leland said. "Just gotta give the man time, that's all."

And then what? Lara thought, but she kept that to herself.

"We'll wait for him here," Leland said, before he led their trailer over to the side of the road.

They "parked" in front of a large red two-story brick building while a couple of Owen's men tied up their horses to a pair of lampposts along the sidewalk. A couple of men, one of them Walter, had already retreated down the street where they climbed off their mounts and began going through the stores. She wasn't sure what they could be looking for. Cherry Point was a ghost town, and surely anything valuable had already been looted long ago.

But not everyone left their trailer behind. The ever-present Leland was there, tying the reins of the leading horses in place. Peterson also didn't go anywhere. The tall and lanky man's constant glances in their direction didn't sit well with Lara, but it was worse for Marie. Lara didn't blame the other woman; Peterson didn't even have the decency to hide his ogling.

Keep your eyes to yourself, asshole, she thought, and wanted to tell him out loud but bit her tongue. Right now, she had to look for her opportunities, and nothing she could see even remotely involved antagonizing Peterson.

If she was going to get out of here without Keo's help, she had a feeling it was going to come down to Leland. And only

Leland. She was going to need the big man's help. The question was: How was she going to get it?

Carefully. Very, very carefully.

And maybe she didn't need to ignore Peterson completely in order to achieve that goal. Maybe she could use him as a stepping stone. Leland had to have seen the way the other man looked at Marie. A blind man could see it.

As Lara and Marie climbed out of the trailer, Leland leading them to the red building, Lara glanced back at Peterson. The other man was waiting on the sidewalk nearby with his back to them.

"You need to keep an eye on him, Leland," Lara said just loud enough to be heard by the big man, and him alone.

"Who?" Leland said.

"Peterson."

"What about him?"

"I don't like the way he looks at Marie."

Leland glanced back at Peterson before chuckling. "Peterson's harmless."

"You need to keep an eye on him," Lara said, staring at Leland.

The big man held open the door into the building for them. "I'll make sure he doesn't do anything he shouldn't. Promise."

"I have your word," Lara said.

"Yeah, yeah."

"Say it."

He gave her an annoyed look, but if he intended for it to be intimidating, it failed. Lara had been around him too much in the last two days to know he was probably the least dangerous human being in Owen's group by a long mile.

When he realized he was losing their staring contest, Leland sighed and nodded. "You have my word. I'll make sure he doesn't come near you guys. Especially her. There. Satisfied?"

"Yes," Lara said, and went inside with Marie, even as her eyes dipped slightly and fell on Leland's sidearm.

The big man was armed with a semiautomatic pistol on his left hip, in a holster. He was left-handed, and while Lara didn't think she could ever in a million years pry that AR rifle he had slung over his shoulder from him, the handgun was another matter. All she needed was a few seconds' head start to grab the gun and pull it out before he realized what she was doing. It had been a while since Lara had held a gun in her hands, but it wouldn't have taken more than half a second to remember how to use one again.

Leland had been wary of her trying something early on, especially yesterday, but he'd seemed to have forgotten all about that today. Not that she made him pay for it. Not yet, anyway. The opportunity she was looking for wasn't here yet, not with the others all within gunshot distance of her and Marie—especially Peterson. Lara didn't like her and Marie's odds even a little bit.

The lobby of the red building used to be a diner Lara hadn't noticed that before, because there was nothing outside but a brick wall and two dirt-caked windows. There hadn't been any writings or signs to indicate an eatery of some sort, but maybe those had been washed, blown, or ripped away by time.

There were booths along the front wall and a counter in the middle. A kitchen behind that, and a hallway that she guessed led to some offices and restrooms farther back. An old jukebox sat in a corner, its window display covered in a generous thick layer of dust. It had been a while since Lara saw a jukebox, and apparently the same was true for Leland, because the big man made an enthusiastic beeline for it.

Marie had walked over to one of the booths to sit down, but Lara remained near the door. She sneaked a quick look outside and could make out Peterson still on the sidewalk, hands on his hips, looking around.

"Haven't seen these in a while," Leland was saying as he brushed at the coat of dust covering the machine in the corner. He coughed. "Damn. A *long* while."

"Plug it in, and see if it'll play something," Lara said.

Leland chortled. "Har har."

"I'm serious."

"Sure you are."

"How long have you been with Owen?"

Leland tossed her an amused *Did you just change the subject on me without missing a beat?* look over his shoulder, but he let it go and said instead, "Long enough."

"That's not really an answer."

Leland turned back to the jukebox. "It's *an* answer."

"I'm not going to stop asking just because you're ignoring me," Lara said.

"A few years," Leland said. "We go way back to The Purge. Him and me, Jackie boy, and Walter. The four of us have been around."

"Jackie told me he and Owen were in Darby Bay when that whole thing went down."

That got a surprised glance from Leland. "The kid told you that?"

"Yes."

"He must have been delirious."

"He wasn't."

"He must be, because that's a no-go topic. For anyone. Even Owen's little brother."

"You didn't answer the question."

"You're asking questions you have no business asking, that's why," Leland said. It was probably the most stern he'd spoken to her.

Careful, be real careful, Lara thought.

"Be smart and don't bring it up again, especially around Owen or Walter," Leland continued.

Lara believed him and let it go. She walked instead over to Marie's booth.

"Okay?" Lara asked, sitting down across from the younger woman, but not before wiping at the seat. A cloud of dust gathered around them anyway, and she let out a small cough.

Marie nodded and turned toward the window next to them. Only two of the booths had window seats. There used to be colorful writing on the glass panes—probably spelling out the diner's missing name—but those were long gone.

Marie quickly looked away when Peterson appeared outside, looking in at them. No, not at them. At Marie. And *only* at Marie—which meant he was oblivious to Lara when she narrowed her eyes threateningly back at him.

Lara reached across the dirty counter and took Marie's hands and squeezed. "I'm not going to let anything happen to you. I promise." Then, when it didn't look as if Marie believed her, "I *promise*."

That got through to her, and Marie nodded. "Is your name really Edna?"

Lara smiled. It was a strange question to ask, especially now. "Why? Don't I look like an Edna?"

"Not even a little bit," Marie said, managing a small smile back.

"I'll tell you later, when this is over."

"So, it's not Edna."

"No."

"And is Bob...Bob?"

"Nope."

"You'll tell me that later, too?"

"Promise," Lara said. She looked over as Leland walked up the aisle toward them. "How long are we going to stay here?"

"As long as the boss wants to," Leland said.

"And how long is that?"

"How should I know?" Leland shrugged. "It'll take as long as it takes."

"Would Walter know how long that would take?"

"Probably. Walter knows everything. Pretty sure he can read the boss's thoughts, too."

"So why don't you ask Walter how long we'll be here?"

Leland slumped tiredly down on one of the counter stools. He waved at a flurry of dust that swarmed him as a result. "Doesn't really matter. Once we're done here, we'll be heading off anyway. An hour. Two hours. Tomorrow. Same difference."

"And then what?" Lara asked, even though what she really wanted to say was, *And then what happens to us when Owen no longer needs me?*

But she didn't, because she already knew the answer. She saw it in the way Owen looked at her, in the way the others avoided her and Marie. And if she missed all the signs, all she had to do was glance out the window at Peterson, on the sidewalk. The man was a walking answer to her and Marie's fate.

"I don't know," Leland was saying. "That'll be up to the boss. Like everything else."

The big man swiveled around in the stool, and Lara thought, *What's the matter, Leland? Don't want to look me in the eyes while you're lying? Because I know you're lying. I know exactly what's going to happen to us when Jackie dies, and so do you.*

She said instead, "I guess it's a good thing you're here to keep us safe."

"Yeah," Leland said. "That's exactly what I'm here to do."

"Thank you," Lara said.

He turned around and gave her a surprised look. "For what?"

"What else? For keeping us safe."

Leland forced a smile and nodded. "You're welcome."

Then, as if he were afraid she might see the truth on his face, he swiveled quickly around in the stool again.

Lara looked over at Marie and saw the fear in the other woman's face. Marie had listened silently, but she was no fool. And, unlike Lara, she had more than just her own life to worry about.

Lara reached across the table and took Marie's hands a second time. She gave the young woman her best reassuring smile.

"Everything will be okay," Lara whispered. "I promise. I *promise.*"

If the terrified look on Marie's face was any indication, she didn't believe Lara.

EIGHTEEN

"You got a plan?"

"You already asked me that. More than once."

"Thought I'd ask again, in case you finally came up with one."

"Are you always this annoying?"

"Pretty much. So, you come up with a plan yet?"

"I do have a plan, yes."

"Let's hear it."

"Go in, get my woman back, kill everyone who gets in the way. Any more questions?"

Bunker chuckled. "That's your big plan?"

"Uh huh."

"It's not much of a plan."

"It's *a* plan."

"That's one way to look at it. What about the other woman?"

"Her, too."

"You sure? You said 'get my woman back' and not 'get the

women back.'"

"I said 'get the women back.'"

"Did you, now?"

"Clean out the wax from your ears, Bunker."

"I'll put that on the list. Right after shower at least once a week."

"So that's what that smell is."

Bunker snorted. "Look who's talking. I should call you Smelly Chan instead of Jackie Chan."

I'm not Chinese, Keo thought but didn't bother saying. He had a feeling Bunker already knew that. The rancher was one of those guys who liked to give out false impressions about himself on purpose. Keo had met plenty of the type while he was working. Some of them did it to gain an advantage, but most—and he thought Bunker fell into this category—just did it for kicks because they were assholes.

"Anything new?" Bunker asked.

"I don't think so," Keo said.

"Then why do you keep looking at it?"

Keo ignored him and continued looking across the four or so hundred meters of open field at the town of Cherry Point.

It wasn't much to look at and didn't appear as if it'd been used for some time before Owen's crew arrived. There was a single main road that cut through the place, with alleyways and smaller streets filling out the sides. The biggest landmark was a water tower on the western end, where Keo could just barely make out railroad tracks through Bunker's binoculars. A group of trees after that and, "a mile or so later" (according to Bunker), was Cherry Point Lake on the other side.

"You sure about the lake?" Keo asked, lowering the glasses.

"I've been there," Bunker said. "Good fishing. You could

throw a stick in the water and fish would try to gobble it up. Place is filthy stock with life."

"'Filthy stock with life?'"

"Meaning, it's fish heaven."

"You have a way with words, Bunker."

"Thanks."

Keo grunted. "So, why hasn't anyone settled the town? It's no oceanside village, but it's pretty damn close."

"Plenty of places out here to choose from, in case you haven't noticed. The problem isn't lack of ideal locations, it's the lack of people to claim all of them. Or haven't you done enough roaming to notice that?"

Bunker had a good point. The openness of the Texas land around them was proof there was more land now than people than ever before. Before The Purge, the roads would have been filled with travelers. The last two days, the only people he'd seen were himself, Yuli, Bunker, and Owen's men. It was a far cry from just half a year ago when Black Tide aircraft buzzed the skies looking to kill Mercerians.

Ah, the good ol' days, Keo thought, handing the binoculars back to Bunker.

"So, you don't like my plan?" Keo asked.

"Like I said, it's not much of a plan," Bunker said.

"What was yours, before we met up in Silver Hills?"

"Follow them, harass them, and kill them one by one until they're all dead and I get all my horses back."

"That might have taken a while."

"Lucky me, I got nothing but time on my hands. No clocks to punch, no bills to pay, no mortgages to save up for. I can do this all year long, if necessary."

Keo sneaked a look at Bunker. Getting his horses stolen by

Owen's men might have been the best thing that ever happened to the rancher.

Bunker's definitely an asshole.

"Yeah, well, I don't have that luxury," Keo said.

"To each his own," Bunker said. "Speaking of being on one's own..." He nodded over his shoulder. "You gonna recruit him to assist your not-so-great-of-a-plan plan?"

Keo glanced back at Yuli, standing with Deux and three other horses behind them. He looked as lost now as he had when Keo saw him on the road yesterday with the bandage over his eyes.

"No," Keo said.

"Probably for the best," Bunker said. "He being blind, and all."

"Ya think?"

Bunker chuckled. "I'm insightful like that."

"Yes, you are."

Keo turned and walked in Yuli's direction.

"Don't forget to tell him about your brilliant plan," Bunker said from behind him.

Keo ignored him and said to Yuli, "You doing okay?"

Yuli "looked" over, responding to the sound of Keo's voice. If he was uncomfortable with the gauze around half of his face, he hadn't mentioned it to either Bunker yesterday or Keo this morning.

"Not really," Yuli said. "I'm feeling pretty useless right now, though."

"It's better this way. You'll be safer."

"I didn't come here to be safe, Bob." Then, quickly, "Keo. I meant Keo."

"You can call me Bob."

"I should call you by your real name."

"Bob's been my real name for six months. It can be for another twenty-four hours."

"Twenty-four hours? So you think this is going to be over by then?"

"It'll be pretty close," Keo said. He pulled the AR rifle from Deux's saddle and stuffed some extra magazines into his pouches. "I need you to stay here with Bunker."

"You're going in there," Yuli said. It wasn't a question.

"I'll bring the women back."

"Both of them..."

"Both of them."

"Thank you, Keo." Yuli paused. He seemed to think hard about what to say next, before he finally did. "I'm sorry I can't do anything to help. I'm so fucking useless."

"You'll be fine," Keo said, and patted the man on the shoulder. "You did good."

"No, I didn't."

"Back there, in Silver Hills. I'd be dead if you hadn't shot out that window. You did good, kid. Not bad, for a journalism student."

That got a bit of a smile from Yuli. "Thanks, Keo. That means a lot."

Keo stared at the young man for a moment. Yuli was staring off in the general direction of Cherry Point and was clenching his hands at his sides. The frustration was written all over his face.

Keo tried to come up with some more words of encouragement, but everything that popped into his head sounded...stupid.

Goddamn, you're bad at this.

Keo said instead, "I'll be back with Lara and Marie before you know it."

"I'll be here," Yuli said.

He turned and walked back to Bunker, using the next thirty seconds or so to get used to the extra weight. He hated carrying so many things at once; if he had his way, he would rely completely on the MP9. Unfortunately, that wasn't possible because he only had two extra mags for the submachine gun. Sixty bullets and the half-mag he had currently loaded. Usually that would have been enough, but he had a feeling it wasn't going to be this time.

Bunker glanced over as Keo approached him. "You guys kissed and said your good-byes?"

Keo smirked. "I got a plan for you."

"You already told me your stupendously dumb plan."

"A new plan."

"A good one this time?"

Keo shrugged. "It's slightly better than the last one, but maybe I'm a little biased."

"Okay. Let's hear it," Bunker said.

Getting into Cherry Point was easy. He'd spotted Owen's men milling about along Main Street through Bunker's binoculars. They were going in and out of buildings, likely salvaging whatever they could before moving on, but there was no pattern to their movements. There was also not nearly enough of them to cover every part of the place, which allowed Keo to insert into the small Texas town without anyone the wiser.

He moved through the back alleys, careful not to make too

much noise. The town was simply too quiet, and anything that didn't fit—like an idiot stumbling into an aluminum trash can and knocking it down, for instance—would have drawn immediate attention. He was grateful for the occasional breezes and rooftop-provided shades, but the lingering heat still made him sweat up a storm inside the tactical vest. He would have ditched it long ago if he didn't need its many pouches to hold his spares.

Keo picked his way through Cherry Point with the Brugger & Thomet leading the way, ready to shoot anything that wasn't Lara. Given the relative silence and lack of civilian life from a distance—and now, up close—he was pretty sure that anyone who wasn't a woman was a justified target.

Shoot first, forget the questions later.

After only a couple of days away from the village, Keo missed the daily cool breezes that came from the Gulf of Mexico. Nighttime was even better, but even the days were bearable. It helped that he always had Lara next to him. She made just about everything worthwhile these days.

There you go again. Getting all soft and shit.

He slipped through the back door of a gas station, made his way through the lobby, and after a quick peek, continued unnoticed out the front. Main Street was long and inviting, but it was also way too dangerous, so he quickly angled away from it and kept to the back alleys.

The AR slung over his shoulder was heavy against his back. He didn't like the extra weight of the rifle and its extra spare magazine. Keo was used to moving fast—he wasn't exactly trudging through Cherry Point at the moment, but it was impossible for him not to notice that he could be moving so, so much faster.

He pushed on through the doubts, relying on the old standby that no one ever regretted bringing more weapons and ammo to a gunfight than necessary. He hoped that was true this time, too.

He went east to west, staying out of the open as much as possible, even if that meant having to take the longer routes to go around buildings in his path. He'd been able to keep track of Owen's caravan as they entered town and knew exactly where they were currently congregated—the western edge. Owen himself wouldn't be there, but Keo didn't give a damn about Mr. Piss Down Your Throat.

He was thinking about Lara—finding her and getting her back—and only Lara. Marie would also be there, since there would be no reason for the bad guys to split the two women up. When he found one, he'd find the other; rescue one, rescue the other. Kill two birds with one stone, so to speak.

It took him a good hour and a half before he finally spotted a couple of Owen's men standing on the sidewalk, chatting about something. Keo turned right and into another alley, the inane conversation drifting away into the background behind him. He passed a Dairy Queen restaurant—a common sight in this part of Texas—and slid by what might have been a small community bank. He only guessed that because the back door was open and there were old greenbacks all over the floor.

Keo stepped over a couple of hundred dollar bills, plastering Benjamin Franklin's wry smirk with dirt from the soles of his boots. He thought about the last time he cared about money. It seemed like another lifetime ago now—

Voices, coming from in front of him.

In front, not from his *left* where he'd last seen the two men.

Keo flattened his back against the corner of the bank and

lifted the MP9, aiming across an open alley at a red brick building. From earlier, he knew that he was almost at the other edge of town. The sight of bright sunlight glinting off railroad tracks up ahead was proof.

He waited to hear the voices again, but they had stopped—

There. A man with a husky voice, speaking to someone that Keo couldn't quite make out. The only reason he could hear anything at all was because the back door in front of him was slightly ajar.

Keo stuck out his head slightly, turned left, and glanced down the alley toward the sidewalk beyond.

Empty—for now.

He hurried across the opening and made it onto the other side without being seen, before tiptoeing silently toward the open door. Slivers of dirt-covered linoleum tiled flooring were visible through the crack, highlighted by stingy pools of light, courtesy of the sun behind him.

Keo peeked inside.

A dark hallway, with a straight look at the front door on the other side. Booths with red polyester upholstery to sit in. Some kind of diner, which meant there should be a kitchen somewhere in front of him.

He slipped inside and pressed his back against the wall, letting the shadows embrace him.

There, the same deep male voice from earlier, coming from just the end of the hallway:

"...deal with it. I don't know anything more than that, and I can't tell you what I don't know. Okay?" Then, louder, *"Okay?"*

Keo waited to hear a reply, but there was none. Either the man was talking to himself—which was unlikely—or whomever he'd been conferring with didn't know how to respond. Either way, Keo wasn't going to wait to find out the answer. He had the advantage right now—no one knew he was even in Cherry Point—and it was time to make the most of it.

He pushed off the wall and slid out of the shadows and glided toward the lobby of the diner—

The Bear Man.

The same large human being Keo had seen before constantly watching over Lara back on the road. The man stood in front of Keo, his back turned to him, while talking to someone Keo couldn't see. Owen's soldier wore a sidearm on his left hip, the pistol almost toy-like against his massive frame.

The man must have either heard or sensed Keo's presence, because he began turning around.

Keo lifted the MP9.

"Hey," the man said. "Who the hell are you?"

Pfft! as Keo shot Bear Man once in the chest. He staggered but didn't go down. That didn't surprise Keo at all, given how much mass the guy was carrying.

So Keo fired two more times—*pfft-pfft!*—at about the same spot as the first one, and Bear Man crumpled to the floor.

Keo hurried forward and out of the hallway, and the very first person he saw was—

Lara, standing next to one of the booths. And Marie, sitting across from her.

But all Keo could see was Lara—

A groaning sound from the floor as Bear Man tried to get up.

You gotta be kidding me.

Keo turned and aimed the MP9.

"Keo, don't—" Lara said, but he pulled the trigger two more times before she could finish.

Bear Man lay still.

Keo looked up and over at Lara. "What?"

"Nothing," she said, and ran to him.

He dropped the MP9 to let it hang from its strap so he had both hands free to grab her. She was sweaty and dirty and smelled like the road they'd been on for the last two days, but he didn't care and held her face in his hands and kissed her as hard as he could. He forgot about however many more men were still outside the diner right now. They might have even heard the shooting and were preparing to bust inside, but he didn't care.

There was just Lara, and she was all he needed.

Not that it lasted forever. Five seconds, maybe even less than that, until she pulled slightly away to smile widely at him.

"You came for me," she said.

"Of course I did," Keo said. "Did you think I wouldn't?"

She shook her head. "No. Never."

He smiled. "Not even for one second?"

"Not even for one second."

She kissed him again but pulled back even faster than the first time and turned to Marie. "Come on, let's get out of here."

Marie had already stood up from the booth, and she hurried over. Keo had forgotten just how small and frail she looked—or maybe that was just the last two days having a noticeable physical effect on her.

"You okay?" he asked the young pregnant woman.

Marie nodded and looked like she was about to cry. She took over Lara's spot and hugged him. He wasn't prepared for that and gave Lara a questioning look.

Lara smiled back before hurrying to the front door. She peered out before locking the deadbolt and rushing back. She crouched next to Bear Man and pulled a Glock out of his hip holster and put it behind her back.

"Let's do that later, guys," Lara said.

After Marie let him go, Keo unslung the AR-15 and handed it to Lara, along with the spare for it. Lara stuffed the magazine into her back pocket and took a quick look at the rifle's fire selector before switching it off safely.

"There's more of them outside," Lara said.

"I know," Keo said, looking toward the door. Then, turning and crouching next to the dead man, "Head for the back."

"What are you doing?"

"Hiding the body."

He grabbed the big man by the legs and dragged him down the hallway before backing up into the arched entranceway that led into the kitchen. He dropped the body and rejoined Lara and Marie, already waiting in the shadows near the rear exit.

"It might buy us some time if someone comes in," Keo said. "A second. Two. I'll take anything."

Lara nodded. He noticed an odd look on her face as she stared back down the hallway.

"You okay?" he asked.

She turned back to him and smiled. "Let's get out of here."

"I'll take point," Keo said, hurrying past them.

"Stay close," Lara said. She was talking to Marie.

Keo thought about telling the two women that Yuli was also here. For a second, anyway. He quickly decided against it.

"Hey, Marie, you know the father of your unborn child?

Well, he's also here, except he took a bullet to the head, and I think he's permanently blind now. Surprise!"

Yeah, that was probably not going to do any of them any good, least of all Marie. And right now, Keo's priority was getting them out of here first.

He leaned out of the ajar back door and took a quick glance around.

Left, right—both empty.

Lara was so close behind him that he could smell the warmth of her breath against the nape of his neck. When he looked over his shoulder, he saw only her crystal blue eyes peering back at him.

"Ready?" Keo asked.

Lara nodded. "As long as you're with me, I'm ready for anything."

"That's my girl."

He slipped outside first, feeling like he could take on the world—and good luck to any poor sap that got in his way.

NINETEEN

"You know what's going to happen, don't you? When this is over. You know, but you just don't want to admit it."

"I don't know anything."

"You're lying to yourself. You know what's going to happen after Owen comes back from the lake without Jackie."

"Jackie's not going to die. That's why you're here."

"I can't do anything for him. I couldn't before, and I can't now. No one could. You guys allowed his injury to get out of control before you found me. I was always just duct tape keeping him in one piece."

Leland shook his head. "Owen's going to come back with Jackie in a few hours—or however long it takes—and then he'll let us know what to do with you two. It won't be bad. Owen's not that kind of guy."

"What kind of man is he?" Lara asked. "The kind that takes two women from their homes against their will?"

"He didn't have any choice."

"Yes, he did. He just chose the wrong one."

The big man shook his head again. "He did what he had to do. For Jackie. He'd do the same for me or Walter. That's why we're a unit. We're family."

Was Portman back at the campground family, too? Lara thought. *Or the ones he sent to kill Bunker but never came back?*

Lara didn't say any of those things out loud, though. Instead, she focused across the diner at Leland. Or at Leland's broad back. He had turned around in the stool to clean his rifle with a rag. The AR was temporarily out of commission as he used a brush on it, but there was nothing wrong with the Glock in his hip holster.

"What do they have on you?" Lara asked.

Leland didn't stop what he was doing. "What's that mean?"

"Owen. Walter. The others. What do they have on you that makes you stay, running around Texas doing God knows what with them?"

"I don't know what you're talking about."

"Stealing horses. Abducting women. Which part of those things don't you understand, Leland?"

"We never abducted women."

"Then what do you call Marie and me?"

"We needed a doctor for Jackie. That's all. Your friend just happened to be at the wrong place at the wrong time."

Lara looked over at Marie, sitting across from her. Her face had paled, and Lara thought, *I don't blame her. Being at the wrong place at the wrong time is not exactly the way I'd like to go, either.*

She returned her gaze to Leland's back. "You don't have to stay, you know. You can leave with us. We can leave together."

Leland stopped cleaning his rifle.

Did I just find something? Lara thought, before adding quickly, "You could settle down. Start over. We did. Anyone could. No one has to know what you've done. You can change your name and begin again with a clean slate. Owen and the others aren't your family. Owen only cares about Jackie. You know that. Stop lying to yourself."

Leland turned around slowly in his stool and squinted at her. "You really believe that, don't you?"

"That you can start over? Or that Owen doesn't care about anyone but Jackie?"

"The first one...."

"Because it's true. But apparently you don't believe it. Why is that?"

"I've done things..."

"We've all done things."

"You?" The corners of his lips tugged like he was on the verge of laughter, but nothing came through. "What have you ever done that's so bad? Overbake a pie?"

"You'd be surprised about the things I've done to survive, Leland."

"Yeah, I guess we've all had to do things we're not gonna be writing home about, haven't we?"

"We have, but we move on. We start over. You can do that now. There's nothing to keep you from doing it, too."

"Not me."

"Not you, because you don't think you can, or because you don't want to?"

"Maybe both."

"Before The Purge, that might have been true. But those days are long gone. It's a big world out there, Leland.

Anyone can get lost if they want to. Even a man as big as you."

He chuckled, but it wasn't the usual Leland chuckle. She would give it half a Leland.

"Not me," he said.

"Yes, you," Lara said. "Even you. All you have to do is leave with us."

"Leave with you?" he said, his eyes widening slightly in surprise. "Why do you keep saying that?"

"Because I want you to believe me. You can leave with Marie and me. Now. Before Owen comes back."

He stared at her for a moment, maybe trying to decide if she was playing games with him. She wasn't, though she *was* trying her damnedest to convert him to her and Marie's side. Lara had turned all the odds around in her head, and it always came out the same way: The two of them weren't going to make it out of Cherry Point on their own. They needed help. They needed Leland. Not just his guns, but *him*. They couldn't do this on their own. She wished that weren't true, but the deck was just too stacked against them.

"Owen's not going to hurt you," Leland finally said.

"You don't know that," Lara said. "Jackie's going to die, and when he does, Owen won't need me around anymore. He won't need Marie, either."

"He'll always need a doctor. It's the smart thing to do."

"What about Marie?"

"What about her?"

"He won't need her."

Leland looked as if he was about to say something—maybe argue the point with her—but he stopped.

Because he knows what's going to happen. He knows it.

Lara got up and took a step toward him.

Leland sprang from the stool, moving way faster than a man his size should have been capable of. "What are you doing?"

"Come with us," Lara said. "You, me, and Marie. We can leave this place. We can leave Owen and Walter and the rest behind."

The big man's eyes left her and darted toward the front door for a brief second.

What's he looking for? Lara thought before the answer came to her. *Peterson. He's checking on Peterson. Why? Because he's afraid Peterson might have overheard our conversation...*

But why would Leland be afraid of that? Maybe because he was *considering her proposition.*

I can turn him, Lara thought. *He's giving me the opening.*

She took another step toward him. "Leland, this is our opportunity, before Owen comes back. We have to go. We have to go *now.*"

Leland held up his hand, meaty palm facing her. "You're jumping to conclusions, lady. Nothing's going to happen when Owen comes back."

"You know that's bullshit. You know what kind of man Owen really is. What kind of men the others are. Walter, Peterson..."

"Walter's a good man."

"What about Peterson?"

"Peterson..." He paused. "We'll keep that scumbag away from you guys."

"You can't watch us forever."

"Yes, we can. Yes, *I* can."

He believes that, Lara thought, even as she took another step toward him.

He might have taken a step back if he could, but he would have bumped into the counter. Instead, he took a few steps to the left to put some space between the two of them. For a second, Lara wasn't sure who was the intimidating presence in the room—her or this hulk of a man with a gun.

"I know you want to, Leland," Lara said. "Help us get out of here. Come with us." She gestured back at Marie. "We need your help."

"I can't," Leland said.

"You can't, or you won't?"

He shook his head. "Look, whatever happens after this, we'll deal with it. I don't know anything more than that, and I can't tell you what I don't know. Okay?" Then, raising his voice slightly, *"Okay?"*

Lara opened her mouth to say something, when the shadows in the hallway behind Leland seemed to shift as if coming alive. Leland must have sensed it, too, because he turned around just before a figure stepped out into the lobby, holding a weapon.

"Hey," Leland said. "Who the hell are you?"

It was Keo, but instead of answering Leland, he fired once —the *pfft!* of his suppressed gunshot barely louder than the sound of someone coughing.

Leland staggered but didn't go down.

Pfft-pfft!

So close. I was so close!

"Ready?" Keo asked.

Lara nodded. "As long as you're with me, I'm ready for anything."

"That's my girl."

Keo slipped out of the back door of the red building first, and Lara followed closely on his heels. She glanced back to make sure Marie was behind her. The younger woman was, and Lara took her hand, and they exchanged a smile. Marie was a bundle of nerves, and Lara hoped her own face gave off more confidence.

"My shirt, Marie, take a hold of it and don't let go," Lara said.

Marie nodded and grabbed a handful of Lara's shirt.

It felt odd to be holding a gun again—even the spare magazine Keo had given her was like a stone in her back pocket—but Lara pushed that queasy feeling away. This was no time for it. They were far from safe; sooner or later, Owen was going to come back from the lake, either with or without Jackie. And even sooner than that, someone was going to discover Leland's body in that diner.

Leland...

She glanced back at the red building one final time. She had been so close to turning the big man, she was sure of it. Another minute—okay, maybe more than that—and she might have made a breakthrough. Maybe. It could also be that she wasn't even close, that Leland was never going to betray Owen and the others.

I guess I'll never know now.

She felt those familiar pangs of regret, but they took a back seat to what was going on right now as they sneaked along the back alleys of Cherry Point, following closely behind Keo. He seemed to know where he was going and never hesitated more than necessary—usually when they came to an alley that exposed them to anyone standing on the sidewalk. It was still bright enough outside that she wasn't worried about nightfall. That was still hours away, and Cherry Point wasn't nearly big enough that they would get caught in here before the sun disappeared.

"How did you find us?" Lara asked Keo. She kept her voice low, just in case there was one of Owen's men nearby.

"I've been tracking you since yesterday morning," Keo said. "From Silver Hills all the way to that campground."

"I knew that was you."

"Of course it was me. Who did you think it was?"

"Some pervert jacking off in the fields."

Keo grunted. "Hey, you have any idea how long I waited? I got bored."

"You came back early from fishing?"

"Yeah. Saw the smoke all the way out in the water."

"How is everyone? Things were moving so fast yesterday at the village I couldn't be sure if anyone had gotten hurt."

"Everyone's fine, as far as I know."

"You don't sound too sure."

"I didn't stick around to get all the facts. My first, second, and third priority was getting my girl back."

"So what are you doing here wasting time with me?"

He chuckled. "You kinda look like her."

"Thank God," Lara said, and smiled to herself.

They continued on, passing a back alley connected to a parking lot—

A muted *crash!* came from behind them, about five buildings down. She knew what that was instantly, because she'd been waiting for it. She just wished it hadn't been so soon: It was someone kicking the diner's front door in.

"Keo," Lara said.

"I heard," Keo said, and began moving faster.

Lara changed up her grip on the rifle and looked back at Marie, still holding onto the back of her shirt. The pregnant young woman made an effort to smile, but it did little to hide the fear running through her face.

"Don't let go," Lara said.

"I won't," Marie said.

Lara turned around as Keo made a left, and soon they were almost jogging between two buildings, one a warehouse on their left, the one on their right—

Footsteps pounding against the hard concrete floor behind them, getting louder.

"Keo," Lara said urgently.

"I know, I know," Keo said.

He sounded calm, because he was calm. This was what Keo did. It didn't matter that they'd spent the last six months or so living in a peaceful village and he spent all his mornings fishing with George and Dusty. He was still Keo, and he would always be Keo.

And right now, that was exactly what she needed.

Keo stopped and turned around and locked eyes with her. "Keep going straight, until you see a place called Dixie's. Past that, and it's open fields. A guy named Bunker will be waiting somewhere on the other side. He's a friendly."

Bunker?

The name sounded familiar, and it took a second or two for the information to register.

Right. That *Bunker.*

"Go," Keo said.

Lara nodded and hurried past him. She hadn't bothered to waste time arguing with Keo. She knew him too well—who he was, what he could do—to believe what he was doing wasn't the right call.

She picked up her pace, Marie holding on to her shirt from behind. Or clutching desperately to the hem of the fabric, anyway. At that moment, Lara wasn't sure if she could even force the other woman to let go.

"Don't let go!" Lara said anyway.

"I won't!" Marie said.

I believe you, Lara thought, smiling to herself.

Then the sounds she'd been waiting for—the *pfft-pfft-pfft!* of Keo's suppressed gunfire from behind them, followed by the *clink-clink-clink!* of his bullets' casings bouncing off the surrounding pavement, seemingly louder than the shots themselves.

Lara glanced back over her shoulder. Keo was leaning around the corner when he suddenly pulled his head back, just before the first *pop-pop-pop!* of semiautomatic rifle fire rang out and the bricks next to his face exploded, clouds of smoke erupting into the air around his head.

Keo must have sensed her staring, because he turned his head and shouted, "Keep going! I'll be right behind you!"

You better be, Lara thought, before running again.

She did her best to ignore the loud *pop-pop-pop* of rifle fire as it thundered and clanged and echoed off the buildings. Compared to them, the return fire from Keo's suppressed submachine gun was almost idyllic, like a child playing with toy guns when the adults were using real ones.

Of course she knew better. Keo wasn't a child, and he

wasn't armed with a toy. She'd seen Keo in tighter spots than this, and she couldn't have found anyone better to put her life in the hands of.

So she didn't worry about him back there.

Not *too* much, anyway.

There, a building called Dixie's Storage was in front of her. It was a large steel warehouse with corrugated siding and two massive twin doors, both of which were wide open. Fading clown images, formerly rendered in bright colors, covered the sections of the wall that she could see.

And there, behind Dixie's, was a field of open grass.

"Keep going straight, until you see a place called Dixie's," Keo had said. *"Past that, and it's open fields. A guy named Bunker will be waiting somewhere on the other side. He's a friendly."*

"Come on," Lara said, and began running as fast as she could toward the warehouse.

"What about Bob?" Marie asked.

"He'll be right behind us."

As the big steel building and what remained of that unfriendly-looking clown came up on her, Lara angled slightly left and ran along its side. She didn't have to check on Marie; she could feel the other woman clutching to the back of her shirt. If anything, Marie was holding on way tighter than necessary, like she was afraid Lara might abandon her. After everything they'd gone through, Lara didn't blame her. Still, it made running more difficult than it should have been.

Once they passed Dixie's, there was literally nothing but a world of knee-high grass slapping at their legs. They could still hear the *pop-pop-pop* of gunfire behind them, the loud noises seemingly ricocheting off every building in the entire town.

That meant that if Bunker was indeed out here waiting, he would be able to hear what was happening—and what was coming toward him.

Bunker and Keo. There hadn't been any time to ask Keo how the two of them had met, but it made some sense that they'd end up on the same team. Both men were on the road hunting Owen's group. Somehow, they'd crossed paths, and even found time to strike up an alliance of some sort. Enough of one, anyway, for Keo to refer to the other man as a *friendly*. That was good enough for Lara.

"Lara!" Marie was shouting. Then, when Lara slowed down just enough to glance back, "Bob!"

Lara looked past the young woman and spotted Keo, blazing a trail alongside Dixie's. He was reloading his submachine gun as he ran. When he saw her stopping to look back at him, he motioned urgently with his hands for her to *go, go, go!*

Dammit, she'd stopped running. Why had she stopped running?

She turned and ran. Her face was covered in sweat and had been since they left the diner behind, and her already-dirty old clothes stuck to her skin. The field in front of her kept going and going. There were hills in the distance, but the road that Owen's caravan had taken into Cherry Point was far to her right and beyond her view at the moment—

"Oh, God!" Marie shouted. "Edna! Edna!"

Lara was going to ask *What?* when she heard them, and turned her head around.

Three men were cutting across the open field toward them on horseback, the sound of their approach like rolling thunder as their mounts pounded the hard ground. As soon as Lara spotted them, one of the riders broke off from the pack—

Keo. The man was going for Keo!

Don't worry about Keo. He can take care of himself. Worry about you and the pregnant girl next to you!

Because there were still two riders left and they kept coming toward her and Marie. She couldn't see their faces over the distance, but she wouldn't be surprised if one of them was Peterson. Or Walter. Or one of the others whose names she didn't know.

Concentrate!

In the next two heartbeats, Lara came to an inevitable conclusion:

We're not going to outrun them. Not on foot. Not on foot!

Lara turned to Marie and shouted, "Get down!"

Marie did, disappearing into the grass behind Lara, even as Lara lifted the rifle and took aim at the two riders.

The men were still too far for her to make out anything more than black clothes coming right at her. She guessed two hundred meters, maybe less than that. The AR had a red dot scope, and Lara did her best to line the crosshairs up with one of the riders. The men must have seen her taking aim, because they quickly lowered their profiles to give her even less to shoot at.

Lara remembered all those days of training, the breathing techniques people had taught her over the years.

Will, then Danny, then Peters, then Keo...

In and out.

In and out...

She squeezed the trigger.

TWENTY

She was prepared for the recoil as the rifle bucked in her hands, but Lara was surprised by how loud the gunshot was. It wasn't like she'd never fired a gun before. She'd learned along with everyone else who had managed to brave the horrors of that yearlong Purge. In the years since, she'd gotten better with weapons—handguns, rifles, you name it. She'd made herself get comfortable with them because of her position.

So why the hell did the loud *pop!* of the rifle firing nearly make her jump?

It was probably that startled reaction that caused her shot to go slightly wide, because instead of hitting the rider she was aiming at, the man remained on top of his horse. If anything, he lowered himself even more until he was almost hugging his saddle.

I missed.

I can't believe I missed!

In the two seconds she wasted realizing she'd missed her

target and trying to figure out why, she had allowed Owen's riders to gain even more ground.

She searched for another shot, but there wasn't one to be found. The men—both of them—were too low now, practically flat against their horses. The biggest targets left were the animals themselves.

I don't want to do this.

She lowered the crosshairs and settled it over the head of one of the charging horses. It was a big black animal with a white stripe running almost exactly down between its eyes. She couldn't see the color of those eyes, but they were big and wide, and she swore they were staring back at her as if they knew she was taking aim at them.

Shoot the horse.

What are you waiting for?

Shoot the damn horse!

She shot the damn horse.

Or, she shot *at* it but missed! Fortunately, her round had come close enough to the horse that the big black stopped suddenly, digging its front hooves into the ground. The rider was caught off guard but held on as the horse spun around and reared up on its hind legs. Owen's man tumbled out of the saddle and disappeared into the carpet of grass.

That works, too! Lara thought as she swiveled her rifle to pick up the other rider.

He had kept coming even after his partner went down.

Lara was taking aim when the man pulled up on his horse. The animal struggled against the reins and whirled around, presenting its flank to Lara. It was a wide brown target, and she could have hit it even without the red dot scope. Except, Lara didn't pull the trigger.

Don't shoot the horse! It's just a horse!

Don't shoot the horse!

She didn't. But before she could retarget the animal's rider, the man unslung his rifle and took aim at her.

Now! Now!

They must have fired simultaneously, because there was only a single gunshot.

Wait. No!

She hadn't fired. She had begun to pull the trigger but never got it all the way back before she heard the loud *crack!* of a gunshot thundering nearby. Then the sight of Owen's rider jerking his head backward before he fell from the saddle and, like his partner, disappeared into the field of knee-high grass.

The gunshot—it wasn't hers! And it had come from—

—*her right side!*

She spun in that direction and was shocked to find a figure standing about twenty meters from her. He was close enough that had she kept running and not stopped, she might have run right over him.

It was a man, aiming a bolt-action rifle not at her but in the direction of the two riders. The gunshot she'd heard seconds ago was his, and he was now moving his weapon but still not pointing it anywhere close to her.

Lara glanced over to see what he was aiming at—

The first rider. The same one that had fallen off his horse when the animal stopped suddenly. The man was picking himself up from the ground when there was another *crack!* of a rifle shot. Again, it wasn't hers, but the figure standing next to her.

Owen's rider turned his body to one side before falling

down—only to pop right back up a few seconds later. The man ran toward his horse, standing nearby, and leapt into the saddle.

Lara waited for the stranger to fire again, but he didn't. Instead, the man lowered his rifle and watched the man take off in the other direction.

I guess he's had enough.

Lara looked back at the shooter, her AR still aimed at him. There were two reasons why she hesitated to shoot: The man had shot at Owen's riders and not her; and two, what Keo had told her:

"Keep going straight, until you see a place called Dixie's. Past that, and it's open fields. A guy named Bunker will be waiting somewhere on the other side. He's a friendly."

The man lowered his rifle and turned around. When he saw she was pointing her rifle at him, he flashed her something that looked like an amused smirk. "You must be Jackie Chan's girlfriend."

"What?" Lara said.

"Speaking of whom," the man said, and looked past her.

Jackie Chan? Lara thought.

Then: *Keo!*

In all the running, then the confrontation with the riders, she'd forgotten all about the third man who had broken off from the other two and charged at Keo.

She turned and saw Keo jogging calmly toward her. There were no signs of the third rider, but Lara could see a riderless horse galloping back toward Cherry Point.

"You okay?" Keo asked as he reached them.

She nodded. "You?"

"Right as rain and twice as sweaty." He nodded past her. "I see you've met my new road buddy."

"Yeah," Lara said, turning back to the stranger.

"Edna," the man said, tipping an imaginary hat at her.

Lara gave Keo a curious look.

He smiled and put a hand on her shoulder. "It's a long story."

"I bet," Lara said. She looked over at Marie, who was just now rising from the ground behind her. "You okay?"

Marie nodded and plucked some grass out of her hair. "I think so."

"Let's get outta here," Keo said.

Bunker, meanwhile, had jogged across the field to the brown horse of the man he'd shot. Lara couldn't see any signs of its fallen rider among all the grass. The animal let out a whinny when Bunker approached and picked up its reins.

"What's he doing?" Lara asked.

"Collecting his horse," Keo said. "That's Bunker, by the way."

"I sort of figured that one out on my own."

"Of course you did."

"He's a friend?"

Keo shrugged. "Friend-ish."

"I don't know what that means."

"It means he shoots at the right people."

"I guess that's all that matters."

Bunker had climbed into the brown horse's saddle and ridden it back to them. "Well? We going to just stand around here chatting all day, or what?"

"What about the rest of your horses?" Keo asked.

Bunker glanced back at the town. "Oh, I'm sure they'll be bringing them over to me soon enough."

Then he turned and rode off across the field.

Keo nodded at Lara and Marie, and they followed Bunker. They weren't quite running, but it was a brisk walk.

"What did he mean? That they'll be 'bringing them over' to him soon?" Marie asked.

Lara glanced back at Cherry Point. "He means they're not just going to let us go. This isn't over yet."

"Yuli?" Lara said. "You brought *Yuli* with you?"

Keo sighed. "I didn't exactly bring him. He followed me."

"On his own?"

"He had legs the last time you saw him, right? Besides, I can't blame the guy. They did take his wife and unborn child. If he'd stayed behind, I would have thought less of him."

Lara watched the reunion taking place in front of her. She wasn't sure if Marie was happy or horrified to see Yuli in his current state. Lara herself wasn't entirely sure. It made sense, like Keo had said, for Yuli to chase after Owen and the others, but to see him with the gauze around his head, covering his eyes...

Maybe he should have stayed at the village. I'm not sure this was what he wanted. Him, or poor Marie.

"He's permanently blind?" Lara asked.

She had lowered her voice when she said it, even though there was probably little chance Marie and Yuli could hear if they could focus on anything other than each other at the moment. Marie was kissing Yuli all over and looked on the verge of tears.

"I don't know," Keo said. "I was hoping you might."

"Where did the bullet hit him?"

"The side of the head. I thought he was dead for a while. It knocked his lights out, and he didn't wake up until a few minutes later."

"He lost consciousness?"

"For a while, yeah." Keo was preparing one of Bunker's horses for her. It was a brown one that he called Gasper. "You wouldn't happen to have an X-ray machine lying around to take a look at the poor guy, would you?"

"I'm not sure there's an X-ray machine within one hundred miles of us, Keo."

"Didn't think so."

"God, he's really bad, isn't he?"

"He's not great, that's for sure."

"Poor kid," Lara said, watching Marie as she whispered to Yuli. Lara couldn't tell if she was laughing or crying.

"He did pretty good back there," Keo said.

Lara looked back at him. "He did?"

"Helped me out in Silver Hills. Not sure I'd be here without him."

"You know he was a journalism student, right?"

"He told me."

"I'm surprised he even knows how to fire a gun."

"Me too," Keo said.

Keo didn't look to be in any hurry and neither did Bunker, who was rubbing down a couple of other horses. Both were his, according to Keo. Bunker had been on Owen's trail for days now, making things difficult for the group after they clashed over the stolen horses.

"Tell me about the little brother," Keo said.

"What do you know so far?" Lara said.

Keo told her, finishing off with, "Will he come after us? The big brother?"

"I honestly don't know what he'll do, Keo. It's not like we were on a date and spent all that time getting to know each other or anything. I don't know how he'll react to this. Or how the others will."

"You said his second-in-command is someone named Walter?"

"Yes."

"What's he like?"

"I have no idea. I have even less of an idea about him than I do of Owen."

"Oh, well. I guess we'll just have to improvise."

Lara smiled. "Like usual."

He returned it. "Like usual."

"You know, there were times when I had doubts you'd actually find me."

"You should have known better than that."

"I should have. And I will, from now on."

Keo slipped an arm around her waist and pulled her to him. He kissed her with the same intensity that always made her weak in the knees. If she ever wanted to know how much Keo loved her, all she had to do was kiss him.

Afterward, Lara leaned her head against his chest. He was so warm and sweaty from all the running, but she didn't mind. They stayed that way for a while, enjoying the moment, and she almost forgot they were not out of trouble, that they were still much, much too close to Cherry Point for her liking.

She looked off into the distance, not that she could see the town from where they huddled. It was somewhere on the other side of a small hill. Lara should have been afraid, but she wasn't. It was Keo. He was here, with her, and she thought they could take on the world if they had to. Maybe it was delusional to think that way, but maybe it wasn't.

Then Bunker had to go and ruin it.

"Hey, I know everyone's happy and all, but we really should get going," the rancher said. "I want to find someplace to hunker down before those boys get their shit together and squeeze one out in our direction."

"You wordsmith, you," Keo said with a smirk.

"You're goddamn right. My momma didn't raise no fool. My poppa, on the other hand... Well, I blame it on all the moonshine."

"He's right," Lara said to Keo. "The remaining ones aren't just going to let this go, regardless of what happens with Jackie."

"See, she agrees with me," Bunker said as he led the horses over to Yuli and Marie. "Can you ride, little woman?"

Marie gave him a confused look. "Ride?"

"Can you ride. This horse here."

"I think so."

"Don't worry. She's gentle. Her name's Nolan. I know, I know, sounds like a gent's name, but she's all woman, I can assure you."

"Okay, I guess," Marie said.

Bunker helped her into the saddle, then did the same for Yuli with another horse.

"How long have you been on the road with that guy?" Lara asked Keo.

"About twenty-four hours, give or take," Keo said. "Why?"

Lara smiled at him. "Because you guys already sound like an old married couple. And I'm kind of jealous, to be honest."

Keo grunted. "It's purely platonic. I'm saving all the bad sex for you."

"You and your sweet nothings."

Keo climbed onto his horse, and Lara did the same with hers. The animal was steady underneath her, clearly used to being ridden, even by a total stranger.

"What's its name again?" she asked Keo.

"Gasper," Keo said.

"What kind of name is that?"

"I dunno, you'll have to ask that guy," he said, nodding at Bunker.

"What's your horse's name?"

"Deux."

"Do what?"

"Deux. Like the French number."

She gave him an amused look. "Why—"

"Horse, part deux," Keo said, shrugging. "It's a name."

"It's...something, all right."

"Everyone's a critic."

He leaned over and smacked Gasper on the rump, and the horse started to trot off. He followed beside her on Deux.

They hadn't gotten more than a few meters before they both heard it, stopping their horses to glance back at the hill. They couldn't see them, but they could hear them just fine— the sound of approaching horses. They were coming from Cherry Point.

"Yo, Bunk," Keo called over to Bunker.

The rancher glanced back. "What is it now, Jackie Chan?"

"They're coming."

Bunker, already saddled, reached over and picked up the reins on Yuli's horse. "Then I hope they're all wearing Trojans!"

The rancher gave his horse a nice tap on the flanks, and his animal took off, leading Yuli's with him. Marie followed behind them, the young woman holding on to both the reins and her saddle horn to steady herself.

Lara and Keo brought up the rear. Lara resisted the urge to look back one more time; she couldn't see them anyway, even if she could hear them just fine. She wasn't, she realized, even a little bit afraid. All she had to do was look over at Keo, riding alongside her, to understand why.

"He knows you're not Chinese, right?" Lara asked Keo.

Keo nodded. "He knows."

"So why does he keep calling you Jackie Chan?"

"Isn't it obvious?"

"Not really..."

"Bunker's an asshole, Lara."

"That's it?"

"You need more reasons?"

She smiled. "I guess not."

She leaned over and gave him a quick peck on the cheek.

He gave her a surprised look. "What was that for?"

"I just felt like it. Why? Do I need a reason?"

He grinned. "No, ma'am."

"Good," she said, and gave Gasper a soft tap on the flanks to get the horse to pick up its pace.

They caught up to the others quickly, with Keo riding

beside her the whole time. She looked over and smiled at him, and he returned it.

Somewhere behind them, Owen and however many men he had left were coming. She found, to her surprise, that she wasn't afraid at all. Instead of fear, she felt a growing sense of anticipation: The faster they finished this, the sooner she could get back to her life with Keo.

TWENTY-ONE

Harlingen was northwest, but they took the southeast road instead. Keo didn't like the idea of making a stand in a city as big as Harlingen. It wasn't the size of Houston or Dallas or even close, but it was home to sixty-five thousand people before The Purge, which was about sixty thousand more than had been in Norman at the same period.

They used the grassy fields to take it easy on the horses but kept the Texas state highway within sight at all times as they traveled. They reached Norman around five in the evening and rode through the place looking for a building—a home, a store, an office—that could help them get through the remainder of the day and, if necessary, the night.

Like most medium-size communities in this part of the state, Norman was wide open and spread out, with almost all of its commercial properties settled around a four-lane road that cut right through the middle. The homes were scattered along the sides—mostly one-story single-family homes with wide-open yards. There was some hurricane fencing, but that was rare; this was one of those places where neighbors regularly crossed over into each other's property without blinking an eye.

They rode through the suburbs but didn't stop. Houses were too dangerous—any one of them could be hiding a nasty surprise, and clearing them out would take too much time. They passed houses of worship, some in better shape than others, and a couple of trailer parks, before reaching the commercial area. Restaurants, car washes, and hundreds of small mom-and-pop establishments mixed in with bigger-named businesses that had somehow found a home all the way out here.

Keo didn't find a serviceable spot to stop and wait for Owen until they were almost out of the commercial area, and the big water tower loomed in front of them like a rocket ship readying for takeoff. It was massive, with a bulbous top and a ladder going up its side. It sat directly across the street from something called Norman Rodeo Grounds—a series of smaller buildings next to a large metal warehouse. Keo had a pretty good idea what the structure was being used for. The big stadium next door, complete with bleachers and billboard advertisings for local businesses, sealed the deal.

He was riding ahead of the group when he stopped Deux and waited for the others to catch up.

Lara was first. "Found something?"

Keo nodded at the water tower, jutting out from a large swath of empty land about half a football field from the road. "Fifty meters high, give or take. It'll make a heck of a good spot for a sniper, don't you think?"

"Depends on who's doing the shooting."

"Not me." Keo looked over at Bunker as the rancher rode over to join them. "Him."

"Me, what?" Bunker said.

"The water tower," Lara said. "You can see almost the entire town from up there."

Bunker peered at the large structure. "Yup. A fella can definitely do a lot of damage up there. Until someone shoots him off it, that is."

"That's why you have to choose a good spot and stay hidden," Keo said.

Bunker smirked at Keo. "Easy for you to say. You won't be up there."

"That mean you'll do it?"

"You're right, it's a fine spot to pick off some nasty *hombres*." He thought about it for a second or two before turning in his saddle to look back down the highway they'd come. "I figure, if I'm fast enough and all sly like, I could take out two, maybe three before they even know where I'm shooting from."

Let's hope, Keo thought, because two—or three—less bad guys for him to deal with was definitely a plus.

"You won't be alone," Lara said. "Keo and I will be down here drawing their fire."

Bunker gave her a doubtful look before turning to Keo. "She serious?"

"She's serious," Keo nodded.

"Why? Don't I look like I can handle myself in a firefight?" Lara asked.

The rancher shrugged. "I don't know you well enough to answer either way. I just met you a few hours ago, in fact."

"We'll do our part, as long as you do yours," Keo said. "By

the end of tonight, you'll have all your horses back. Worst case, by the end of next morning."

"Promises, promises," Bunker said.

"Speaking of horses..." Keo nodded toward the fairgrounds. "I'm willing to bet that big metal warehouse is a stable. We'll clear it out and store the horses inside. They'll be out of harm's way while we take down Owen and however many men he still has left out here."

"Sounds like you got everything figured out, JC."

"Trust me, Bunker, this isn't our first rodeo. No pun intended."

"Hey, pun all you like, no skin off my nose."

Bunker glanced back at Yuli and Marie, sitting on their horses in the back. The couple hadn't interjected or even said a word, with Marie sticking close to Yuli as if she were afraid he might fall off his saddle. Keo wasn't too worried about that. Yuli had remained on his mount through the long ride from Cherry Point, despite not being able to see a lick.

"What about them?" Bunker asked.

"They'll stay with us," Lara said. "Marie will watch Yuli."

"All of this is assuming the *mucho baddo hombres* will know where we are."

"They'll find us," Keo said.

"Why are you so sure of that?"

"Listen, Bunker."

Bunker did. There was a slight breeze, and somewhere back in the commercial area of Norman, a metal object *clanged* against something over and over again. Other than that noise, there was nothing to hear.

"What am I listening for?" Bunker finally asked.

"Exactly," Keo said. "We've made it pretty easy for them to

follow us here from Cherry Point. Oh, they'll be careful, maybe they'll even wait for nightfall to attack, but they're coming one way or another."

"And then what?" Yuli asked. It was the first time he'd spoken, and all three of them turned to look at the young—and, at least for now, blind—Mexican. "What happens when they find us here?"

"We make sure they don't leave Norman," Keo said.

There were exactly five buildings next to the large two-story metal warehouse that was, as Keo had guessed, a stable. The smaller ones were offices for the people that managed the Rodeo Grounds business. The stadium, flanked by aluminum bleachers, had a large dirt floor in the center that was once covered with horse prints, but that was years ago, and no one had used the place since.

Keo and Bunker cleared out the stables, which didn't take nearly as long as Keo had expected. There were large windows ringing the top of the warehouse, allowing plenty of sunlight to drown the interior. That had kept ghouls from creating permanent nests inside, though there was lingering evidence in some of the darker corners that they hadn't always avoided the place.

When they were done, they brought the horses in and put them into the individual stables. Bunker then jogged across the street and climbed up the water tower, while Keo returned to one of the offices where Lara and the reunited Yuli and Marie were waiting for him.

They had chosen the only two-story building among the group. The first floor was a lobby with couches for visitors and extra offices along a back hallway that led to a rear exit, now locked with a deadbolt. Keo walked through and up the stairs, the hard aluminum steps *clanging* loudly under his boots. He liked that. In the middle of the night, with no one making a sound, that *clanging* was going to come in real handy as an early warning system.

Lara was waiting upstairs, standing next to one of the windows that faced the highway about thirty meters away, on the other side of a large gravel parking lot that extended almost the entire length of the business grounds. The AR that Keo had given to her back at Cherry Point leaned against the wall nearby. With the blinders opened, sunlight poured into the room, but they were noticeably softening. He guessed they had about an hour before nightfall.

There were a half dozen or so trucks parked outside, spread out across the lot. All the vehicles were so old and covered in dirt, mud, and whatever else had blown through the town in recent years that Keo and Bunker hadn't bothered to check if any of them were still working, never mind locating still-usable fuel.

"Can you see him?" Keo asked.

Lara nodded and pointed out the window. Keo squinted and could just barely make out Bunker scaling the ladder that extended up the skinny base of the water tower. "Skinny" when compared to the giant balloon on top, anyway.

"All of this because they took his horses?" Lara asked.

"He really, really likes his horses," Keo said. "Maybe a little *too* much. Me, I wouldn't have gone through so much trouble for horses."

Lara smiled across the window at him. "But you'd do it for a woman."

"Hey, have you tried cuddling with a horse?"

"Glad to know I'm better than a horse."

"Most definitely." Keo glanced over at the back hallway. There were more offices in the rear, including a bathroom and supply closet. "How're the lovebirds doing?"

"Marie's scared," Lara said.

"About Yuli?"

"Him, her, their unborn child. She's scared."

"Understandable. What about Yuli?"

"I'm not sure. It's hard to read someone when there's gauze over half of their face."

"He didn't say anything?"

Lara shook her head. "Marie's taking care of him. She asked Yuli about the village, but he didn't know either. Or maybe he couldn't remember. I don't know which. How was it when you left?"

"Burning," Keo said.

"Was it very bad?"

"Bad enough that there might not be a village there for us to return to."

"God, that's terrible."

"The others were trying to fight it with water from the ocean, but..." He shook his head. "There's a reason firefighters use fire hoses and hydrants are located on sidewalks next to buildings."

"When they took us, the village looked okay. The clinic was burning, but it didn't look that bad."

"I guess it spread quickly."

"Everyone lost their homes?"

"I don't know for sure, but if I had to guess..." He nodded.

"Houses can be rebuilt, Lara. The others already did it once from scratch. They can do it again."

"I guess that's true. But everyone's okay?"

"I don't think anyone was hurt. Scared, but okay when I left there."

"Good. At least there's that."

"Why did they burn the clinic, anyway?"

"Owen told me it was an accident, but I think he did it to distract the others. To keep them from following us." She smiled at him. "I guess he wasn't counting on you."

"It's going to take a hell of a lot more than just a little fire to keep me from coming after you."

"You said it was a big fire."

"Not big enough. You know how far I had to run before I finally found Bunker and got my hands on a horse?"

Lara sniffed the air. "Is that what that smell is? All that running you did?"

Keo grinned. "Something like that."

"When was the last time you showered?"

"It's been a while. Why? Do I really stink that badly?"

"You reek." She took a silk handkerchief out from her pocket, then picked up a water bottle sitting on the floor nearby and wetted it. "Come here."

Keo came over, and she wiped his face with the fabric. He wrinkled his nose and asked, "What's that smell?"

"Evaporated ghoul blood."

"Ugh."

"Don't be such a baby." She cleaned him down to his neck before noticing that he was smiling at her. "What are you smiling at, mister?"

"Reminds me of the first night we spent at the village together."

That pulled a smile from her, too. "I remember."

"Best bath of my life."

"Really."

"Absolutely."

"I'm honored."

"You should be." Keo noticed that she wasn't carrying the Glock pistol she had taken from Bear Man back at Cherry Point. "What happened to your sidearm?"

"I gave it to Marie, just in case. I hope she doesn't have to use it." She stepped back. "There. All cleaned up. Mostly."

"Nice."

She opened one of the pockets along his cargo pants and shoved the handkerchief inside. "Don't say I never gave you anything."

"Speaking of which..." He unslung his tactical pack and rummaged through it until he found the extra SIG Sauer he'd taken from Ronald back at Silver Hills. He handed the handgun, along with two spare magazines, to Lara. "Try not to give this away too, okay?"

She took the gun. "I'll do my best."

"You remember how to use it, right?"

"It's a gun, Keo. You pull the trigger, and it goes bang."

"Good enough."

He zipped the pack back up and left it on the floor. Keo looked out the window and toward the water tower again. Bunker had made it to the top and was moving along the railing that circled the massive ball. He might as well be an ant up there.

"How good is he?" Lara asked.

"He's pretty good," Keo said. "If he can take out a couple of Owen's boys, that'll increase the odds in our favor."

"You really think he'll ride right through town and straight at us?"

"I'm hoping that's what he does. But like you said, it'll depend on what happened with Jackie. You still don't think he'll live through the day?"

Lara shook her head. "He was pretty badly off even before they found me. He didn't get any better after that. I don't think Owen ever had any illusions Jackie was going to get any better."

"So, Cherry Point."

"Cherry Point. They spent their summers there with their mom, apparently."

"Owen was taking them there so he and Jackie could... What, exactly?"

"Maybe to relive their glory days. Maybe he just wanted to fish with Jackie one more time. I don't know, Keo. But I don't think Jackie came back from that lake with Owen."

"So, you've met him. This Owen guy."

Lara nodded. "Yes. Of course. Why?"

"Someone told me he was a real piece of work. A dangerous man."

"Who told you that?"

"One of his men. A guy named Ronald."

"He's not wrong," Lara said. "He is dangerous, Keo. He's very dangerous. He killed one of his own men with his bare hands. You met him. The dead guy on the side of the road."

"The one you left your message on."

"That's him."

"Nice work with that, by the way."

"It was spur of the moment, and I didn't have a lot of time. My big worry was that you wouldn't find the body."

"I almost missed it." Then, "So Owen killed him?"

"He beat him to death." Lara told him about the "disagreement" that led to Granger's execution. "Whatever this Ronald told you about Owen, you should believe him. He's very dangerous."

"Noted."

"Does that change anything?"

"With Owen?"

"Yes."

"Maybe."

"How?"

"Now I'll shoot him the first chance I get. No talking." He patted the submachine gun slung in front of him.

"That's probably for the best," Lara said.

"What else can you tell me about him?"

She smiled. "Why? You writing a book?"

He chuckled. "It's always a good idea to know as much about your enemy as possible before you have to go into battle against him. I think some smart guy named Sun-something wrote that long ago."

"Jackie told me their father was in the Army. That he was a Green Beret."

"Owen, too?"

"I don't think so. Jackie said something about Owen going into the Army, like their dad, but then he went somewhere else later. He became a buddy?"

"A buddy?"

She thought about it for a moment. "No, not buddy. He

said buds. That Owen went into buds? I didn't know what he meant. I still don't."

"Hunh," Keo said.

"You know what that means, don't you?"

"Owen was in the U.S. Army, then he went into buds, you said?"

"Something like that. It means something to you?"

"He was probably talking about BUD/S," Keo said. "B-U-D-slash-S."

"What is that?"

"Basic Underwater Demolition/SEAL."

"Seal? Like the Navy SEALs?"

"Like those guys, yeah. You go into BUD/S to qualify for becoming a SEAL."

"I thought only Navy guys become SEALs."

"Anyone can go through selection. You just have to switch over to the Navy first."

"How do you know so much about this?"

"I used to be an Army brat, remember?"

"I forgot about that."

"Did Jackie say if Owen graduated BUD/S?"

Lara shook her head. "He didn't."

"That's too bad."

"Why? Does it make a difference if he graduated or not?"

"Well, if he got through BUD/S, that means he's a pretty badass motherfucker. Only about one in four guys that go through selection pass muster. Didn't you have a SEAL in Black Tide?"

"No. At least, not that I know of. Danny and Will were Rangers, and there were some Marine Force Recon guys, but I don't think we ever had a SEAL." She added, a few seconds later, "Maybe Peters."

"Peters?"

"He never really said what he used to do, but there were rumors..." She shook her head. "Anyway. You still haven't told me if knowing all this about Owen makes any difference with what's about to happen tonight."

Keo thought about what Ronald had told him, but it was that one line that really stood out then, and still did, now:

"You don't want to...fuck with him. He'll kill you. He'll fucking kill you and piss down your throat."

Apparently, Ronald had good cause to make that threat.

Lara was watching him closely. "Keo?"

"Nah," Keo finally said. "It doesn't make any difference."

"You sure? You took a while to answer..."

"I'm sure."

She didn't look as if she fully believed him, probably because Keo himself wasn't sure if *he* believed it. He smiled at her—he thought it was pretty convincing—before reaching over and taking her hand and pulling her over to him.

Keo kissed her on the lips, then the tip of her nose, then her forehead. She pressed her cheek against his chest, and he smelled her hair. Sweat and dirt and something else that didn't belong, but he couldn't care less.

"Keo," Lara said. She was almost whispering.

"Yeah?"

"What are we going to do after this? Are we going back to the village?"

"Do you want to?"

"I don't know. After what you told me, there might not even be a village to go back to."

"The people will still be there."

"But will they be happy to see me? After what happened..."

"It wasn't your fault."

"Wasn't it?"

"Not even a little bit. It was Owen's fault. If they want anyone to blame, they can blame that dickhead."

"They might not see it that way."

"Yeah, well, I can always beat it into them."

He couldn't see it, but Keo imagined her smiling at that.

"Let's not do that," she said.

"Are you sure?"

"Pretty sure."

"Okay. But only because you say so."

"I'm not one hundred percent sure I want to go back anyway, even if the whole place hadn't burned down."

"No?"

"I thought I'd want to, but the more I think about it..." She paused for a moment. "Maybe it's time to move on."

"Move on to where?"

"Anywhere. It's a big world. Texas is just a small part of it. Maybe it's time we leave the state."

"Sure. We'll do whatever you want to do."

"It should be both our choices. We're a team, aren't we? *We* should decide, not just me."

"Do we have a name?"

"A name?"

"Every team needs a name."

She didn't answer him for a few seconds. Then: "How about Bob and Edna's Spectacular Traveling Show?"

"Sounds good."

"So?"

"So?"

"Do you want to move on or go back to the village?"

"It depends..." Keo said.

"On what?"

"What do you want to do?"

She laughed. "I hate you."

"I know you do," he said, and held her tighter.

TWENTY-TWO

Thirteen bad guys. Fifteen bad guys. Twenty bad guys?

Bunker said one thing, and Lara said another. What mattered was that the number had dwindled to somewhere between five and ten. Ish.

Close enough, I guess.

And then there was the SEAL.

Not that Owen's past really mattered all that much to Keo. SEALs, like Green Berets, Rangers, and any other Special Forces operators went down just as easily as Joe Schmoe from the neighborhood when you put a round into them. Okay, maybe you'd need an extra—or two, or three—to make sure they stayed down, but they'd go down just the same.

So Keo wasn't too worried about Mr. Piss Down Your Throat as an individual. He was more concerned with the guys he'd be bringing with him. One was wounded but not out of commission. Bunker had said he'd shot a third man outside of Cherry Point, but the man hadn't stayed down. Lara had confirmed the story.

Seven, or eight, or nine probable bad guys—one definitely gimpy and another a nonfactor. He had a sharp-shooting rancher on his side and a tough lady who knew how to handle herself.

It wasn't great odds, but it wasn't the worst Keo had faced.

I'll take it.

Besides, unlike all those other times, Keo had something on his side tonight: A very good reason to win. It wasn't just his hide on the line; it was his future. *She* was his future.

He stared across the semidarkness at her, sitting across the window from him. Streams of pale moonlight shone into the second floor of the office building between them, but neither one of them were in the light's path. Not that it was difficult to make out her face; her long, blonde hair; and the crisp blue of her eyes...

God, she's beautiful.

Except for the lonely pool of light, the rest of the building was dark but not quite as bleak as the outside world. He could still make out the four-lane state highway whenever he glanced out the window through the vertical blinds. They kept it open, which allowed light in and for them to see out, but wouldn't necessarily look obvious from the road.

The only sounds in the entire world that his ears could pick up were his own calm breathing and Lara's nearby. He couldn't hear Marie and Yuli in the third—and last—room down the hallway on the other side of the floor. Their job was to stay there until all of this was over. The last thing he wanted was a scared pregnant woman and her blind husband running around getting in the way.

With nothing to do, they waited.

And waited...

Midnight came and went, and there were no signs of Owen and his goons. Was it possible they might have gone right past Norman after all? Or maybe the bad guys really had lost their tracks during the day?

Both of those scenarios were possible, but unlikely. The world was too empty, too devoid of life, that you could find someone—or a group of people fleeing on horseback—without really trying. Keo had found that out himself when he'd tracked Owen's group to the campgrounds and then later to Cherry Point.

It'd been easy. Incredibly easy, in fact.

So no, he didn't think Owen had lost their trail earlier in the day. The more likely scenario had the former SEAL biding his time and taking things slowly. Would he wait until morning? In the man's shoes, Keo would. It was the logical thing to do. Why attack a fixed position in the middle of the night when your targets knew you were coming? After everything Keo and Bunker had done to him, Owen would know by now that he wasn't dealing with amateurs.

He looked across at Lara again. If there was any fear in her, he couldn't see or detect it. She was serene, as if they were back at the village, sitting on their porch, listening to the waves crash against the beach. He wished they were there now instead of out here. This was dangerous, and he hated putting her in danger.

Lara must have sensed him staring, because she turned her head, crystal blue eyes locating him easily. "What are you staring at, mister?" she asked. It wasn't quite a whisper, but low enough that he wouldn't have heard if the world inside and outside the building wasn't so quiet.

Keo smiled. "You."

"What do you see?"

"My future."

He couldn't quite tell her reaction despite the two of them sitting so close together, but he thought she looked pleased with the answer.

"You do realize that you are never, ever going to get rid of me if you keep talking like that," Lara said.

"So, my plan's working."

"I think so."

"Good. I was starting to think—"

The first *crack!* of a rifle shot rang out.

It echoed like thunder, rippling across the Texas countryside for the next few seconds.

About fucking time! Keo thought even as he stood up, back sliding against the smooth wall behind him.

Lara did the same. "Bunker?"

He nodded. "That's his rifle."

Keo leaned toward the window. He didn't need to squint between the white PVC slats because of his angle—he had a perfect view through the vertical valley between the blinds and the window frame, and at the parking lot outside.

Moonlight glinted off the abandoned vehicles sprinkled across the gravel clearing between their building and the highway. And there, across the street, was the massive water tower with its round top—

Crack! as Bunker fired again, the muzzle flash from his rifle sparkling briefly in the darkness, then disappearing well before the sound of the gunshot itself.

Keo refocused on the flat asphalt, gray against the night, and followed it back toward the main commercial area of Norman, where Bunker's shots had been aimed. He wondered how long it'd been since Owen's group reached town and slowly but surely made their way up toward this part of the city. That had taken a lot of patience. Maybe even more than Keo could have mustered.

"You see anything?" Lara asked. She was leaning against her side of the wall and looking out, but in the opposite direction as him. This way, they had eyes on both sides at all times, in case Owen did something crafty like go around Norman and come up on them from behind.

Keo shook his head. "Nothing yet. You?"

"I don't see any movement out there." Then, "You think it's possible Bunker might have fired for no reason?"

"Doubtful. At least not twice."

"You've only known him for a day. Maybe he's not as pro—"

Pop-pop-pop! as someone opened up with a semiautomatic rifle. Keo glimpsed muzzle flashes coming from a squat building about maybe two hundred meters from their location. He looked up and over at the water tower as rounds struck the side of the domed structure and ricocheted off with loud *ping-ping!* echoes.

"Never mind," Lara said.

Keo smiled but kept his eyes outside and up the street. He wasn't too worried about Bunker. The man would have had to be a total idiot to leave himself exposed up there after taking his first two shots. The smart thing would be to shoot and move around the walkway and use the bulbous top as a shield before his targets could return fire. Keo was pretty sure that was exactly what Bunker had done, even if he couldn't see all the way out there to be sure.

"What was that?" Lara asked when three more *pings!* rang out.

"Water tower," Keo said. "They're shooting at Bunker."

Lara slid across the window and squeezed in next to him so she could watch the muzzle flashes from up the road. There were more than one—three separate points of fire letting loose —and they were on the move, leapfrogging from business to business as they picked their way down the highway. Keo couldn't see the men themselves in the darkness, but it was clear they were taking turns providing covering fire for one another.

"They're good," Lara said.

"They're not amateurs," Keo said. "It's a good thing neither are we."

"Are you including me?"

"Why not?"

She smiled and gave him a peck on the cheek. "Stay frosty," she said before hurrying back across the window to her spot.

Keo grinned. "'Stay frosty?'"

"Something Danny used to say all the time."

"Ah. The lack of a bad joke before or after the phrase threw me off."

"Speaking of Danny, it'd be nice to have him here right about now."

"It'd be nice to have one of your Warthogs here right about now."

"You're right. Those would be better," Lara said.

The *pop-pop-pop!* of rifle fire, almost instantaneously followed by the *ping-ping-ping!* of their rounds striking the outer metal layer of the water tower, continued outside.

Owen's men were using single shots, conserving ammo. No one was shooting wildly; they knew what they were doing and had the ammo to get the job done.

"Do you think Bunker got anyone?" Lara asked.

"One," Keo said. "Maybe two."

"Why are you so sure he even got one?"

"He shot first. And he wouldn't have done that if he didn't get one of them in his crosshairs."

"I hope you're right."

Me too, Keo thought, but he said, "Anything behind me?"

"Still nothing. What are you seeing?"

"They're leapfrogging between buildings, getting closer—"

He stopped in mid-sentence when the gunfire suddenly ceased and there was an eerie quiet outside that lasted.

The silence fell like a brick and lasted for five seconds...

Ten...

Thirty...

A full minute went by.

Then two minutes...

"What's going on?" Lara finally whispered.

Keo shook his head. He hadn't taken his eyes off the cluster of dark structures up the highway. Not that he could see much of anything. There wasn't enough moonlight for him to even make out the business signs that he could earlier in the day. The second floor of the office they were in gave him a good view, but it also presented him with a lot of rooftops.

Five minutes of silence, and still nothing. He couldn't see or hear—

The *crack!* of Bunker's rifle shattered the calm, followed by the *ping!* as the round punched through a hard, metal surface. But it wasn't the sound of the gunshot that startled Keo; it was the result of its impact: *It had come from just beyond the parking lot outside!*

He was certain the *ping!* was from Bunker's bullet striking the metal shell of a car, one that was parked less than a hundred meters from Keo's location. As if to confirm that guess, at least two—maybe three—rifles returned fire on Bunker, the rain of *ping-ping-ping!* bouncing off the water tower, creating multiple sparks across the street.

Here we go!

The thought hadn't completely finished in Keo's mind before he spotted figures—dark and black and moving *fast*—darting across the parking lot in front and below him!

Two—no, *three.*

Keo spun in front of the window and opened fire with the MP9 on full-auto. Glass shattered, his rounds chopping into the PVC blinds and cutting them apart as he rained down bullets onto the front yard.

One of the figures fell and a second stumbled, but the third kept going (*Shit!*) until he had vanished underneath the window. Keo didn't bother looking for the third man and instead spent the last of his remaining bullets putting down the stumbling figure.

He immediately sidestepped away from the broken window, ejected the mag, and slapped in a new one. He was prepared to spray the ground a second time to make sure both bodies stayed down when Lara acted first, moving in front of the window and firing twice into the parking lot.

Pop-pop! and another one of the figures, already trying to get up, slumped back down to the ground and lay still.

Keo grinned, thought, *That's my girl.*

Lara quickly slid back behind cover and looked across at him. "Just two?"

Keo shook his head. "A third guy made it through."

"Shit."

"Stay here," Keo said.

"What?" Lara said.

He pushed off the wall. "And stay out of sight."

She looked alarmed. "Keo, where are you going?"

Keo glanced toward the stairs across the floor. He hadn't heard the front door opening below them, not that the third guy (*Owen, is that you?*) could have just entered unopposed. The front and back door had deadbolts that Keo had made sure were in place before he came up. That left the attacker to shoot or break his way in, and either option would have made a lot of noise. Noises that Keo hadn't heard yet.

"I'll be right back," Keo said, and jogged across the room.

He saw something moving out of the corner of his eye and turned, the MP9 swinging up instinctively, but it was just Marie in the hallway looking out at him. She was clutching the Glock Lara had given her with both hands, and he wasn't sure who was more startled—her or him.

"Is everyone okay?" Marie asked.

"Get back inside," Keo said.

"But—"

"*Now.*"

She nodded, turned, and hurried back down the hallway.

Keo reached the stairs and glanced down. Pitch black. When he looked up and across the room, he saw Lara watching him silently.

"I'll be right back," Keo said.

"You better," she said.

He turned and was rushing down the stairs when he heard the *crash!* of a door breaking. The sound was too muffled and echoey, all signs that the third guy was coming through the back instead of the front door.

Sneaky little bugger.

Keo hopped the last set of stairs and landed on the first floor in a crouch. He snapped up to his full height a second later, the Brugger & Thomet in front of him, and turned left toward the opening into the back hallway. He'd moved fast enough that he was certain he'd gotten down before whoever had kicked open the back door could get all the way through the long corridor and reach the lobby.

He hoped, anyway.

It was pitch black on the first floor, and if not for the fact Keo's eyes had adjusted to the darkness in the hours since nightfall, he wouldn't have been able to see a damn thing with the blinders still covering the two windows at the front. The tiled flooring was slick against his boots, but Keo was used to it, and glided toward the hallway.

His forefinger tested the pull of the submachine gun's trigger, and he became aware of a slight increase in his heartbeat. What was this, his first gunfight? Why was he suddenly so anxious? Was it the prospect of facing off against an ex-SEAL?

If one of the two dead guys outside in the parking lot wasn't Owen.

If the man had even been out there at all and hadn't just sent three of his lackeys ahead of him.

There were a lot of ifs there.

Well, two, anyway.

It wasn't bad enough that the entire building was dark, but it had to be stiflingly hot as well. He was already sweating when he raced down the stairs and hadn't stopped since. Perspiration dripped down his forehead and cheeks and jaw, and his clothes clung to his skin.

Definitely need a shower after this, Keo thought as he kept moving a foot at a time toward the hallway—

Gunfire from his right, coming from one of the windows!

He dropped to the floor, slamming chest-first into the cold (*Well, at least something's cold!*) tiles as glass shattered and bullets *zip-zip-zipped!* over his head, followed by the *pek-pek-pek!* of those same rounds slamming into the wall across the room behind him.

Jesus Christ!

He rolled to his right, the thoughts *It was a trick. He kicked the back door in knowing I'd hear and go right for it. But he never came inside. He was waiting at the window the whole time for me to walk into the open like the big dumb idiot I am!*

The shooting didn't stop until Keo clumsily flopped his way into a patch of dark shadows and pulled himself up from the floor. He bumped his back against a wall, keeping the window and its shredded blinds in front and slightly to the right of him.

The shooter was already gone, disappeared from what remained of the window.

Nice one, pal. You almost got me. You almost—

Aw, man, Keo thought when he felt wetness running down the length of his left arm.

He'd been shot, and there was a hole near his shoulder blade that shouldn't be there. No, not hole, but *two* holes—one in front and one in the back. Dark liquid dripped out, already forming a puddle on the floor. He'd left behind a trail of blood without realizing it and could just barely make it out now in the semidarkness.

He rested his head against the wall. There hadn't been any pain before—just a slight, buzzing numbness—but that had changed when he noticed the wound. Keo laid down the submachine gun and pulled out the handkerchief Lara had used to clean him with earlier. It still smelled like vaporized ghoul blood, but he was glad to have it. Keo tied it around his shoulder and pulled it tight to stanch the bleeding.

He picked the MP9 back up and scooted along the floor until he was closer to the second window—the undamaged one to the right side of the front door. He'd spent way too much time in one spot for his liking. Keo slid up the length of the wall, until he was back on his feet, and refocused on the room.

The door was to his right, on the other side of the still-intact window. In front and to his left was the entrance into the back hallway. Keo had a feeling Mr. Clever was going to return to the back door after his little stunt. It would make sense, since climbing in through the broken window, with all those shards of glass, wasn't going to be a very good trip for anyone.

Keo knelt down on one knee and waited. The world around him was suddenly very quiet again. Impossibly and eerily quiet.

For now...

TWENTY-THREE

He was back to breathing calmly again and had been for some time now. This wasn't anything special. He'd done this before. Too many times to count. Another day, another dollar, another gunfight. So what else was new?

In and out...

It had been nearly five minutes since he'd heard anything from Bunker. Or, more precisely, Bunker's rifle. The bolt-action made a very distinct sound when it fired compared to the easily recognizable *pop* of a semiauto AR, which was what most, if not all, of Owen's people were carrying and had been filling the night with ever since the fight began.

In and out...

The lack of evidence that Bunker was even still out there and kicking—and more importantly, shooting—was...not good. The only plus Keo could see was that Bunker had taken out one, maybe two of Owen's goons.

One, for sure. Two, hopefully.

In and out...

And then there were the two dead bozos on the other side of the wall to his right. Bunker may or may not have notched a kill when he started shooting, but Keo could at least be 100 percent certain about the bodies on the gravel parking lot. One of them might have even been Owen himself.

What is this, your attempt at Captain Optimism?

Hey, why not? Someone's gotta claim the title.

Even as he tried to convince himself one of the two dead outside was Owen, he didn't really believe it. He didn't know how he knew—or how he could be so sure of it—but Keo just did. He didn't think a guy who had made it through the wet and mud and misery of BUD/S would die that easily. Would he?

Here's hoping...

...but probably not.

He knew at least one thing for sure: Whoever was still out there, he was a clever little bugger. He had lured Keo out into the open and almost took his head off. They'd gotten a round through his shoulder instead. That same someone wouldn't be retreating now. Nosirree—

"Keo?" a voice whispered.

He glanced left toward the back of the room.

Lara, halfway up the stairs, staring back at him. If not for her blonde hair and blue eyes, he might not have been able to make her out in the darkness. How had she gotten all the way down there without him noticing? Or, more importantly, *hearing* her footsteps?

Shit. Maybe I'm more hurt than I thought.

Did I just go deaf, too?

No, he couldn't have gone deaf, because he'd heard her

whispering his name. Of course, there was no telling how long she'd been doing that—

"Keo," Lara said again, still whispering.

He lifted a finger to his lips to shush her, then pointed toward the back hallway. Lara nodded, understanding.

Keo gave her the *A-OK* sign before indicating the ceiling.

He couldn't tell if she was relieved by his confirmation that he was fine (It wasn't a complete lie; he was still capable of moving, even if he was having doubts about his hearing, so he was fine *enough*.) because beyond her hair and eyes, he couldn't read the expression on her face.

But she nodded a second time and disappeared back up the steps. This time, he heard the *clangs* as she went up. Why hadn't he heard those before? Maybe he had...

Oh, who are you kidding? You didn't hear shit before, pal.

Well, that's no good.

He didn't breathe easier until she was gone. He hated the thought of her down here, in danger. Not that he didn't trust her ability to defend herself—she had, after all, cold-bloodedly gunned down that wounded man out in the parking lot earlier. (*That's my girl.*) Keo just didn't need the extra burden. If it was Owen out there, sneaking around in the dark, Keo had a feeling he was going to have his hands full.

It didn't help that he was doubting his own senses. Shit. Did he really miss her coming down the steps? How in the world—

He glimpsed movement a split second before the silver canister landed with a echoey *clank!* against the tiled floor and bounced back up before *clanking!* a second time. It didn't go back up a third and instead rolled toward him, spewing white clouds out of one end with every inch it gained.

Oh, you sonofa...

Not just plain smoke, but tear gas. He knew that right away when his eyes began stinging and the scar along his left cheek tingled like it was trying to rip itself off his face. The stench of vinegar filled up his nostrils, and the first acidic taste flicked at his tongue. He'd been tear gassed before and knew the signs. He also knew that the worst was yet to come.

Keo stumbled back, letting the submachine fall and hang off his shoulder by the strap, while he tore loose the handkerchief he had been using to stanch the bleeding on his left arm. He continued staggering, fighting to keep his balance, even as white clouds continued to belch out of the canister that had finally stopped rolling in front of him, almost exactly in the middle of the room.

Hurry up! Hurry up!

His heartbeat had accelerated, every beat pounding like a snare drum even as his chest constricted, as if his rib cage were clamping down on every organ in his body. He wanted desperately to stop moving—just *stop*—and fall to his knees and try to fight the seizures, but that would mean giving up. On Lara. On Yuli and Marie, too, because all three of them would be in danger if he went down here and now.

No. He couldn't let that happen. He *couldn't let that happen.*

He had retreated so far that his back bumped against the wall; which was good, otherwise he might have already sank to his knees without the extra support to stay upright. Keo forced his hands to move, to tighten the bloody handkerchief around his head, over his nose and mouth. He could smell and taste his own blood in the fabric as it pressed against his lips, but it was a hell of a lot better than gas.

Covering up half his face did nothing to save his eyes, though. They were probably red and bulging by now, and tears were welling up around the sockets, not that he could confirm or deny. Unlike Yuli, he hadn't gone blind, even though he wanted badly to snap his eyes shut.

Thick white smoke filled up the first floor around him. Goddammit, there was a lot of smoke. Keo didn't think one single can could produce so much. Then again, maybe the darkness—and the general lack of light—just made everything look thicker than it really was. Or maybe his eyes had actually fallen out of their sockets, and he wasn't really seeing anything at all.

He doubled over, grabbing his gut, wanting to throw up.

But he didn't. Somehow, he kept himself from vomiting—

Something stepped out of the smoke. A creature in black, striding through the swirling clouds like some monster from a nightmare.

No, not a creature. Not even a monster.

A man, wearing a gas mask.

Hey, that's cheating! he wanted to shout and laugh, but all he could muster was a series of wheezing coughs as he struggled to keep his eyes open even as tears streamed down his cheeks.

Christ, it burned. *Everything* burned.

Brown eyes peered through the twin lens of the gas mask at Keo. He couldn't see anything else of the man because of the smoke and black clothing. He could have been looking at just about anyone, but he knew—he didn't know how he knew, he just did—that this wasn't just anyone.

Owen.

It was in the way the man walked—calm, with purpose—

and the way he gripped the knife in his left gloved hand. (Keo tried to remember if Lara had mentioned anything about Owen being a leftie, but he couldn't recall.) The stock of a rifle poked out from behind one shoulder, and though the man wore a gun belt, the pistol remained undrawn. He could have taken out the handgun or unslung the rifle and finished Keo off without even having to show himself.

But he hadn't. He'd chosen instead to walk up to Keo with a knife. It wasn't a particularly big knife, either. About six inches of stainless steel with a black matted handle—ten to eleven inches, give or take, of total length. Keo himself would have gone for something longer and bigger, like the Ka-Bar he'd lost somewhere back during all the action in Cherry Point, though he hadn't realized it until much later.

Or a gun! Like the submachine gun hanging off his shoulder!

Even as Keo dropped his hands to grab the MP9, the man (*Owen. That's fucking Owen!*) lunged at him. He was fast, or maybe Keo was just moving slower than usual thanks to the effects of the gas (*Yeah, that's it! That's the reason! It's definitely not because he's faster than you!*). Before Keo could even put his hands on the Brugger & Thomet, the blade of the knife drove into his right shoulder.

Owen's forward momentum sent Keo reeling backward, and he crashed into the wall again. Not that he had very far to go, but the impact still sent shockwaves through his body and only increased the savage pain coming from Owen's blade as it dug its way into his flesh, as if the man was determined to drive every inch of steel all the way through Keo and into the wall behind him. Of course that was never going to happen, not with the knife's guard bunting up against

Keo's shoulder. The blistering contact made Keo scream out in agony.

Or, he thought he screamed, anyway. Keo couldn't be sure of anything, not with all the gas in the room trying to claw out his eyes and pieces of the blood-soaked handkerchief somehow having gotten into his mouth as he bit down on it to fight back the intense pain.

Keo had forgotten about the submachine gun. He couldn't find it with his hands anymore, though he was pretty sure it was still hanging off his shoulder by the strap. So why couldn't he locate it? If it was still there—

Owen pulled out the knife to cock his hand back—a spurt of blood arced through the air between their bodies—and Keo gave up on finding the MP9 and grabbed Owen's wrist with both his hands just as the man tried to plunge the blade back into Keo.

The knife froze in the air.

For a heartbeat or two, anyway, before Owen put his other hand around the knife handle and began pushing it down despite Keo holding on.

It was clear now that the man was dead set (*Ha! Dead!*) on eviscerating Keo up close and personal. Not that the whys of it mattered, because at the moment all Keo could do was hold on and push back...and he was losing.

He was losing!

Owen was gaining, pushing Keo's hands back and at the same time lowering the knife inch by inch by inch toward—

Keo's chest. The very, very sharp point of that knife was focused squarely on Keo's chest. A little movement to the left and that blood-covered steel would go right into his heart. Keo thought he could survive a lot of things—hell, he was still standing after getting shot and stabbed once already tonight—but he wasn't sure he could walk away from a blade plunged straight into his heart.

And right now, a foot of smoke-filled air separated Keo from the point of the knife. Just a foot.

A measly, lousy foot.

Owen hadn't said a word since he attacked. Not that he needed to say anything. Those hard brown eyes peering out from behind the glass lens spoke volumes. Keo didn't see anything that looked like actual hatred in those eyes, but he could make out steely (*Ha! Steel! Like the steel he's about to plunge into your heart?*) determination.

The foot had become ten inches of space separating Keo from death.

Nine inches...

He was bleeding badly from both shoulders. The blood squirting (*Jesus Christ, it's really squirting outta there!*) from his right looked worse than the small dribbling from his left for some reason, not that Keo cared enough to figure it out. He thought he could hear the *drip-drip-drip* as his blood made its way down to the tiled floor around his feet, but that was probably all in his head. Besides, he could barely hear anything above the pounding in his chest. His ears were still ringing for some reason, and his eyes were filled with tears.

But those were going to be the least of his problems when that knife entered his heart. This man wanted Keo dead, but Keo couldn't allow that. Once Owen was done with him, he'd march up the stairs for Lara, and there was no guarantee he would want to keep her alive this time. If Jackie was dead, like Lara had guessed, then the big brother wouldn't need her anymore.

Seven—no, six? Was there just six inches between him and the knife now? Jesus Christ, how strong was this guy? Keo had both hands pushing back, but the man was gaining anyway. It didn't help that Keo was already wounded.

Yeah, that's it. That's the reason you're losing.

Slowly, so painfully slowly, the knife was getting closer...

...and closer...

Five inches.

Wait, five inches? How did they get to five—

Four inches.

Fuck!

There wasn't going to be a happy ending for Lara if he died right here, right now. All he needed to do was look into the eyes of the man trying to kill him to know that with 100 percent degree of certainty.

Three inches...

Those weren't kind eyes. They were a killer's eyes.

And he couldn't allow them near Lara.

Not now, not tomorrow, not ever.

Two...

Not *ever*.

Keo let go of the knife completely—*and jerked his body to the left at the same time.*

Thunk! as the knife drove into the wall next to Keo's still-sliding body, the sharp blade striking the wooden frame underneath.

Unfortunately for Keo, he'd moved too fast and was out of control, and despite his best attempts, he lost his footing and went sprawling to the floor.

Get up! Get up now!

He was trying to do exactly that when he saw the submachine gun dangling from its shoulder strap, somehow still slung over his shoulder despite everything that had happened.

There you are!

Keo grabbed for it now, even as his legs continued to pathetically try to raise him up from the floor—

The first boot landed against the back of Keo's kneecap and sent him reeling back down. Even as he fell, Keo managed to twist slightly and squeezed the trigger while swinging the MP9 wildly from floor to ceiling, praying he might hit some part—*any* part!—of his attacker.

The *pffi-pffi-pfft!* of gunshots filled the lobby just before Keo's back slammed into the cool tiles.

He was flat on his back but had somehow held onto the submachine gun while falling. But not for long. A boot landed against the back of his wrist, and he swore something might have snapped. Or a lot of somethings. There was exploding pain, but the only thing Keo could focus on was the MP9 flying out of his hand and disappearing into the still-thinning smoke around them.

No, no, no!

He'd lost the submachine gun, but he still had his holstered Glock, and Keo frantically reached down for it with his right hand. A blur of a black shape moving in front and above him (*Above? Right. Above. Because you're on your back on the floor! You should really get up now!*) as Owen moved in for the kill.

Those brown eyes peered back at him from behind the glass lens as Owen pointed something at Keo—

A gun. Owen had finally drawn his sidearm and had it pointed at Keo's face.

Keo's hand, only halfway to his own handgun, froze.

So close. I was so close...

But it hadn't been close enough. Owen was faster. Stronger. And the fucker was wearing a gas mask that kept him from choking with every breath he inhaled.

Blood dripped from Keo's shoulders, the knife wound on the right side already creating a sizable puddle on the floor underneath him. He waited for the man to say something. A joke at his expense, maybe. Or a final good-bye. A one last *"This is why I'm killing you, motherfucker"* speech.

Instead, the man stayed quiet, and the only signs of life were those brown eyes squinting behind the lens of the gas mask. The gun remained pointed at Keo's face, the hand holding it steady as a rock.

Steady as a fucking rock.

The first *bang!* struck Owen in the chest, and the second one hit him at about the same area even as the man was stumbling backward. Owen pulled the trigger as he did so, returning fire on whoever had shot him.

Bang-bang-bang!

Keo lost count of how many times Owen fired and how many times whoever had just saved his life kept shooting—

Lara. It had to be Lara! She had come down to help him.

That's my girl!

Owen had been shot twice, but for some reason, the man refused to go down. Not that Keo just lay there and watched the whole thing. He finished drawing his own Glock and shot Owen's still-moving body in the chest.

Again and again and *again*.

Eventually, Owen went down (*Thank fucking Christ!*), and Keo stopped pulling the trigger. He rolled over onto his chest and looked toward the back of the room.

There was something on the stairs, sitting down.

Keo jumped to his feet and ran over.

Lara was holding her left thigh with both hands. There were holes in the wall above her head that hadn't been there before, and parts of the banister were cracked.

She was looking at him. "You've been shot."

"So have you," Keo said.

He crouched in front of her and took a closer look at her wound. Blood seeped through her fingers, but she didn't seem to notice them. Keo ripped off the handkerchief he still had covering half of his face and pressed it against her wound.

Lara was staring at the body across the room. "Is it him?"

"Who?" Keo said.

"Owen."

"I don't know. Maybe. I'm not sure."

"It has to be him."

"Forget him. We need to get you upstairs."

He helped her up to her feet. She cringed, finally acknowledging the pain, but still didn't cry out.

"Keo," Lara said. "You're bleeding so much."

"I'm fine; I barely feel a thing," he lied. "But I need to fix this leg of yours first."

He helped her up the stairs a step at a time. He only glanced back at the body crumpled in the middle of the lobby once. He still didn't know if it was Owen or not, but it probably was. He'd find out sooner or later, but for now, he couldn't care less.

Right now, all that mattered was making sure Lara was out of harm's way.

TWENTY-FOUR

She'd been shot before, but this time it was a little different. There was some pain, but most of it was just numbness and the occasional stinging sensation as Keo worked on her. It wasn't too bad of a wound, though an inch more to the left and it would have missed her completely. Except it didn't, but she could think of a hundred ways it could have been worse.

She might not have gotten down there in time just as the gas-masked man was ready to shoot Keo, for instance. She could have stayed on the second floor, like he'd told her, even ignored the fighting and screaming she could hear coming from below. Then there was the line of bullets that had punched through the floor and embedded themselves into the ceiling above her head. Even if she could ignore all those things, she still wouldn't have been able to turn a blind eye to the smoke in the air that, even now, clawed at her face.

Lara spent her time alternating between learning to breathe again and trying not to choke on the tear gas that clung to her clothes and hair. It was in her eyes and nose, and she couldn't imagine how much harder it had been for Keo in the thick of it downstairs. Up here, they had some reprieve as the gas began to thin out, but even so, it took everything she had not to throw up.

She coughed instead and watched Keo as he cut a hole in her pants leg with some shears he'd taken out from his backpack. He did it cautiously, afraid of nicking skin underneath. She was amazed he could be so calm in his current state. She'd seen him fighting down there, then saw him on the verge of being killed. And yet, here he was, completely unfazed. If he was still feeling the effects of the tear gas, it didn't show on his face. His hands were steady, as was the rest of him.

He's amazing. God, he's so amazing.

"You doing okay?" he asked her. His eyes were bloodshot, and there were specks of blood on his cheeks. Maybe his, or the man he was fighting. Or both of them.

She coughed. "I'm fine."

"You're not fine. You've been shot."

"I've been shot before."

"I don't like that. You need to stop getting shot, woman."

She smiled. "I'm trying."

"Try harder."

"It's not my fault people keep shooting at me. You should know something about that."

He grunted. "This isn't about me. Now sit still."

"I'm trying."

"Try harder."

"Yes, sir," she said, and gave him a mock salute.

He grinned and continued cutting a wide enough hole in her pants to see what he was dealing with. He grabbed a bottle of lukewarm water out of the same pack and cleaned the wound, before using a clotting bandage from the first-aid kit to stanch the bleeding.

Lara wanted to tell him to stop, to let her work on *him* first, because she could see that he was also bleeding. But he wouldn't allow it. So instead of fighting him, she let him finish his work. The faster he got it done, the faster he would let her focus on him in turn.

He handed her the same handkerchief—Leland's—that she'd given to him earlier, that he'd used to stop the bleeding while they were on the stairs. She pushed the silk fabric against her mouth and nose to spare herself from some of the lingering tear gas in the air. She could still see small wisps of smoke drifting up the stairs to the second floor across the room.

When he was finally done, Keo sat down in front of her with a heavy sigh. "There. All fixed up."

"Now it's your turn," Lara said.

"Don't worry about me. I'm okey-dokey."

"You're not okey-dokey. You're bleeding."

"You should see the other guy."

"I did."

"Oh yeah, forgot about that."

He blinked at her, then wiped at a bead of sweat. His hands were covered in blood. Hers, his—who else's? His eyes were still unnaturally bloodshot.

"Keo?" she said.

"I'm feeling a little light-headed," he said.

"Let me—"

"I think I'm going to faint."

"Wait—"

He toppled sideways, his head hitting the smooth floor with a painful *thunk!*

"Keo, you idiot," Lara whispered as she scooted the short distance over to where he lay.

She grabbed the same first-aid kit he'd used on her leg and took out a bundle of bandages. Blood was seeping out of his shoulders—both of them—and running down the length of his exposed arms. She wrapped Leland's handkerchief around the lower half of her face before going to work on Keo.

She pulled up his sleeves to reveal his wounds—two, one on each shoulder. Thanks to the moonlight coming in through the window next to them, she was able to tell that one was the result of a knife, while the other one was a bullet that had gone through. They both looked bad—especially the blood running down his arms and pooling underneath him—but everything about Keo told her he'd survive this.

He was unconscious at the moment, which was probably for the best given how much blood he'd lost and what he'd gone through downstairs with the tear gas. His breathing was shockingly regular, though, but maybe she shouldn't have been so surprised. Keo had taken more punishment than any man she'd ever known; hell, he'd taken enough punishment for *ten* men.

And he was still standing. Or, in this case, lying down.

But alive. And if she had anything to say about it, he would stay that way.

"Edna?" a voice whispered.

Lara wiped at the blood along Keo's left arm with a pad of antiseptic towelette before she glanced over at Marie, just barely visible at the entrance of the back hallway. The young woman looked out tentatively, as if afraid of revealing too much of herself. She had smartly grabbed a hand towel to cover up her mouth and nose, but even so her eyes blinked rapidly, still feeling the effects of the dissipating gas that had made it up to the second floor.

When Marie saw Keo, she gasped. "Oh, God. Is he—"

"He'll be fine," Lara said before the other woman could finish. "I need you to come here, Marie."

Marie rushed over and kneeled on the other side of Keo. She cringed when she realized she'd kneeled right in a pool of Keo's blood. But to her credit, Marie got over it quickly and, after coughing a bit, said, "What can I do?"

"Where's Yuli?" Lara asked.

"He's in the room." Then, "What can I do, Edna?"

"Lara."

"What?"

"My real name's Lara, remember?"

"Oh. I forgot."

"Here," Lara said, handing her a bundle of moist disinfectants. "I need you to clean his face and any exposed skin you can reach."

Marie took the towelettes but gave her an alarmed look when Lara stood up. "Where are you going?"

"I need to make sure he's dead," Lara said.

"Who's dead?"

Owen, she thought, but said, "I don't know. Whoever Keo was fighting downstairs."

"Is it over? Is it all over?"

God, I hope so, Lara thought.

She said, "I don't know. Just stay up here with Keo, okay? Keep an eye on him and shout if something happens."

"Like what?"

"If he bleeds again or his breathing becomes erratic. Anything that isn't normal."

"Okay," Marie said, her voice far from convincing.

But Lara didn't have time to help the other woman get over her doubts. She had been honest with Marie—she needed to make sure the man downstairs was dead. Not just him, but to make sure there was no one else left to come up here. She wished she had heard something from Bunker, but he had gone silent after the barrage of semiautomatic rifle fire.

She drew the SIG Sauer from her holster, then swapped out the half-empty magazine with a fully-loaded one. She also retrieved the AR rifle she'd left behind earlier before hobbling over to the stairs.

"Edna," Marie said. "I mean, Lara."

Lara looked back.

"Be careful," Marie said.

"I'll be right back," Lara said, and turned and headed downstairs.

***

She didn't like leaving Marie alone on the second floor with an unconscious Keo, but she liked how quiet everything was around them even less. There were no sounds whatsoever from outside, as if the entire world had simply decided to stop existing. The thick metal walls around them didn't help, but she thought even without them it would have just been as silent in all of Norman right now.

Where was Bunker? Where were the rest of Owen's men? Had they killed each other while Owen was in here with Keo? Was the dead man downstairs even Owen at all? Maybe it was Walter. Or Peterson? Or...

That was the problem. There were so many questions

swirling around inside her head and no answers. It was the reason she couldn't just stay upstairs with Marie and Keo and wait it out. She couldn't afford to; if there was even one of Owen's group left, he remained a threat to all of them.

Too bad Bunker was out of commission. He was probably dead. After all, once he opened up on Owen's group from up the water tower, they knew exactly where he was and had concentrated their fire on him. How could he have survived all that? There was the walkway that he could move around, but there were only so many safe spaces available to him.

She stopped thinking about Bunker. Dead or alive, he couldn't do anything to help her right now. And right here, right now, she only had herself to rely on, because even Keo—the most reliable man she'd ever known—was temporarily unavailable.

She moved slowly down the stairs, her skin tingling against the lingering tear gas in the air. Most of it had dissipated, thanks to that blown-out window in the lobby, but too much still remained that her eyes continued to water and she had to keep fighting the urge to stop, double over, and throw up.

Get it together. Get it together!

She did, using the puddles of blood on the steps to guide her on the way down. Not that she needed the hints. It was dark, and nightfall wasn't going anywhere anytime soon, but she could see well enough in the semidarkness to move around with some confidence.

The heavy AR rifle in her hands didn't hurt. She was accustomed to the weight of it, especially with a full magazine, and her forefinger was in the trigger guard. She wasn't exactly practicing "proper trigger discipline," as Peters would say, but she didn't care. If there was anyone downstairs, it was unlikely to be Bunker, the only "friendly" in all of Norman. He would have called up or made noises to let them know he was coming.

God, she hoped she wasn't wrong and ended up shooting Bunker by accident instead.

There were a lot of *ifs* and *maybes* going around in her head, and she couldn't cross any of them out until she got downstairs. She took the metal steps one at a time, listening to every single sound, disliking the heavy *clank!* her boots made each time she descended. She had avoided being detected earlier because the man Keo was fighting with was too busy with him to hear her coming down. She didn't have that element of surprise this time.

Lara paused briefly, counted to five, and on *five*, ran down the rest of the steps instead of taking it one at a time. She reached the bottom quickly, lifted the rifle, and looked through the red dot sight. She sucked in a deep breath, thankful for the protection of Leland's handkerchief that kept her from swallowing too much of the still-present tear gas in the air.

But there was nothing to shoot.

Thank God, there was nothing to shoot.

She stared across the room at the front door. It was still closed and, for all she knew, still locked. The dark hallway to her left remained pitch black, hidden from the revealing moonlight coming through the broken window. There was a large puddle of blood in the middle of the first floor, and moonlight glistened off the smooth side of a canister lying nearby.

But there was no body.

Where the hell was the body?

She'd shot Keo's attacker. She was sure of it. She'd shot whoever was down here with Keo at least two times. Probably three or four times. Then Keo had shot the man, too. Altogether, they must have put six to eight bullets into the dark figure, if not more.

So where the hell was the body?

Lara ran into the lobby, stopped on a dime, and swung toward the hallway. Suddenly, she couldn't even smell or feel the effects of the tear gas anymore. Her heart was racing, and every ounce of her concentration was pointed at the dark hallway.

Blood.

There was a trail of blood leading from the center of the room and into the corridor, which then disappeared into the darkness beyond. Whoever she and Keo had shot, the man had picked himself up and walked away. He hadn't dragged himself, because that was inconsistent with the pattern on the floor. A body being dragged—either by himself or by someone else—would have left a wider swath of red.

There was so much blood. Way more than one man should have been able to bleed out. Someone who lost that much should be dead.

So why wasn't he dead?

Lara didn't wait to find out. She made a beeline for the hallway, the rifle pointing her way, her forefinger against the trigger. Her instincts were to open fire, to pour some rounds into the dark passageway and hit whatever was in there. She had a full magazine, and she could cover a lot of ground. When the AR was empty, she could switch to the SIG right away instead of wasting time trying to reload.

It would have been easy. It would have been the smart thing to do.

But she didn't, for whatever reason, and hurried across the lobby, keeping the bloody tracks to her left so she wouldn't do something stupid like slip on them. They were still very wet, very shiny against the random streams of moonlight that did manage to touch them.

The pain along her left thigh, where she'd been shot, had waited for this moment to come roaring back. Or maybe it was always there, but she'd managed to block it out as she came down the stairs, and then later, moved across the lobby. Trying not to gag against the tear gas had probably lent a hand, too.

Now, she couldn't ignore it. But she didn't let it stop her. She was going to be suffering from aches and pains for days to come anyway, but to get there she had to survive tonight first.

Just get through tonight first...

Nothing moved within the shadows in front of her. Nothing shifted or even stirred. There were just pockets of darkness when she was outside the back hallway entrance and still nothing when she took her first steps inside.

Lara paused briefly to get control of her breathing. Her heartbeats sledgehammered against her chest, so loud she could barely hear anything over them. She willed the beats to slow down, but it was like trying to stop the ocean with her hands.

Keo, why aren't you here with me right now? I could really, really use you right now.

It wasn't just his abilities, but his presence. He brought out the best in her, made her think she wasn't the total failure that she knew she was.

Medical school, Will, Black Tide, Darby Bay, Gaby...

Keo made all those things go away; and in return, all he asked for was her.

God, she wished he were down here beside her right now.

But he wasn't. He was upstairs, trying not to die, while

Marie watched over him. And Lara was down here, alone, making sure no one went up there to harm them. To harm him.

She pushed on, avoiding as much blood on the floor as she possible—the ones that she could see, anyway—but finding it a hopeless task after a few steps. She could hear the *slurp* when the soles of her boots stepped over a puddle.

Then another, and another...

There was so much blood. How could one man bleed so much and still keep going?

Finally, after what seemed like hours of walking in the darkness, Lara reached the end of the hallway and the closed metal door. There was very little light, but she could make out the bloody handprints on the smooth door, left there when someone (*Owen. It has to be Owen.*) pushed the door open to exit. The deadlock was busted, the handle barely hanging on.

Lara used the barrel of her rifle to ease the door open. It did, slowly—inch by inch, by inch—

—she threw her shoulder into it and lunged outside—

And almost tripped over a body on the ground.

She was covered in sweat, and there was the smell of blood in her nostrils, but the sudden presence of tear gas-less air was like a reprieve from death row. She sucked in a grateful lungful and swung around.

She faced left, then right, then front and back—looking for something, *anything* that could be a threat.

But there was nothing.

There was just her, in the back of the building, surrounded by a dead town.

When she was absolutely sure there wasn't anyone—or any*thing*—hiding in the shadows, she turned back to the body.

It was a man in black, clutching a gas mask in one hand,

while he lay on his side. Blood seeped out of multiple wounds along his chest and serpentined around the many tiny pebbles that made up the gravel floor underneath him.

Lara leaned against the wall and pulled the handkerchief down and sucked in another couple of deep breaths, letting the clean, warm air fill her lungs. They had made it through the night. There were moments when she didn't think they would (Small, fleeting moments, but moments nonetheless), but they had.

They had...

She focused on the body again. Its back was to her, but even without seeing the face, she knew it was the same man she'd shot in the lobby. The same person that Keo had added a few rounds into just for good measure. How the hell had he gotten up from all of that and walked out here? What kind of willpower did something like that take?

Lara slung her rifle and drew the SIG Sauer before crouching next to the body. She reached over—

She stopped, her hand in mid reach.

Her hand was shaking. Why was her hand shaking?

Because finally, *finally*, the ordeal she'd had to endure for the last forty-eight hours was about to be over.

Finally.

She grabbed the body by the shoulder and turned it over onto its back.

A pair of brown eyes looked up at her.

No...

Brown was the wrong color. It should have been gray.

Hard, gray eyes.

The dead man wasn't Owen.

TWENTY-FIVE

She hurried back into the building, nearly slipping on all the blood on the floor as she rushed through the dark hallway. There was still no one in the lobby, and the door remained closed, with just that one blown-out window to represent any kind of threat. Lara made sure of that first—that no one had snuck inside while she was outside—before heading for the stairs and taking the steps two at a time, even if doing so made her grimace, the pain shooting from her wounded thigh even more pronounced now.

Marie was where Lara had left her, kneeling next to Keo. She looked up, holding the Glock that Lara had given her with one hand. The younger woman still had the towel wrapped around the lower half of her face, even though Lara could barely smell the tear gas on the second floor anymore.

Marie relaxed when she saw Lara. "Everything okay?"

"Everything's fine," Lara lied.

She walked across the room, past Marie and Keo, and went to the window. She stood next to it, away from the open, and peered out. It was just as quiet and empty out there as it had been when she last checked before heading downstairs. The two bodies on the ground directly below her hadn't moved. For a second or two, an image of them getting up and walking away flashed across her mind's eye.

But no, there they were.

Was one of them Owen? It was possible, but she didn't think so. Would a man like Owen, a former Navy SEAL, go down that easily? In front of her, while trying to run for the front door? It seemed so...anticlimactic. The only way to know for certain either way was to go out there and look at their faces up close, which wasn't going to happen tonight.

"Lara?" Marie said behind her. "Are you sure everything is all right?"

Lara glanced back and nodded. "Everything's all right now." She looked at Keo's unmoving form. "How is he?"

"He seems fine, but I don't know. I'm not a doctor like you."

I'm barely a doctor, Lara thought, but she said, "You should go back into the room with Yuli."

"Are you sure?"

"Yes. Go on."

Marie got up. "Why don't you guys come into the room with us? Isn't it safer in there?"

Someone has to stay out here to shoot Owen when he tries to come up the stairs, she thought, but said, "We'll be fine out here. Besides, it's too hot to stuff everyone into the same room all night."

Marie nodded and said, "Okay," before she disappeared into the back hallway.

Lara heard a door open, then close a few seconds later.

She walked back to Keo and picked him up by the armpits and dragged him over to the far wall, placing him between the corner and the destroyed window. She laid him down on his back, then grabbed a pair of extra dirty shirts from his bag to make a pillow for his head. Lara settled on the floor next to him and placed the AR to her right, the muzzle facing the stairwell directly across the open space from them. She kept her handgun in her lap.

Just in case.

Because he was out there, somewhere. The man in the gas mask that she and Keo had shot wasn't Owen. It was Walter. There was no mistaking the two; they had at least ten years between them—Walter was much older. Owen was more athletic, whereas Walter was bigger and heavier.

So where was Owen? Maybe one of the two dead men lying in the gravel parking lot outside the window right now was him. God, she wanted desperately to believe that. It wasn't like she had seen the men's faces when Keo shot at them, then she finished off the second one. It was too dark at the time. It still was. The only way to know for sure would be to go outside.

Dammit. She should have done that earlier. All she would have had to do was walk around the building and

Expose herself.

No. That wouldn't have been a very good idea. In fact, it would have been very stupid...if there was someone out there, waiting for a clean shot. Maybe the same someone who had killed Bunker and taken his place up in the water tower.

If Bunker was dead.

If there was someone else still out there.

If...

Too many ifs. That was the problem. The only sure thing was that it was safer in here, on the second floor of the office building. If they wanted her—or Keo, or Marie, or Yuli—they would have to come get them. If they had anything that could reach them from a distance, they would have used it already.

A grenade. A rocket launcher. *Something.*

But none of those things had happened. No one had attempted entry after Walter, and there hadn't been a single shot—or any signs of life in all of Norman, except for her slightly ragged breathing—since the last gunshot was fired.

God, she hoped it was all over, but she didn't think so. How could it be, if she didn't know Owen was one of the dead bodies? Maybe Owen was the first target Bunker had taken out. Or the second one.

"Do you think Bunker got anyone?" she remembered asking Keo.

"One. Maybe two," he had said.

"Why are you so sure he even got one?"

"He shot first. And he wouldn't have done that if he didn't get one of them in his crosshairs."

That made sense. A lot of sense, actually. Bunker wasn't just a "rancher," he was someone used to violence. He was also fearless, if the stories she'd heard about him were even half true. The man had stalked Owen's group—over a dozen men—across Texas because they had stolen his horses. Not *all* of his horses, just *some* of them. The only reason Owen had needed her was because of Bunker, who had shot Jackie during the theft.

If that first kill by Bunker had been Owen, would Walter and the others still carry out the mission? Maybe. She didn't know these men well enough. She thought she knew Leland, thought she could turn him, but...

He's dead. Keo did what he had to.

Move on.

There was nothing to do now but wait. She hated to wait, but it was better than getting into a gunfight with an ex-Navy SEAL. Keo hadn't seemed all that impressed when he found out about Owen's past, but Lara had been. She had seen ex-Special Forces guys like Danny and Will in action, and they weren't close to the elite level of a SEAL. It did make her wonder, though, how someone like Owen had ended up with Buck's group. The man was a Mercerian. Or he used to be, anyway, until being one was hazardous to your health. Danny had made damn sure of that in the aftermath of Darby Bay.

She looked over at Keo, snoring lightly next to her. So lightly, in fact, that she had to really listen to even pick up the sounds. She could see the slow but steady rise and fall of his chest under his shirt, and that did wonders to comfort her. A few minutes later, she leaned over to make sure his bandages were in place and that he was in no danger of bleeding out.

Keo looked so peaceful, like he was back at their house in the village. She wondered if he was dreaming; and if he was, of what.

She found herself smiling while watching him sleep. It was so rare to catch Keo in such a tranquil state. Usually he was alert, always aware of his surroundings. There was a constant wariness about him that she used to mistake for suspicion. But she eventually understood that it wasn't suspicion that kept him at arm's length from the others; it was anticipation. Despite George's village being everything they could have hoped for and more, Keo never really believed it would stay that way. She didn't blame him, because Lara had thought the same for the longest time.

It had taken over six months, but Owen's arrival proved Keo right.

Owen...

The man was still out there, somewhere.

Maybe plotting, biding his time.

Or maybe making his way to her building right this second.

That last thought made her glance toward the destroyed window even as her hand clutched the pistol in her lap. The gun was heavy because it was carrying a full magazine. In the years since The Purge, she had become intimately aware of the weight of a fully-loaded firearm.

There wasn't very much wind tonight, and the humid air continued to float into the glassless window. That helped to vent the room of what little remnants of the tear gas remained, which wasn't very much at all. Not enough for her to bother covering her face, anyway.

Perspiration dripped from her forehead, and Lara wiped at it before doing the same to Keo's sleeping form. He stirred slightly when she touched his cheeks with a fresh towelette, and something that almost looked like a smile creased his lips.

Lara sat back, her eyes glued to the stairs across the dark room from them.

Sooner or later, Owen was going to show himself.

Sooner or later, the man was going to come here and finish what his men had started.

Sooner or later...

Sooner...

...or later...

But he didn't.

Owen didn't appear an hour later.

Or two hours after that.

He didn't show himself as the sun rose in the east, and he remained absent when the crickets came alive among the vast fields that surrounded Norman.

Morning sunlight poured in through the window, chasing away the remains of last night's tear gas.

And Owen still didn't make an appearance.

Lara stood up, the SIG Sauer in her hand. She hadn't slept all last night, and every bone in her body ached as she straightened her legs. She clutched and unclutched the gun, making 100 percent sure the grip was true.

Because this could be a trick. Owen could have waited for morning, for her to let down her guard. He might have guessed she would try to stay awake all night in case he attacked. It was an incredibly big if, but she couldn't discount it outright. She couldn't afford to. There were too many things at stake. Too many lives.

Lara walked to the window and peered out at the bodies in the parking lot below. They were still there, in the same awkward position they had fallen last night. She could see the faces of one of them. It was Peterson, the man who had ogled Marie relentlessly. He lay on his back, eyes closed. Keo had shot him.

The one Keo had also shot but she had finished off lay on his side. The problem was that his face was turned in the wrong direction and she could only get a tiny glimpse of his side profile. If she squinted hard enough, the second dead man *could* be Owen. The hair was the same color, and the body shape was about right...

She walked back to Keo and kneeled next to him. He was still asleep, his wounds secured. He was in no danger of leaving her last night and seemed to have only gotten stronger this morning, the rise and fall of his chest more pronounced. That was good. The thought of losing him after everything they had gone through was more than she could bear.

Lara leaned down and kissed him on the cheek, then got up and walked to the stairs.

She didn't go down right away. Instead, she stood at the top and listened, but there was just the sounds of crickets coming in from the windows behind. Small wisps of lingering tear gas tickled at her cheeks, but not enough to bother her.

She went down.

The lobby was as empty as it had been last night, and now with the bright splashes of morning sunlight, all the blood gave it the appearance of a slaughterhouse. To her surprise, Lara wasn't the least bit bothered by the sight. Maybe it was because she had primed herself for it. Or, maybe, she had just seen something like it too many times before.

Is that a good thing?

Probably not.

She walked across the room and to the front door, giving the back hallway a quick glance as she passed it. The door at the end was closed, not that that meant anything. The lock was gone, destroyed when Walter kicked it in last night. Anyone could have come in at any time, though it didn't look as if anyone had.

It didn't *look* as if anyone had, anyway.

She gripped the gun tighter when she reached the front

door. The deadbolt was still in place, and Lara slid it free and swung the door wide open. Sunlight hit her full in the face, and she blinked a couple of times, letting her eyes get used to the sudden brightness. Maybe it was the lack of sleep or the fact she was just suddenly very tired and feeling unafraid and just *wanted to get it over with already*, but she didn't take any precautions before stepping outside.

She walked past Peterson's body and over to the second one. Lara didn't bother turning it over. All she had to do was circle it to get a good look at the face.

Shit.

It wasn't Owen, but another man she'd seen among the group. She didn't know his name or remember if anyone had ever mentioned it while she was around. Unlike Peterson, the man's eyes were open, and he was staring at her boots.

Lara glanced around at Norman. A slight wind had picked up, pushing away some of the stifling heat, but not enough to keep her from sweating under the baking sun. She looked toward the water tower, but all she could see was the bulbous head silhouetted against the thick, bright cloudless sky—

"Good morning!" someone shouted.

That startled Lara and she reflexively clutched the SIG at her side. It took a few seconds before she realized the voice had come from the water tower itself. All the way from the top. And it had sounded like...

"Bunker?" she shouted over.

"No, it's the Easter Bunny!" Bunker shouted back.

Lara smiled and started jogging across the parking lot—and almost fell on her face. Right. The bullet hole in her left thigh. She hobbled the rest of the way instead.

She could make out more of the water tower and the

walkway that circled it as she crossed the street. There was definitely someone up there, sitting down. It was Bunker, of course. She recognized his voice. Besides, if it wasn't Bunker and was one of Owen's men—or even Owen himself—they would have shot her by now.

Lara gimped her way across the highway and got close enough to the tower that she could finally make out Bunker's sitting form. She stopped, shielded her eyes, and grinned up at him—not that she thought he could see it. He was too high up and still too far away for her to see what kind of shape he was in, but his voice had sounded strong earlier.

"Bunker!" Lara shouted. "You're alive!"

"Barely!" Bunker shouted back down. "What happened to your boyfriend?"

"He's sleeping last night off!"

"Good ol' Bob, always half-assing it."

Lara grinned. "He had a rough night!"

"So did I. And you, too, from the looks of it."

"Can you get down?"

"Yeah, but not yet."

"You need help?"

"I'd say yes, but seeing your condition, I think it's best if I do it myself. It might just take a while, is all."

"But you're okay?"

"I wouldn't say that, but it could have been a lot worse. I'll take the win."

Me too, Lara thought. *Me too.*

"All right," she said. "I'm going back to check on Keo."

"You mean Bob?" Bunker asked.

She smiled. "Bob, I mean." She started to turn, but stopped halfway and looked back up at him. "Bunker!"

"Yeah?" Bunker called down.

"Did you get him?"

"Who?"

"Owen. Did you get him last night?"

"I have no idea," Bunker said. "I got someone. Two some-ones, actually. I take it he's still unaccounted for?"

"I can't find his body."

Bunker didn't say anything for a moment. She couldn't quite make out his face, but she assumed Bunker was thinking.

"Bunker!" Lara said.

"Go check on your boyfriend," Bunker said. "I'll stay up here and keep an eye out in case anyone shows up."

"Are you sure?"

"Sure, I'm sure."

"All right," Lara said. She turned to go again.

She felt better with Bunker up there, watching her back with a high-powered bolt-action rifle. As she limped her way back across the highway, then through the gravel parking lot, she couldn't help but wonder about Owen's whereabouts. Bunker said he'd killed two last night. One of them could have easily been Owen.

God, I hope one of them was Owen.

Please let one of them be Owen...

TWENTY-SIX

"We get them all?"

"Almost."

"'Almost?'"

"There's one missing."

"Who?"

"Owen."

Keo sat up on the floor and leaned back against the wall. Both shoulders let him know all about the ass-kicking he'd gotten last night by sending jolts of pain through his arms and into the rest of his body.

Okay, okay, I get it.

He might have grimaced a bit because Lara reached over and put a comforting hand over his. "You okay?"

"Hunky dory," Keo said. "So, Mr. BUD/S is missing?"

Lara nodded. She sat in front of him eating a bag of MRE with a spork. The alluring aroma of beef stew filled the entire second floor, though it would have been stronger if the window to his right wasn't still blown out from last night's gunfight. He could just barely detect some tear gas still mingled in the air, but not enough to elicit a cough.

"We couldn't find his body anywhere," Lara said.

The *we* she was talking about included Bunker and Marie. Yuli, as far as Keo knew, was still blind.

"So who was the guy we shot last night?" Keo asked.

"Walter," Lara said. "He was Owen's right-hand man."

"And Owen himself is nowhere to be found?"

She shook her head. "We looked everywhere. Bunker doesn't think he was ever in Norman last night."

"Then where was he?"

"We don't know. That's the mystery."

"Hunh," Keo said.

Lara held out some of the beef stew. Keo opened his mouth and took a bite. He chased down the chunk of beef with a generous portion of fudge brownie bar that had come with the meal.

"Drink some of this," Lara said, handing him a bottle filled with an electrolyte powder beverage.

Keo did, before asking, "You okay?"

She smiled. "I should be asking you that." She held out some more of the stew. "I spent all morning trying to figure out why Owen isn't here."

"What did you come up with?"

"I still don't know."

"So what *do* we know about the man?"

"I know that everything he did, it was to keep Jackie alive until he could get his brother to Cherry Point. Beyond that..." She paused briefly. "That's it. That's all I know with any certainty about the man."

Lara put the spork back into the entrée bag and seemed to drift off for a bit.

"What?" Keo said.

"Maybe that's why Owen never showed up," Lara said. "He wanted to get Jackie to the lake. Everything else after that..." She paused again. Then, "Maybe he doesn't care."

"I don't understand."

"Me. Us. Maybe he doesn't care about what happens to us."

"Because everything he did, it was for Jackie. To get his little brother to the lake where they spent their childhood."

Lara nodded. "Does that make any sense?"

"A little," Keo said. He took another sip of the mixed drink. "From what you told me, this was never anything personal for Owen. At least not when it comes to you and me. But what about Bunker? The rancher shot his little brother."

"It was Jackie's fault, though. Or maybe he blamed himself."

"A lot of maybes..."

"Yeah. Too many."

"Here's another one. Maybe he was here and his body is still somewhere out there. Bunker said he got two of them last night?"

She nodded. "We found two bodies farther up the highway, where he first opened up on them."

"So two bodies accounted for, just like Bunker said."

"Uh huh."

"And neither one of them was Owen."

"Right again."

"And the two outside, in the parking lot? The ones we put down?"

"One was a man named Peterson, but I don't know the other one."

"But it wasn't Owen."

"No."

"Maybe he's hiding," Keo said, but even as he said it, it sounded stupid. A man like Owen, who had done the things he had, with his kind of past, wouldn't be "hiding" from a gunfight. Especially if his brother was dead and he blamed Keo, Lara, and Bunker for it.

"You really think that?" Lara asked, apparently also sharing his doubt.

"No, not really." Then, when something else occurred to him, "Maybe you were wrong about Jackie. Maybe he's still alive."

"More maybes."

"Is it possible?"

"It's possible," Lara nodded.

"Maybe you did a better job on him than you thought? Saved his life without realizing it?"

Lara shrugged but didn't reply.

"But you don't think so," Keo said.

She shook her head. "Nothing was going to save him, Keo. Not me, not a team of the world's best doctors. He was just in too bad a shape when they got him to the village. I've seen people die. Too many people for my liking. Friends, enemies..."

Lara set the beef stew packet down between them and stared at it. She didn't say anything for a while, and Keo didn't force her to. He could tell she had been thinking about this all night and morning. She hadn't gotten much sleep last night, if any; he could see the fatigue on her face, the puffiness around her eyes.

Finally, she looked back up at him. "He's dead. Jackie. What I don't know is how that affected Owen." She looked toward the window. "For all we know, he just arrived and is waiting for us out there..."

Keo looked toward the open window with her, but all they could hear was the sound of horses whinnying loudly somewhere outside.

"That's Bunker," Lara said. "He found where Walter and the others had stashed their horses before they launched their attack." She looked back at Keo. "Speaking of which, he invited us to go back with him."

"Who?"

"Bunker."

"Go back where?"

"His ranch." She smiled. "Although, I think he's just looking for someone—namely yours truly—to make sure he doesn't keel over on his way home."

"He told me it was a big ranch."

"That's what he told me, too. But you know guys, always exaggerating about sizes."

He chuckled. "It couldn't hurt. A change of scenery, I mean."

"You tired of George already?"

"Nah. George is fine. I'm just tired of fish."

"I thought you liked fishing."

"I like beer, too, but I don't like drinking it *every* day."

She gave him a surprised look. "You never told me that."

"About the beer?"

"The village. I always thought you liked it."

"I did, because you liked it."

"That was the only reason?"

"Not the only reason, but it was one of the reasons. The biggest reason."

She crawled over to sit against the wall next to him before letting out a big tired sigh. Lara folded her knees up to her chest and glanced over. "A big, sprawling ranch with a lot of open field sounds good right now. I can learn to raise horses, and you can...find something to do."

"Oh, I'm sure I can find something to do," Keo said.

"Something that doesn't involve guns, I mean."

"That's going to limit my options."

"You'll figure something out."

"What about cleaning guns?"

"No."

"Storing them?"

"How about no guns at all?"

He grinned. "So, we're going to pretend that Bunker's ranch is La La Land and immune to the outside world, is that it?"

Lara put her chin against her knees and sighed. "Yeah, I felt stupid as soon as I said that." She pursed a smile. "But a girl can dream, can't she?"

"Yes, she can," Keo said.

He reached over and pulled her closer. She leaned her head against his shoulder, most likely forgetting about his wound there. He grimaced but didn't let her see it.

"Dream away," Keo said. "You deserve it. And I promise to do my best to make it come true."

Bunker had seen better days, but Keo could say the same about himself and Lara, and Yuli. Marie looked the least pathetic among the five of them. She'd gotten through her ordeal in generally good shape, while Yuli didn't appear as if he was ever going to get his vision back. Lara had no answers and nothing to test him with to be sure one way or another.

But Yuli was alive, and he still had a beautiful wife and a baby on the way. He might stay blind for the rest of his life, but at least he'd have that. These days, after everything that had happened to the world, Keo called it a win.

At the moment, though, Keo was more worried about himself and Lara. The possibility that Owen, Mr. Piss Down Your Throat himself, was still out there somewhere left him a little nervous. More than a little nervous, actually. It didn't sit well with him at all, and Keo made sure he was armed and ready when they finally left the Norman Rodeo Grounds.

They were headed "home," but only for Marie and Yuli. Keo and Lara thought they owed the couple at least that much. As for them, they would head north as soon as possible, returning to Bunker's ranch and, as Lara said, "take it from there."

That was fine with Keo. He didn't really have any attachments to the village anyway. He liked it well enough, including its people—one dog and its owner in particular—but home for him was always with Lara. He didn't say that out loud, of course; it sounded way too sappy even in his own head.

They left Norman about two in the afternoon, which would give them plenty of time to reach the village before nightfall. According to Bunker, it would take two days of "easy riding" to get back to his ranch. Again, that was fine with Keo. He wasn't in any hurry. His wounds weren't that bad, though he didn't discount the strong painkillers Lara had spread around as being the reason. The meds were part of the bundle Owen's group had taken from the village and Bunker had found in the packs left behind with the horses.

Bunker himself rode alongside Keo and Lara, while they pulled nearly a dozen horses behind them. The rancher had found five in all, hidden away inside a warehouse about half a kilometer from the Rodeo Grounds. There were exactly five for the five dead bodies they had been able to account for. Only three of the horses were Bunker's, which left one more still out there. But Bunker, who hadn't gotten through last night scot-free, wasn't that anxious to go looking for it.

"I think I'm done," Bunker said when Keo asked him. Keo figured that had a little something to do with the rancher's wounds. The return fire by Walter's men last night had chipped away at the water tower Bunker was moving around and sent shrapnel flying everywhere. Some had found homes in Bunker's right cheek and arms. Lara was the one who had pulled them out of him piece by piece this morning.

They rode on the shoulder of the same stretch of highway they'd taken two days earlier, the sun still bright and hot above them. At least there was a nice breeze this afternoon to make all the knee-high grass that populated the wide-open fields around them sway back and forth. Not enough to overcome the heat, but it was better than nothing.

Around four in the afternoon, with the village still far off, Lara pulled up to Keo and Bunker after talking with Marie for a bit. "Let's take a break, guys."

Keo glanced back at the couple. "Everyone okay?"

"They're fine. Just tired."

They found a pair of trees and let the horses graze around

them, while the humans sat in the shade and watched the sun burning away in the cloudless sky. The nice breeze from earlier was gone, replaced by the same insufferable Texas heat that Keo had been dealing with for the last two months. Except this time he didn't have an ocean literally in his front yard to jump into and go for a nice swim to cool off.

Every now and then, Keo caught Lara gazing off into the fields, as if she expected to see something out there.

Or someone.

He reached over and took her hand, and squeezed. "Hey."

She looked over. "Imm?"

"He's not out there."

"Who?"

"You know who."

She forced a smile and nodded.

"If he was going to show himself, he would have long ago," Keo continued. "I think you're right. All of this was for Jackie. And now that his brother's dead, I don't think he cares about us anymore."

"Would explain why just Walter and the boys came after us last night," Bunker said.

"How?" Lara asked.

Bunker was leaning against the tree next to them, chewing on a piece of grass. His right leg was heavily bandaged, and he limped around more than he walked, and had been all morning. "If what you say is true, then Owen doesn't give two damns about these guys. It was all about his little bro. Walter, on the other hand, might feel differently. We did kill two of their guys in Cherry Point. He might care about that."

Three guys, actually, Keo thought, remembering Bear Man in the diner.

He said to Lara, "He could be right."

"He could be," Lara said, though Keo didn't think she completely believed it, even if he knew that she wanted to.

"Well, one thing's for sure," Bunker said, "if he comes after us, he'll be outgunned."

"Will he?" Keo asked.

"Five against one. I know my math."

"One ex-SEAL against three gimps, one blind guy, and a pregnant woman," Keo said. "I'd love to be outgunned by those kinds of numbers."

Bunker grunted. "Speaking of being outgunned, you wanna hear something curious about that water tower I was on all night?"

"That you still stink despite being so close to all that water?" Keo asked. "That's not curious, Bunker. That's just punishment for your traveling companions."

Bunker snorted, but Keo caught him sniffing himself briefly and trying not to be noticed doing it.

"What about the water tower?" Lara asked.

"There were bones up there," Bunker said.

"Bones?"

"Ghoul bones."

"You sure they were ghoul bones?" Keo asked.

"Of course I'm sure. I was born at night, not last night."

"What were ghoul bones doing up there?" Lara asked.

"Beats the hell outta me," Bunker said. "Probably some sap crawled up there one night, trying to get away from the creepy crawlers. Wonder if he was one of those bones still hanging around on the walkway, or if he made it down."

"That is curious," Lara said.

"Told you," Bunker said to Keo.

"Don't encourage him," Keo said to Lara.

"Lesson learned." She leaned toward Keo and rested her head on his shoulder. "Let him come," she said quietly, as if she meant for only him to hear. "It doesn't matter if he's alone or if he has more men with him. We'll deal with it. Like we always do."

Keo smiled. He liked the sound of that. "Damn straight."

He leaned over and kissed her. She returned it with a smile of her own.

"Ugh, disgusting. I don't need to see this," Bunker said next to them, before getting up and limping away.

Keo ignored him and concentrated on Lara.

"So..." he said.

"So..." she said.

"What's our next move?"

She shrugged. "We'll improvise. We're good at that."

Keo grinned. "Yeah, we are, aren't we?"

She kissed him back and he wrapped his arms around her.

He looked off at the empty fields, burning under the hot scorching sun around them, and felt as if he could take on an army all by himself.

Not that he had to, because Lara was by his side.

Made in the USA
Lexington, KY
15 May 2019